ELLE GRAY

BLAKE WILDER

FBI MYSTERY THRILLER

A SHOT TO KILL

A Shot to Kill

CHAPTER ONE

Wingate Hotel, Downtown District; Seattle, WA

My eyes flutter, then open, and I find myself staring at a strange ceiling. A bolt of adrenaline shoots through me, and my heart kicks into overdrive as I sit up. My head is pounding, my mouth is drier than the Sahara, and there's a sick, greasy sensation churning in my belly. But in a flash, my entire body tightens when I realize I'm not alone. Turning to my left, I see him lying on his stomach, one arm at his side, the other flung haphazardly above his head. The thin sheet is not quite covering his obviously bare backside, and he's softly snoring, caught in the grip of sleep.

A quiet gasp bursts from my throat when I look down at myself and realize that I'm naked. Not partially clothed. Naked. I clap my hands over my mouth and quickly try to sort out how I ended up here. How I let this happen. I run my fingers through my hair, trying to smooth it out as I struggle to put the fragmented pieces of last night together in my sleep-deprived, hangover-addled mind. And when all those pieces start falling into place, I groan softly. *Dear God, what have I done? I think I might throw up.*

DEA Agent Sonny Garland, the charming Matthew McConaughey doppelgänger, mutters and stirs in his sleep, sending a fresh wave of near panic surging through my veins. Thankfully, he doesn't seem to be waking up, so I carefully slip out of bed. As swiftly and quietly as I can, I find my clothes, which have been scattered all over the floor, and pull them on. One of my shoes is under the bed and the other on a table across the room, so I snatch them up. I'll put them on later. It wouldn't be the first time I had to make the walk of shame barefoot. I find my bag underneath his pants and grab it, stuffing my badge and weapon into it.

Holding my breath and moving on tiptoes, I head for the door. I need to get out of here. But when I hear the rustling of the sheets and a grunt behind me, I grit my teeth and try to keep the absolute mortification washing through me off my face.

"Sneakin' out on me, huh?"

Turning around, I offer him a smile I hope can pass as sincere.

"Not sneaking out. I just need to get to the office. I was going to text you later," I reply quickly. Probably too quickly.

Slowly, I turn around to find him sitting up, his icy blue eyes fixed on me. Sonny offers me that wide, magnetic smile that is probably what got me into this mess in the first place, and despite my best efforts, it puts a flutter in my heart. I can't lie. He's a gorgeous man. He's intelligent, witty, and incredibly charming. On top of all that, he seems to be a genuinely decent, nice guy.

But sleeping with him was not part of my game plan when we met for drinks last night. We met to discuss next steps for his case with the motorcycle club running drugs for the Arias Cartel in

Arizona. That was all that was supposed to happen. Business. We were supposed to be forming the skeleton of an action plan for an op. That was supposed to be it. Obviously, I somehow went off script. Embarrassingly way off script.

"I didn't take you for the love 'em and leave 'em type, Blake Wilder."

"That's not what this is. I just have to get to work," I tell him, then add lightly, "Not all of us can lie around watching trashy movies and ordering room service all day."

He grins. "Hey, I'm working. I'm up here on official DEA business."

"Yeah, how long do you think your bosses are going to let you get away with coming up here when your office is down in Arizona?"

"As many times as I need to come up until we can figure out how to smash that MC-cartel connection," he says. "My bosses were impressed with what your team did, and they're hopin' to have you all back down to finish the job."

"I remember you giving me that little speech at the Emerald last night."

"Did I?"

"You did."

"Wow," he says and rubs his head as he chuckles to himself. "Well, just because I said it once already doesn't make it any less true."

"I suppose not," I say. "Anyway, we'll talk later. I need—"

"To get to the office, yeah. You gave me that little speech already," he teases.

Sonny slides out of bed and stands up, showing off his taut, toned, and very naked body. My cheeks flushing and my face growing warm, I quickly turn around. His slow, drawling laugh rings in my ears, making my face so hot, I wouldn't be surprised if it burst into flames.

"Really, Blake? After last night, you're going to be shy now?" he asks.

"Can we just… not talk about last night?" I respond. "And while you're at it, do me a favor and put on some clothes."

"Yeah, sure."

I hear the rustling of clothes, and as he dresses, I plot the most efficient way for me to get out of here without seeming rude. As last night's events come into sharper focus, I can't honestly say I didn't have a good time or enjoy Sonny's company. It's just… going home with a man I barely know isn't really my style. That's just not something I do. And the fact that I'm here right now, in his hotel room, trying to creep out without waking him, makes this more than a little awkward. Truthfully, I'm kind of ashamed of myself.

"All right. I'm decent," he says in his syrupy sweet drawl.

I turn around to find him standing there shirtless and wearing nothing but a pair of jeans. Clearly, we have different definitions of the word decent. I do my best to keep from gawking at the hard angles and planes of his chest and abdomen without looking like I'm keeping myself from gawking. Like I said, he's a beautiful man, and I'm not blind.

"When can I see you again?" he asks.

"Well, you're coming by the Chapel to talk about—"

"When can I see you in a non-work-related setting?" he clarifies.

The heat in my face ticks up another couple of degrees. I'm not sure if a person can actually die from excessive mortification, but I think I'm on the cusp of finding out.

"Listen, Sonny, I'm not sure that's a good idea," I say.

"What do you mean? We get along well, and we had a great time last night."

"I just… I'm not sure it's appropriate."

"We don't work together. I'm not your superior, you're not mine. How is our getting together off the clock inappropriate in any way? We are grown-ups, Blake."

"I just… it just is."

He frowns and runs a hand through his shaggy dirty blond locks, frustration on his face.

"Blake, I like you. And I got the idea that you like me back. I don't do this sort of thing with just anybody—"

"No?"

"No," he says, his tone serious. "There is an undeniable chemistry between us. I don't understand why you're freaking out, but last night was really good. And I'm not talking about—this," he says, pointing to the bed. "I'm talking about at the bar, when we were both relaxed and just vibin'. We had a great time, and I'm not ashamed to say I want more of that."

My gaze falls to the floor as a thousand thoughts rocket through my mind. He's right. When we were at the Emerald last night, just sitting and talking, we did have a great time, and I really enjoyed his company. I can honestly say I haven't enjoyed a man's company that much in a very long time. And that's kind of the problem. When I enjoy a man's company, when I drop my guard and open up to him, nothing good has ever come of it.

"You don't even know me," I say.

"That's something I'd like to remedy."

"I don't think it's a good idea."

"What about last night?"

"Last night was… what it was. And you're right—I had a good time. I enjoyed being with you," I tell him. "But I think last night is all it was."

He recoils, and a stunned expression creeps across his face. If I had to guess, I'd say it's because Sonny doesn't get turned down very often. Going even further, I'd say he wants to see me again, not because he likes me, but because I'm available and in his proximity. He says he doesn't take women home regularly, but am I supposed to take him at his word?

That being said, I bear some responsibility for being where I am right now. I'd had a few, sure, but I was fully cognizant of what I was doing when I came back to his room with him. And nothing would have happened last night if I didn't want it to. It was fun. I enjoyed spending time with him. And now it's time to move on and let that memory live in our collective past.

"Wow," he says. "I guess I was wrong about you being the love 'em and leave 'em type."

"I guess you were."

He eyes me closely. "I don't believe you. I don't believe you're really that way."

I shrug. "I'm not sure what to tell you then. Like I said, I enjoyed hanging out with you last night. We scratched a mutual itch. But that doesn't mean I'm looking for a full-blown relationship."

He stands there, eyeballing me in silence for a moment. I can tell he wants to keep arguing that there is something between us. And perhaps there is. But I'm not in a place where I want to explore it right now. I can see him grappling with his self-control while trying to keep the disappointment off his face. Ultimately, he gives me a frustrated nod.

"All right," he says. "If that's the way you want things, then I'm not in a position to say otherwise. You do you, Blake."

"I think keeping things professional will be for the best. For both of us."

"You say that like you're trying to talk yourself into it."

"I'm not."

He sighs. "If that's really the way you want things to be, I guess that's your choice. I don't agree and think we'd be great together, but I'm not going to force something on you that you so clearly aren't sure you want."

"I appreciate that, Sonny," I say. "It's nothing against you. You really are great. It's just… I'm not really in a place to start a relationship."

"It's not you; it's me, huh?" he says wryly.

"Something like that."

"Fair enough. I understand."

"Thank you," I reply. "I appreciate that."

"Sure," he says, sounding resigned.

"Then I guess I'll see you at the Chapel later."

"Yep. Guess I'll see you there, and we can keep things all professional-like and pretend none of this ever happened. Copy that."

His tone is suddenly curt, and he's not even trying to hide his disappointment. There's a part of me that feels bad and another part of me that's honestly disappointed because there actually is something about him I find compelling… something I'm incredibly attracted to. If I'm being honest with myself, I'd say he's right: there is a connection between us. If there wasn't, I wouldn't be standing here in his hotel room right now.

But this is ultimately the right decision. For both of us. He's upset now, but I'm confident he'll see it in time.

"All right. Have a good day then," I say.

"Yep. You too."

I walk out of his room, letting the door close softly behind me. And as I head for the elevators, I'm battered by waves of guilt, shame, and even a touch of disappointment for closing myself off and shutting Sonny out the way I did. But it's for the best.

And if I keep repeating that, eventually, I'm going to believe it.

CHAPTER TWO

Maxwell Building, Downtown District; Seattle, WA

I GLANCE AT THE PANEL ON THE WALL BESIDE THE DOOR. The red light is on, telling me she's in with a client. I'm sitting in one of the two plush chairs in the small room. The other is against the wall across from me, and each chair has a small, round table with a couple of magazines on top next to it. Other than that, the room is empty. The light wood paneling on the walls gleams in the dim light, framed black and white pictures of bucolic scenery hang on the walls, and the carpeting beneath my feet is thick and soft.

Everything about the room is meant to evoke calm. It's meant to put you in a relaxed, contemplative, and open state of mind, which is, of course, beneficial for therapy. And yet, because it's so barren and silent, it evokes the opposite in me. It makes me tense and has my nerves stretched tauter than a bowstring, and when my phone chirps with an incoming text message, I jump. Turning my phone over, I see in the preview pane the message is from Sonny.

"Great," I mutter.

I call up the message, hoping against all hope it's about something related to his case. That hope is quickly dashed. I should close out of my texts, but morbid curiosity and that pang of disappointment that gripped me before compels me to open it.

I'm not going to keep badgering you, but I just want to say we have a real connection, Blake. When you find yourself in a place to consider it, give me a shout. I'll wait. But not forever. ~ Sonny

"Come on, Sonny. Don't do this. Don't make this more difficult than it has to be," I mutter to myself as I close my phone.

Dr. Isabel Azar's office is on the seventeenth floor of the high rise. Sitting in the lobby, waiting for my appointment time, I glance out the large windows that give me a view of downtown Seattle. It's a partly cloudy day out there, but with the last vestiges of summer in the air, it's nice. It would be a nice day to sit outside and have a leisurely lunch. It would sure be a hell of a lot more preferable to sitting in this lobby waiting to be poked, prodded, and dissected.

It was DD Church who recommended Dr. Azar to me when she noticed I was having a hard time moving past a recent case we worked in New Orleans. Actually, recommended probably isn't the right word: *ordered* me to go is probably more accurate. I'm sure from Church's perspective, getting me to agree to start some counseling was probably a lot like feeding a pill to a cat. She finally had to threaten to bench me until I agreed to go and get my head back on straight.

Obviously reluctant at first, I did my own research and learned that Dr. Azar works exclusively with law enforcement personnel, seeing members of the Seattle PD as well as agents from some of the federal agencies in the area. She's got a pretty solid reputation and is credited with pulling people out of their darkest places and helping them turn their lives around. Everything I've read speaks of her in the most glowing of terms.

This is my third session with her, and so far, I'd say she's living up to her billing. She's smart, intuitive, and has a great sense of humor. She's also got an easy way about her that makes sessions seem more like a conversation than an interrogation. But she's also tough and doesn't let you get away with anything. She won't let you hide behind rationales and excuses and will call you out when you try. She believes in the healing power of being uncomfortable.

Being that I graduated with a degree in the same field, I can see what she's doing when we talk. It's kind of like one magician watching another and knowing all the tricks. But I recognize the value in one therapist seeing another to gain some clarity and perspective. Most therapists I've known have a counselor of their own. Finding their center, having a clear mind, and being well-grounded is critical to the work they do.

As for Dr. Azar, she's clever and insightful. She's also got a very light touch and can deftly elicit information that you never intended to give her. She's good at earning trust and being able to get people to open up without making it seem like they're spilling all their secrets. She's got qualities as a therapist I approve of and admire. Talking to her hasn't always been fun, which is kind of the point, but our conversations are productive. And I like her. A lot.

The light goes off, and a moment later, the door opens, and Dr. Azar leans out, a smile stretching her thin, heart-shaped lips when she sees me.

"You came back," she says approvingly.

"Did you doubt me?"

"I wasn't sure after our last session."

"Well, here I am."

"Here you are indeed," she says. "Come on in."

I step into her office, and she closes the door behind me. I hear the click of her turning on the light outside, telling her next appointment she's in session. Unlike the spartan confines of her waiting room, Dr. Azar's office has a well-lived-in appearance. It's comfortable. It's even a bit cluttered, which makes it seem almost homey.

To my right is a sitting area, which has just two deep, plush chairs sitting across from each other, with a coffee table between them. A desk to my right sits in front of a large picture window, offering the same view of Seattle as the waiting room. A pair of massive bookcases line the wall across from me, the shelves stuffed with not just books but a variety of knickknacks from various places she's traveled. Her degrees and certificates hang on the wall between them.

There are also framed pictures of her family, which I find to be an interesting touch. Most therapists, at least the few I've seen, tend to keep their family well away from their office. Most don't like mixing their personal and professional lives. Dr. Azar is different. She has a very handsome husband and two beautiful children. I can tell she's proud of her family and doesn't mind showing them off. It humanizes her in a way most therapists don't like to be humanized. It's one of the reasons I think she and I have been able to click so well in such a short period of time.

"So, Blake, how are you?" she asks as she sits down.

"I'm fine. I'm good."

"It sounds like you're trying to talk yourself into it."

A rueful expression crosses my face as I take a seat. Dr. Azar is a tiny woman, no more than five-three and petite. But she carries herself in a way that makes her seem bigger. She has a presence about her. A gravitas. Her obsidian hair is tied back into a braid that falls to the middle of her back. Her eyes are the color of honey and always seem to see more than you want to reveal, and she has a warm, tawny complexion. She has a kind face, but there is something just below the surface that tells you she is not a woman to be trifled with.

"So, catch me up on your week," she says.

As Dr. Azar opens her notebook and clicks her pen, I slowly and reluctantly catch her up on the past week as honestly as I can. I even tell her about waking up in Sonny Garland's hotel room, a confession that elicits a smile from her. As I speak, she is jotting down some notes, which seems superfluous to me since she records our sessions. When I'm finally done talking, she sits forward.

"So, you like this Agent Sonny Garland," she states, not a question.

"I didn't say that."

"You didn't have to," she replies. "I know you well enough already to see that you don't go home with somebody you don't have a connection with. You're not, as they say, that kind of girl."

A wry chuckle bubbles out of my throat, and I look down at my hands. There's not much I can say to that. There's not much I want to say to that.

"We'll circle back to this burgeoning relationship later," Dr. Azar says.

"There's no burgeoning relationship—"

"We'll circle back to all that later," she interrupts. "What I want you to tell me right now is how you are processing the trauma from your last case. Are you still having the nightmares?"

I clear my throat and wring my hands together. "They're not as bad. But… yeah."

"I can only imagine that watching somebody take their own life has to be… difficult," she says. "But you've mentioned this isn't the first time you've seen a person die while on duty."

"No, it's not. I've even had to take their lives. It's never easy."

"I imagine it's not. But those other cases you've been able to move forward from… even on those occasions when you've had to take a person's life," she says. "Why do you think you're stuck on Garrett Arceneaux's death? What is keeping you fixated on that?"

"I… I really can't say. Probably because I was powerless to stop him?"

"Can I offer up a different opinion?"

"Sure."

"I think you're hung up on Garrett Arceneaux because, yes, in part you were powerless to stop him," she says. "But I also think it's staying with you because that's how you feel when it comes to Kit. You believe you're powerless to protect her, just as you were unable to protect him."

I shake my head. "He was a serial killer. I don't see how he equates with my sister."

"Well, from what little you've told me, your sister kills too."

The comparison offends me. To suggest my sister is the sort of monster Garrett Arceneaux was is appalling to me. The logical part of my brain calms me down—tells me that Dr. Azar isn't actually suggesting my sister is no different than a serial killer but is trying to make a larger point. So, rather than bite her head off, I sit back.

"It's… different. They are different. Kit is nothing like him," I say.

"Is it different, Blake? Garrett Arceneaux killed for pleasure—perhaps revenge. But you said he took an undeniable pleasure in it. Your sister, according to you, killed for money. May still kill for money, although it's now under the color of governmental authority," she replies. "I think you are making a distinction without a difference."

"My sister is not a monster."

A patient smile curls the corners of her mouth. "Of course, she's not. She's a victim. Just as you say, this Garrett Arceneaux was—a victim of his upbringing, I think you said. Which, if you recall, is also what you said about your sister."

I open my mouth to respond, but close it again with an audible click of my teeth. I can't argue with her because I did say those things to her. I just haven't actually considered it that way before. The protective big sister in me hates it, but the clinician in me has to admit, albeit a bit grudgingly, that it's an interesting insight.

Dr. Azar sits forward. "I'm of the opinion that Garrett's suicide is sticking with you because in some ways, on some levels so deep you probably don't even realize it, you see a lot of your sister in him. And watching him take his own life made you feel powerless. You wanted to protect him but couldn't. And I think you see Kit in much the same way. You still carry a tremendous burden, mostly of guilt, for not being able to protect her when she was taken."

I twist the ring around my finger, considering her words. She might be right. It makes sense. But I'm not sure what I'm supposed to do with that.

"But there's something else you need to really understand," Dr. Azar says.

"What is that?"

"It's not your job to protect your sister. And it's certainly not your fault she was taken. You were just a little girl yourself. If you'd been in a position to try, both of you may have been murdered right alongside your parents."

"I can't help but think it's somehow my fault."

"It's not. She's a grown woman, Blake. She's capable of making her own choices," she says. "Kit sounds a lot like you. She obviously takes pride in her work and sounds just as passionate. That's her choice. You need to stop treating her like a little girl and recognize her as the grown, intelligent, dedicated woman she seems to be. I think if you do that, it will not only take a tremendous burden off your shoulders, it will improve your relationship with her markedly."

I sit back in the chair, grimacing like Dr. Azar just hit me in the stomach with a sledgehammer. Of all the things I expected her to say, telling me I infantilize my sister was probably the last thing on the list. Hell, it wasn't even on my list.

"I don't think I treat her like a little girl, Dr. Azar."

"Constantly telling her to check in with you, trying to keep tabs on her, consistently telling her she shouldn't be doing a job she's obviously passionate about—yeah, you really do treat her like a little girl," she responds.

I run a hand over my face as her words echo through my head. I can be a bit overprotective. A bit overbearing. And it annoys Kit. But when I found out she was alive again and had been working her entire life to get back to me, I told myself I needed to do what I'd failed to do when she was just a kid and protect her.

But hearing Dr. Azar's rather stark opinion puts a different spin on things for me. It never occurred to me that I was infantilizing her—that I was smothering her—or that I was not seeing her as a grown woman with the agency. I thought I was just being a big sister. Sitting here with Dr. Azar, I can now see that fine line—and see just how far over it I am.

"You've given me a lot to consider," I finally admit. "I don't think I ever really saw any of this in quite that light before."

"Good. I'm glad you're going to think about it. And I think when you do, if you are open and honest with yourself, you'll come to the same conclusions."

"Yeah. Perhaps."

"Good. Then I will give you some space to think about it. So, let's move on," she says with a mischievous glint in her eye. "Now, tell me about this handsome Agent Garland…"

CHAPTER THREE

Chief Wilder's Office, The Chapel, SNAP Team HQ, Industrial District; Seattle, WA

"Blake Wilder," Astra gasps. "I am shocked. Truly shocked."

"Trust me when I tell you that nobody is more shocked than I am," I reply.

"I'm not so sure about that. I'm so shocked I don't even have a snarky remark on deck."

"Wow. You must be pretty shocked."

"Believe me. I am."

I lower my gaze to the top of my desk and brush away some imaginary dust as my cheeks grow red and warm. I debated long and hard with myself whether to tell Astra about my awkward morning or not. But she has the uncanny ability to sniff out my secrets. She's got a sixth sense for them. And when she catches a whiff of one, she's even more ruthless an interrogator when it comes to digging a confession out of me than she is to our suspects. I've never been able to keep things from Astra, and trying to hide something like this would be an exercise in futility. It drives me nuts.

But I also tell her things because I value her input. She has a unique perspective and sees the world differently, which I treasure. Other than Kit, she knows me better than anybody else on the planet and always cuts through my BS to the heart of the matter. She tells me the truth, whether I like it or not. And to me, somebody willing to not sugarcoat anything and tell you the truth of things is the mark of a good, true friend. It's tough to hear and may hurt my feelings sometimes, but I would rather have somebody give me a hard truth over a sweet lie.

She gives me a wide, mischievous smile. "I am so proud of you."

"I'm not sure this is something to be proud of."

"Trust me—it is. You loosening up a little and having some fun not only makes me proud, it makes me want to throw a freaking party."

"Yeah, well, enjoy it now because it's not happening again."

"Blake, Sonny is a decent guy, and it's obvious that he's pretty crazy about you. Not to mention he's drop dead gorgeous," she says. "Why wouldn't you see him again?"

"Because, according to Dr. Azar, I am 'emotionally unavailable'," I say with air quotes.

Astra shrugs. "Well, I could have told you that."

"Thanks for that."

Astra laughs. "What do you want me to say? In all the years we've known each other, I've watched you shoot men down like you were getting paid for it."

I lean back in my chair and frown. I should have figured she'd come down on Dr. Azar's side in all of this. Turning to the window, I stare at Lumen Field in the distance and try to put some order to the chaos in my mind. My head has been a mess since leaving Dr. Azar's office, and my thoughts have been bouncing around all over the place like somebody turned a giant box of rubber balls over inside my skull.

Sonny does seem like a decent guy. But he's been in our orbit less than a month, and I know better than most that people have secrets. People have agendas. I've seen firsthand that people betray and that people kill. Knowing all I do, having seen the things I've seen, and having endured the things I have, how can I ever trust anybody?

I turn back to Astra. "How do you do it?"

"Do what?"

"You and Benjamin. Having done this job and dealing with the people we deal with on a daily basis, how did you let yourself be open to him? How did you learn to trust him?"

Astra shook her head. "I just did. There came a point where I decided that I was tired of the cheap one-night stands and crappy situationships. I wanted something real, a foundation, something I could rely on. There's no manual or how-to guide, Blake. You just have to do it. You have to decide you don't want to be alone anymore and just … let somebody in."

"Easier said than done."

"It's actually not. It's a choice. Just as shutting everybody out and keeping them at an arm's distance is a choice," she says pointedly.

It's a fair point, but honestly, I've been so closed off for so long, I fear I wouldn't be able to open that door even if I wanted to.

"Think about it. Good guys don't come around all that often, and Sonny, underneath all that swagger, seems like a decent guy," Astra says. "And I think on some level, you must think so, too, since you slept with him."

The door to my office opens, and Nina sticks her head in. She tucks the bubble gum pink stripe in her otherwise dark hair behind her ear and smiles.

"Your appointment is here," she says.

I quickly glance at the files on my desk. They're so scattered, I don't even remember who we're meeting with this morning.

"Opal Rivers," Nina says as I find the file.

I take a quick moment to scan through it, absorbing as much as I can, then nod. "Great. Can you show her in? Thank you, Nina."

"You got it."

Astra turns to me. "Any early standouts in the race for this job?"

"None. Not a one of them has impressed me yet. You?"

"I kind of liked that guy, Brent."

"That's just because he laughed at your jokes," I reply.

"That is an important part of the job."

I chuckle as the door opens again. A woman a few inches shorter than my five-nine frame strides in, her gait quick and efficient. She's got an almost military-like demeanor. Her obsidian-colored hair is in a tight bun, and her hazel-gray eyes are sharp, flicking around my office quickly as she sizes it—and me—up. I suddenly realize she's interviewing me as much as I'm interviewing her. Opal's complexion is warm, giving her a vaguely exotic look which I'm sure is from her mother, who is Middle Eastern.

Standing up, I lean across my desk and extend my hand. "Unit Chief Blake Wilder," I say. "This is SSA Astra Russo, my number two."

"Pleasure to meet you both," Opal replies as she shakes Astra's hand.

"Please, have a seat," I say.

She sits down just as briskly as she walks, her hands folded in her lap, her back ramrod straight. I retake my seat and stare at her for a moment.

"Deputy Director Church recommends you highly," I start.

"I have a lot of respect for her," Opal replies. "I didn't work with her directly, but our paths crossed often at HQ."

Opal's voice is clipped, her tone curt. Everything about the woman from the way she walks to the way she talks seems designed for maximum efficiency. She's almost like a droid. I can see why they love her back in DC.

"You have a degree in Criminology from Florida State and a Masters in the same from Miami," I read from her file. "After a stint with the Miami PD, you went to Quantico—"

"I worked as a field agent for several years at my first post in San Antonio. After that, I headed up the resident office in Flagstaff, Arizona, overseeing an office of three other agents. After that, I worked as legal attaché in Vancouver where I oversaw an office of five," she cuts me off. "But all this is in my file, which, given your reputation for thoroughness and detail, you've no doubt read several times already. So, we can skip the bona fides and cut straight to the real questions you want to ask."

Astra and I exchange a look. The corners of her mouth are flickering upward in a smile she's desperately trying to suppress. Opal Rivers is blunt. Direct. And unafraid to speak her mind. She's got a no-nonsense demeanor, and judging by the things DD Church has told me, is loyal to a fault. All admirable qualities, to be sure.

"All right," I say. "I see a marked shift in your resume from field work to administrative duties. And yet, I see nothing that indicates you want to climb the ladder within the Bureau hierarchy. You're not on an upper management track. Why is that?"

"Because I don't care for the ladder-climbing and think that I'm more useful in an administrative capacity," she replies.

My chair squeaks softly as I lean back. Opal is returning my gaze, unflinchingly, but there's more to the story than what she's saying. She obviously doesn't understand that I'm well aware of why she removed herself from fieldwork. I lean forward again.

"And did the situation in Flagstaff have anything to do with that?" I ask.

Her cheeks redden slightly, and her face tightens as the memory of that day, no doubt, flashes through her mind. I get the sense it's never too far from her conscious thoughts. Enduring trauma has a way of sticking with us. To her credit, she doesn't run from the truth and gives me a curt nod.

"It has everything to do with it," she replies. "I was forced into a position where I had to take the lives of two young men. It wasn't an agreeable experience, and not one I care to repeat, if it can be avoided."

"You were cleared of any wrongdoing," Astra notes. "Not only that, you received a commendation for your actions that day. You saved the lives of two other agents."

"Be that as it may, two young men lost their lives at my hands. My soul is already burdened by that, and I have no wish to add to it," she replies. "Those of us who work behind the scenes, doing the administrative work, have just as much value to the Bureau as those of you who are out there kicking doors in."

She's not wrong. We need administrative support to do our job effectively. There just aren't many agents I've met who don't pine for some action. But then, I suppose having to kill a nineteen-year-old and an eighteen-year-old would dull the shine off that desire for excitement. Everything I read says that Opal's actions were justified. If she hadn't acted when—and how—she did, two agents would most assuredly have lost their lives. But I also understand the lasting mental and emotional trauma she's suffered in the aftermath.

"And do you understand what this job entails?" I ask.

"My understanding is that you're seeking a case manager to triage incoming cases and requests for assistance as well as liaise with personnel from other agencies," she says. "Having been a Legat in Vancouver, I've got extensive experience as a liaison, having often coordinated Bureau resources with the RCMP and other Canadian agencies."

That's a big plus and experience the other candidates we've talked to didn't have. But I also need to ensure whoever becomes our case manager will be a good fit with the team. Culture and morale around here are everything to me. As if picking up on my thoughts, Astra turns to Opal.

"Our unit is a bit different. We're a little unorthodox," she says. "We—"

A small smile creases Opal's thin, bow-shaped lips. "I've heard the stories. But I also know that your team is highly effective and has closed some major cases. People in DC speak about your team almost reverently. Some people, anyway," she amends.

"And do you think you can fit in with our more… relaxed atmosphere?" I ask.

"I do," she replies.

"Why do you want to be part of this team specifically?" Astra asks.

"I think I can be an asset to your team," she replies. "And I would like to be part of a team that's making a real difference in the world. Even if my capacity is behind-the-scenes support, I'd like to do my part to make this world a little safer by working on the cases your team takes on and goes after: the worst of the worst."

I'm skeptical. She seems pretty rigid, and I'm not sure she'd react favorably to how loose we are around here. I have doubts that she'd be a good fit culture-wise. But she's got an impressive resume, has all the skills I'm looking for, and checks all the boxes. She's head and shoulders above the other candidates we've interviewed.

Astra glances at me, and the downward curl of her lips makes me think she's having the same thoughts I am. Leaning back in my chair again, I look to the bullpen beyond the window and watch as the team laughs and jokes around with one another, reinforcing my initial sense and stressing the importance of the family we've built. But we didn't start this way. At first, I was a little resentful and felt like Rick and Mo had been foisted upon me. In those early days, Mo was just as rigid and unyielding as Opal seems to be. Now, they're integral parts of our team… of our family.

"All right. I think I've heard enough. Your office will be the last one on the left," I say. "When do you think you can be ready to start?"

"I can be ready to start whenever you need me, ma'am. The home office already knows I'm looking to transfer. My superior said he'll expedite it."

"It's just Blake. Please," I reply. "We don't stand on formality here."

She nods but seems clearly uncomfortable with the lack of pomp and circumstance. But she seems willing to give it a try. We all get to our feet and shake hands. I'm a bit uneasy and fear I'm trying to jam a square peg into a round hole. But if Mo can come from a stiff, rigid, white-collar background and fit in with us like she's been here all along, perhaps Opal can too.

"Terrific. Then we'll see you soon, Opal."

CHAPTER FOUR

The Chapel Bullpen, SNAP team HQ, Industrial District; Seattle, WA

"ALL RIGHT, LISTEN UP," I SAY AS I STEP TO THE TABLE in the bullpen.

The conversations stop, and everybody turns to me and Opal, who is standing beside me.

"This is Opal Rivers, and she is going to be our new case manager. She comes to us highly recommended by DD Church as well as the folks at DC HQ," I introduce her. "She brings a wealth of experience including heading up a resident office and as the Legat of the Vancouver resident office. Give her a warm welcome."

Everybody welcomes Opal, properly introducing themselves and getting acquainted with the woman who will be in charge of scheduling our lives from now on. Or at least, she'll have a big hand in scheduling our lives from now on. Opal is smart, well put together, and organized, and I'm hoping she'll have as good a feel for how to prioritize our case load and where to send us as I think she will. I'd rather not have to exercise my veto power since that could lead to some awkward and tense situations.

I'm sure Astra and Dr. Azar would say this is just my Type-A, control-freak nature speaking, but I do retain final approval privileges on whatever cases she assigns us to. It's my team and my reputation on the line, so it's ultimately my decision. But I'm hoping she'll deploy our resources wisely enough that I won't have to intervene much, if at all. I mean, that was the point of hiring her in the first place—so I can take the administrative work off my plate and simply focus on, as Opal says, getting out on the streets and kicking in doors.

As Opal is introducing herself and the team is welcoming her into the fold, the buzzer sounds shrilly, drawing my attention to the security monitors. My heart stutters, then beats in a drunken rhythm when I see Sonny at the front gate.

Her eyes on the monitors as well, Astra leans close to me, a wicked smile on her lips. "Oh Romeo, Romeo, wherefore art thou—"

"Shut it," I say.

I walk over to the console and press the button that opens the front gate, then watch as he drives through. My mouth is bone dry, but I have to blot my palms on my slacks. We haven't spoken since I slunk out of his hotel room the other morning, and seeing him at the gates makes me feel all kinds of awkward and tense.

"This is going to be fun," Astra whispers.

"Don't make me shoot you."

When he parks and walks to the front door, I hit the button that unlocks it, allowing him in. Sonny strides into the room, offering everybody a smile with his usual disposition, which is pretty accurately reflected by his name. But when he gets to me, that sunny disposition suddenly clouds over, and a frown flickers across his lips.

"Chief Wilder," he says, his tone icy.

"Agent Garland," I reply. "Opal, this is DEA Agent Sonny Garland. We recently collaborated on a case with him down in Arizona. Agent Garland, this is Special Agent Opal Rivers; she is our new case manager and liaison."

"Good to meet you, Agent Rivers," he drawls.

"Good to meet you too, Agent Garland—"

"Sonny, is fine."

"What was the case you all collaborated on?"

"Drugs. We had a motorcycle club moving product into the prisons for the Arias Cartel," he says. "These fine folks helped my team smash that connect. Unfortunately, a rival MC has risen up to take their place."

"Sounds like you're playing a game of whack-a-mole," Paige says.

Sonny chuckles. "That pretty much sums it up."

"What do we have on this rival MC?" I ask.

"The Road Prophets—they're a little more hardcore than the last club. Better organized," he replies without looking at me. "Most of their membership were in the military, they're heavily armed, and they will shed blood without thinking twice about it."

"They sound like a lot of fun," Astra says.

"Life of the party types," he says. "They're violent—but even worse—they're smart. Very smart. The club president, Rico Nagy, is a former Army major. He did almost twenty years in the service but was believed to be running a smuggling ring—"

"What was he smuggling?" Astra asks.

"Artifacts mostly, out of Iraq and Afghanistan. Some pallets of cash also went missing under his watch. The Army couldn't definitively tie him to any of it, of course, so they couldn't prosecute. They did have enough to discharge him—albeit honorably," he tells us. "After being mustered out, Nagy came home to Tucson and founded the club. He attracted a lot of disgruntled veterans, and it wasn't long before they ruled Tucson and started to branch out. They ate up territory, and after some bloody fighting, took over Phoenix as well. Now, they're running drugs, guns, and girls for the Ariases."

"Wow. Why didn't the cartel just start working with these guys in the first place? Sounds like their product would have been in better hands," Mo says.

"Probably because they were trying to keep a low profile. At first, anyway," Sonny answers. "I guess now, they figure they're already on our radar, so they don't care as much. Now, they're working with the group that will be able to protect their product better."

"Is this all confirmed?" I ask.

"If you count the two agents who turned up dead this morning after they'd been tasked with shadowing the Ariases' new business partners as confirmation, then yeah. It's corroborated."

"I'm sorry for your loss," I say sincerely.

"Yeah. Me too."

The DEA has been getting hit hard in their war against the cartels lately, and it's understandable that Sonny's mood is a little brittle at the moment.

"Anyway, my bosses want me to work with you all to put together an op to take down the Road Prophets," he tells us. "And if there's any way we can blow a hole in the Ariases' operations here stateside, they'd like to do that too. What can we do about gettin' that done?"

I perch on the corner of the table and frown. "Blowing up the Road Prophets is going to be a lot easier than taking out the cartel, simply because they're based across the border. I'm not sure we're even going to be able to put much of a dent in their operations. Not without significant assistance from the Mexican government."

"And with relations between their government and our government being what they are, we shouldn't count on much help there," Astra notes.

"There has to be a way. They've taken out five of my agents in the last year—four of them in the last two months," Sonny drawls. "We can't let them get away with this."

"We won't. But we need to be smart about how we go after them," I tell him. "If we go in half-cocked and without a coherent game plan, we'll just up their body count."

Sonny sits back in his chair and glowers, grumbling to himself. I understand his frustration. What it feels like when you lose your people. All you want is to go right at the people who took them from you head on. There will be no convincing him, but I'm right. The Arias brothers are sophisticated, smart, and ruthless—even more so than other cartel bosses we've gone after. Other cartel bosses might hesitate slightly when it comes to taking out a federal agent, not wanting the heat that comes with it. But the Ariases do not hesitate to kill, be they federal agents or not.

Opal turns to me. "I'm going to need a couple of days to dig through all the relevant case files and get up to speed—"

I shake my head. "This op predates you, so we're going to work on this. But if you could start going through the rest of the files on your desk and triaging those, that would be great."

Opal frowns, clearly not happy to have the decision taken out of her hands, and I can see already there might be some issues moving forward, which makes me a little uneasy. She is clearly as much of a control freak as I am, which might lead to us butting heads. While I want somebody in that position who takes charge, isn't afraid to speak their mind, and is willing to give it to me straight, I also need somebody who knows when to back off. Time will tell if Opal is or can be that person, I guess. We just need to get a feel for each other's rhythm and how we handle our business.

Before I can say something to smooth out any ruffled feathers, my phone buzzes in my pocket. I pull it out and frown, not recognizing the number. That's nothing new, so I connect the call and hold the phone to my ear.

"Blake Wilder."

As I listen to the voice on the other end of the line, I feel myself growing paler, and my heart sinks with every word he speaks.

"I'll be right there."

I disconnect the call and drop the phone into my pocket, then look up as I try to clear my head. Everybody is looking at me curiously.

"I have to go," I say.

CHAPTER FIVE

Mountainview Medical Center, Downtown District; Seattle, WA

I FIND MY WAY UP TO THE CRITICAL CARE UNIT AND BADGE MY way by the hospital's security guard at the door. The overhead fluorescent lighting gleams off the stark white walls and tile, and the air in the corridor is thick with the smell of antiseptics. My boots echo hollowly off the floor, each footstep sounding like an explosion in the otherwise silent ward.

After a couple of wrong turns, I finally arrive at room four-thirty-two. Two large men I recognize, Ling and Hui, a couple of Fish's loyal foot soldiers, flank the door. Their faces are drawn and pale, their eyes filled with fear and worry, which sets my heart racing. Ling's lips tighten, a slash across his face, and he gives me a nod as he opens the door for me.

"Thank you," I say softly.

Ling closes the door behind me as I step into the private room, and I gasp at what I see. A single lamp on the nightstand burns, leaving most of the room around me cloaked in shadow. In the soft glow cast off by the lamp, I see Fish lying beneath the thin blanket on the bed. A large, thick bandage is wrapped around his head, and he's hooked up to a battery of machines that are keeping him alive. He's been intubated, and the machine beside the bed is pumping up and down with a mechanical hiss that reminds me of Darth Vader. His body bristles with what seems like a thousand tubes and wires, and he looks frail and small lying in the bed.

"My God. Who did this to you?" I whisper.

Stepping to the side of the bed, I take his hand in mine and give it a squeeze, hoping that he can feel me. Hoping that he knows I'm here with him and that I can somehow not just reach him, wherever he is, but encourage him to come back.

"I'm so sorry," I say quietly. "I'm so sorry this happened to you."

Tears slip from my eyes and race down my cheeks as my emotions overwhelm me. Fish, otherwise known as Huan Zhao, isn't a large man. But he's got such a flamboyant personality and carries himself with such confidence, he always seems larger than life. In a way, he's always somehow seemed… immortal. But seeing him lying in the bed, barely clinging to life, is a stark reminder of his mortality. And the mere thought of him passing—of not having him be the regular fixture in my life he's been for years now—is almost too much to bear.

Our relationship is… complex. The crime boss and the FBI agent. That's all most anybody sees. That's all most people will ever consider him—even now that he's gone legit, for the most part, and actually serves on Seattle's city council. But he's far more layered than anybody knows, and as I've gotten to know him over the years, I've seen so many different facets to him. He's become family to me. In some ways, he's become a surrogate father figure.

It's strange, yes. But at his core, Fish is a good man. One of the best I've ever known.

Most people will never understand him or this relationship we have. My relationship with him has led some people to assume that I'm corrupt myself—that I'm in the pocket of one of Seattle's most notorious crime bosses. My relationship with Fish has been the subject of much gossip and consternation within the Bureau and yet, despite the fact that it's been investigated to death and not even the barest hint of impropriety has ever been found, those people will forever continue to think I'm all mobbed up.

I stopped caring what people thought a long time ago. Like I said, Fish is one of the best people I've ever met, and that is most definitely a hill I'm willing to die on. I would say he's reformed and turned his life around, but moving out of the shadows and going legit has always been his master plan. He simply had to accrue a fortune and bring much-needed stability to Seattle's underworld before he was able to do it. He finally did it. When he was elected to the city council and was embraced by most within the community, he officially conquered that mountain. And now that he's at the summit, somebody gunned him down for his efforts.

The door behind me opens, and Trevor Kondo steps to the side of the bed beside me. Neither of us say anything for a long moment, letting the weight of the moment settle down on our shoulders and in our hearts. Trevor and I are cordial, but our relationship has always been frosty. He doesn't like the fact that I'm law enforcement—he's naturally predisposed to see me as the enemy. I don't begrudge him that. I understand. He is a criminal, after all, and asking him to like me is like asking cats and dogs to get along. But beyond that, I've always gotten the feeling he resents how close Fish and I are. It's like he's jealous.

I've always thought it was silly. His place in Fish's world is unquestioned. Trevor is his right-hand man, but in truth, he's more than that. Fish found Trevor, an orphan living alone on the streets, and took him in. He essentially raised him, put him through school, and showed him the ropes of his burgeoning business. Fish has always treated Trevor more like his son than anything. Trevor has been with Fish for a long time and is always by his side.

After finishing his education, Trevor was there, running Fish's underground casinos, working as an enforcer, or doing whatever was required as they built Fish's criminal empire. Whenever Fish does finally remove himself from the darker side of Seattle's underworld, it's expected that Trevor will take up the reins. I just hope when that day comes, he runs it with the same integrity and honor Fish always has. It's another strange thing for me to say given the businesses they dabble in. But it's true.

"Thank you for calling me," I finally say.

"Of course," he replies. "I figured you would want to be here."

"What happened?" I ask.

"It was a drive by," Trevor replies, his tone somber. "He was coming home after a city council meeting, and his driver had just dropped him in front of his building when somebody cruised by and opened up. I don't know more than that right now."

"His injuries?"

"He caught two rounds in the chest, one in the abdomen, and one in the head. That is the one that is most worrying. The doctor says the bullet caused massive swelling and bleeding in the brain," he tells me, his voice curt and precise. "They say they have done what they can, but they are not sure he will ever wake up. They say it's up to him now."

"He'll wake up," I say, my voice thick with emotion. "He has to wake up."

Trevor says nothing. I take a moment to slow my heart and try to clear my mind. Right now, I need to focus. There's no question in my mind that I'm going to hunt down the person or persons who did this to Fish, and to do that, I'm going to need a clear head.

"Do you have any suspects?" I ask, knowing his information will probably be better than anything the SPD can provide.

"Take your pick," Trevor replies dryly. "You know as well as I do that he's got a list of enemies longer than your arm."

"But why now? Why did they pick *now* to pull the trigger?"

He shakes his head. "His mind has not been on his businesses—his real businesses—as I am certain you are aware, since it is at your encouragement. He has been more focused on his other business projects as well as his agenda with the damn city council."

I turn to him, my jaw clenched. "Why do I get the feeling you're blaming me?"

"I am not blaming you, Agent Wilder," he says, using my title like an epithet. "I am just saying, once you came into his life, he became almost obsessed with going legit."

"I think that plan was in place long before he met me."

"If it was, he never mentioned it to me."

It's abundantly clear that Trevor blames me for the fact that Fish is lying in this bed connected to all these machines, barely clinging to life. I obviously disagree with his assessment of the situation—vehemently—but this is neither the time nor the place to have that argument. This isn't about us. It's about one thing and one thing only: Fish, and finding the person or persons who did this to him. That's it. That's all that matters right now. That's all I care about.

"All right, so nobody stands out to you right now?" I ask.

He shakes his head. "No. Not right now."

"Has Fish had problems with anybody recently? Any threats?"

"No. Nothing unusual. And I would have heard something," he says.

"Maybe. But then, maybe not."

Trevor's face softens. "Listen, I know what Fish means to you. He means just as much to me," he says. "But let me handle this. I will find the—"

I shake my head. "Absolutely not. Bloodshed and chaos are not what Fish would want. Most definitely not in his name when he spent so long and sacrificed so much to put order to the chaos."

"How can you presume to tell me what he wants?"

"I know what he wants because he told me what he wants," I respond. "And what he wants is peace and order within the community. He wouldn't want you to destroy that."

Trevor glowers at me, then turns away, his face etched with anger. The attack on Fish is affecting him deeply—I can see that. It's affecting me deeply too. But the answer to this senseless violence is not with more senseless violence. It would be a betrayal of everything Fish has worked so hard to build and every sacrifice he's made. Fish deserves better than that.

"I will find the person who did this," I tell Trevor. "I give you my word."

Trevor says nothing. He doesn't even look at me. I turn back to Fish and feel my heart fracturing as I look at him. I've never seen him look so weak or vulnerable in all the years I've known him, and it's gut-wrenching. Reaching out, I take his hand again and give it a squeeze.

"I'll find them. I promise you I'll find them," I vow.

CHAPTER SIX

The Emerald Lounge, Downtown District; Seattle, WA

THE SLOW, SOMBER RHYTHM AND NOTES OF THE SONG THE band onstage is playing fit perfectly with my mood right now. Makes me think coming here for a drink to take the edge off was the right decision. After leaving the hospital, I briefly considered going back to the Chapel, but I wasn't going to do anybody any good there. My head and heart just aren't in the work right now.

I'm not deluding myself about him. I know exactly who and what Fish is and what he's done in his life. He's certainly nowhere close to being an angel, but he's not nearly the monster some make him out to be. And he's never been anything but good to me. He's looked out for me when I wasn't looking out for myself. There aren't many people in my life who've had my back the way Fish has. He's always there without hesitation and never asks me for anything in return.

Having grown up without a father figure in my life, it's not hyperbole to say that's the space Fish came to occupy in my life. That's why seeing him lying in that bed, hovering on the edge of death, has stirred up all those unresolved emotions surrounding the murder of my parents I'm apparently still carrying all over again.

I drain the last of my scotch and am just about to signal for another when Astra slides into my booth and sets a fresh glass down in front of me.

"Your timing is impeccable," I say.

"It always is."

I raise my glass to her, and Astra taps hers against it, the sharp ping of our glasses meeting ringing in my ears. We take a sip and sit, listening to the music for a couple of minutes before Astra turns back to me.

"I thought I might find you here," she starts.

"I'm predictable."

"Sometimes," she says. "When you don't return my calls or texts, the odds of you being down here throwing a few back is pretty high."

I take another sip of my scotch and stare into the deep, amber liquid. "It's Fish—"

"I heard already," she says gently. "Are you okay?"

I shrug. "I'm better off than he is."

"What's the word on his condition?"

"He's in a coma. Right now, it's just wait and see."

"I'm sorry, Blake. I know what he means to you."

"Thanks, Astra. And thanks for coming down, but I think right now I just need—"

"No. You don't need to be alone right now."

I sit back in the booth and cup my glass between my hands. "You should go home and spend some time with Benjamin. I know he doesn't see enough of you."

Astra chuckles. "He's out of town at some architectural conference. Try again."

"I'm not good company tonight."

"Are you ever? I mean really?"

Despite my sour mood, a laugh bursts from my mouth. "You're awful."

"Hi, have we met?" she replies. "You know you love that about me."

"Yeah, maybe so."

"So, since you have no valid excuses, it looks like you're stuck with me tonight whether you like it or not," she says. "Therefore, I say we tie one on and get ourselves good and schwasted."

"As good as that sounds, I have to get my head on straight and go back to the office tomorrow. I'd rather do it without a hangover."

"Party pooper."

The corners of my mouth flicker upward, but the melancholy that's gripping me swallows the good humor Astra was able to summon in me. I run a hand over my face and do my best to pull myself together. If I'm going to find the person who tried to murder Fish, I need to be at my best. Fish deserves no less.

"How did things go at the office after I left?" I ask.

"Fine. More or less."

"More or less?"

"Sonny tried to take over. He's anxious to get us down to Arizona to work on his problem," she replies. "But Opal wasn't having it and put him in his place, reminding him that our task force isn't required to do his bidding and that she's got a stack of requests for assistance three feet high on her desk. She's fiery. I like her."

I grimace. "How did he take it?"

"About as well as you'd expect."

"Stormed out of the building, huh?"

"Bingo."

I sigh and rest my head in my hands. "I'm going to have to call him."

"You really should," she says. "When I said you shouldn't be alone tonight, I didn't mean you had to be with me."

"Yeah, we're not going there."

Astra smirks. "Can't blame a girl for trying."

"I think the fact that he throws temper tantrums when he doesn't get his way is a big red flag. I'm not interested in being with somebody like that."

"I wouldn't say he had a temper tantrum. And honestly, I can understand why he's so anxious to get this started… his people are being killed," Astra replies. "If you were in his place, you'd do the same thing if your people were being killed. I mean, look at what you're doing right now for Fish. It's kind of the same thing."

I take a sip of my drink, letting it roll around on my tongue as Astra's words bounce around in my mind. She's not wrong. I'm ready to burn down everything to find Fish's attacker. I guess it really is no different from Sonny wanting to do the same to get some justice for his team. Put in that light, I get it. I suppose I can't hold his outburst at the Chapel against him.

"Sure, but it doesn't make getting together with him any better of an idea," I say.

"If you're really going to shut him out, you should at least be honest about your reasons for doing so instead of hiding behind artificial excuses."

"How is it not being a good idea an artificial excuse?"

"Because the real reason you aren't opening up to him is that you're scared."

"I'm not scared."

She grins. "You can't lie to me. You haven't been with somebody in a long time because you're scared. Plain and simple."

A wry expression crosses my face. "If that's true, and I'm not saying it is, could you blame me? The last man I was truly with was spying on me. Not only that, he tried to kill me."

"I hear you. And that was… unfortunate."

"That's one way to put it."

"But one bad experience—even one as horrible and traumatic as that—shouldn't dictate the rest of your life. You shouldn't let it shut you down forever," she says. "I have a feeling that if you were working as a counselor, you would tell your patients the same thing. So, maybe you should take some of your own hypothetical advice."

"Hypothetical advice, huh?"

"Physician, heal thyself."

"Well, I'm not a physician."

"In my hypothetical, you are."

"I see," I reply, and we share a laugh.

"At least, think about what I've said," Astra adds. "I really think it's important that, even if it's not with Sonny, that you allow yourself the freedom to open your heart. I think it will benefit your life in ways you can't even conceive of right now."

"I will. I'll think about what you said," I promise.

"Good. I hope you do."

Like Dr. Azar, Astra makes some really good points that allow me to see things in ways I haven't allowed myself to consider before. It's not always what I want to hear, but it's important that I hear these things all the same.

"I really am sorry about Fish," she says softly.

"Thanks, Astra."

"Whatever you need from me, I'm in. One hundred percent," she says. "We are going to get the people responsible for this."

I raise my glass, and she taps her against mine. "Yes, we are."

CHAPTER SEVEN

The Chapel, SNAP Team HQ, Industrial District; Seattle, WA

"I WANT TO APOLOGIZE FOR LEAVING SO ABRUPTLY yesterday," I say. "As I'm sure you've all heard, Fish was injured in a drive by shooting."

The looks on the faces of everybody around the table tell me they all already know. Opal is the only one who seems to be out of the loop. Maybe once she's become more integrated into the group, we'll talk about it. Or maybe she'll just pick it up through osmosis. She doesn't need to know the details of my relationship with him right now.

"How is he doing?" Paige asks.

"No change," I reply.

"I'll say a prayer for him," Nina says.

"Thank you," I respond. "But right now, the best thing we can do is get to work."

Before I can add anything to that, Opal raises her hand and motions to the three files sitting on the table in front of her.

"On that note, I've identified three cases that should be a high priority for us," she says.

"I appreciate you diving in like that, but right now, our only priority is finding out who shot Fish and bringing them in," I tell her.

"All due respect, Chief Wilder, but my understanding is that the Seattle PD is on that case, and as far as I know, they've not invited us in," Opal says.

"Not yet. But they will."

"Until they do, I think it would be a better use of our time and resources to focus on cases we've actually received requests for help with," she replies. "To that end, we have a possible serial killer in Los Angeles, a series of child abductions in Cincinnati, and a high-end robbery crew operating in Miami—"

"I appreciate your diligence, Opal. But let's put a pin in those cases for the moment," I say. "We will revisit them once we've found the person or persons who attacked Fish."

Opal's lips curl down, and her face tightens. "With all due respect, Chief, you brought me in to triage cases and deploy our resources efficiently. I hardly think working a case the SPD is handling and hasn't invited us in on is doing that."

"I understand where you're coming from—"

"And I understand this is personal. I don't know this Fish character, but I get that he means something to you, which is all the more reason it is a bad idea to force your way into this case and instead, focus on the cases we can actually assist with. I am certain if the SPD requires help, they will come knocking on our door."

"Opal—"

"Isn't this why you hired me, Chief? To efficiently direct resources?"

"Yes. It is," I say, my voice low and hard. "But I also told you there would be times when we needed to handle something outside the caseload on your desk. Did I not?"

The tension in the bullpen is palpable, and everybody else seems to be looking anywhere but at the two of us. I understand that Opal is trying to mark her territory—trying to be assertive and carve out her place in the chain here. And I respect that. But right now, I don't have the time, nor am I in the mood for it.

"I appreciate your diligence, Opal. But as the chief of this unit, I have final say," I tell her. "And right now, I am saying this case is our top priority."

Opal opens her mouth as if to argue but quickly closes it again and lowers her gaze to the top of the table in front of her. I sigh. Pulling rank isn't usually my style, and I do everything in my power to avoid it. I find it tacky. But Opal seems to respect the chain of command. She obviously doesn't agree with my decision, but she's not going to rock the boat too hard.

Astra catches my eye and subtly motions toward my office, silently telling me she wants to talk. She's obviously going to take issue with my demeanor but doesn't want to cut me off at the knees in front of the rest of the team.

"Excuse me," I say.

I turn and walk to my office and a moment later, Astra comes in and closes the door behind her. As I perch on the corner of my desk, she braces herself on the back of the chair in front of me and leans forward. I can already tell by the look on her face that I'm not going to like what she has to say. Or perhaps that's my own guilt about lashing Opal in front of everybody talking.

"You didn't have to neuter her in front of the team," she begins.

"I didn't mean to neuter her. I'm just not in the mood, nor do I feel like justifying myself to somebody I hired like five minutes ago."

"To be fair, you hired her to do exactly what she's doing. She wasn't wrong about that."

I pinch the bridge of my nose, trying to stave off the dull thud behind my eyes. Astra's not wrong. Neither was Opal. And as loath as I am to admit it, this case being so personal is clouding my judgment and leading me to make rash-slash-bad decisions.

"You seem to have a plan in mind," I say.

"I do."

"Let's hear it."

"Of the cases she triaged, the child abductions in Cincinnati are the most worrisome and should be addressed immediately," she says.

Crossing one ankle over the other, I look down at the tops of my boots. Whenever we have a case involving children, we pretty much drop whatever we're doing and handle that. And she's right. This shouldn't be any different. I push my hair back and let out a loud breath.

"All right. You're right," I admit. "Both you and Opal are right about letting this get too personal for me. I'm making some bad decisions."

"You're making emotional decisions, which is understandable, given what happened. But I do recall you telling us that we need to separate the emotions from the job. On more than one occasion, actually."

I glance at her with a wry twist of my lips. "Thanks for throwing my words back in my face."

"Hey, you can always count on me."

"Yeah, I know I can," I respond.

"So? Should we prep the team for a trip to Cincinnati?"

"*You* need to prep the team for a trip to Cincinnati," I tell her.

"Blake, what did we just say about emotional decisions?"

"This one is clear-headed. You are right: we need to get on the child abductions right away. And I want you to lead the team," I reply. "I'm going to stay behind and work on Fish's case. I'm also going to nab Nina since I might need some tech expertise."

Astra purses her lips. "You sure about this?"

"About you leading the team? I have some doubts, but I'm reasonably sure you can do it. If not, you'll have Paige there to back you up."

She laughs and gives me the finger. "You're a jerk."

"Yeah, but that's why you love me."

"You're lucky I do," she says, then grows serious. "Are you sure about this? I mean, we can go handle what's out in Cincinnati then come back and hopefully, the SPD—"

"I have little to no faith in the SPD. You know that. I'm going to work the case and get ahead of them," I tell her. "I'm going to find out who did this to Fish."

Astra holds my gaze for a moment then nods. "All right. But how are you going to get onto the case? I don't see the SPD welcoming you with open arms."

"I'll find a way."

The door to my office opens, and Paige sticks her head in. "Chief, Agent Garland is here."

I roll my eyes and let out another long breath. "Wonderful," I mutter. "Okay, send him in. Thank you, Paige."

"You got it."

Astra gets to her feet and gives me a lopsided grin. "I've got a team to prep, so I'm going to give you two a little alone time."

"Don't say it like that."

"Like what?" she responds innocently.

Sonny comes through the door and gives Astra a nod. She scoots out and closes the door behind her, leaving me alone with him. The air in my office is instantly thick with the weight of unspoken words and emotions. I can't deny that I'm attracted to Sonny. I like him. But having given it some thought, I realize that Astra is right… I'm scared. Just the idea of opening up to somebody and trusting them again terrifies me. And I just don't know that I have it in me to get over it and try again.

"Hey," he says, finally breaking the awkward silence.

"Hey."

"Paige told me about your friend. I'm sorry."

"Thanks."

He leans against the chair Astra had just been leaning against, his icy blue eyes fixed on mine. I swallow hard and remain perched on the corner of my desk trying to figure out how or where to start. It strikes me, not for the first time, that I'm absolutely awful when it comes to relationships.

"Anyway, I wanted to talk to you about finishing putting together the op we started and getting your team down to Arizona," he says.

And just like that, he switches into business mode, the moment for anything more out the window. At least this is footing I'm more comfortable on.

"Right," I say. "We're going to need to put a pin in that for the moment."

"What are you talking about?" He stands up straighter, his jaw flexing as he grits his teeth. "Blake, you told me you were going to help. I've got agents being murdered, and we need some help—help you promised you'd give me."

"And we *will* help you. I give you my word. But right now, my team has a child abduction case in Ohio that I'm assigning them to. Children take precedence," I tell him.

"Assigning to them," he says. "And what are you going to do?"

"I'm going to work on Fish's case," I reply, unable to keep the emotion out of my voice.

Sonny's face softens, and he runs a hand through his hair. He turns and looks out my window for a long moment, a thoughtful expression on his face.

"Look, I'm sorry," he says as he turns back to me. "I know I'm letting this case get to me personally. I don't mean to take it out on you."

"Yeah, well, there's a lot of that going around."

"I don't mean to demand that you drop everything to help us. I understand why you'd prioritize abducted children over my case. It's more pressing. I get it," he says. "And I don't know much about your relationship with this Fish guy, but I understand he means a lot to you. I can see it all over your face."

"I guess we're in the same boat."

"I guess we are."

"Unfortunately," I say.

"I also can't help but think this thing between us isn't making any of this any easier."

"Probably not."

"Look, Blake, I like you. I've been pretty clear about that."

"You have."

"I'm sorry if I'm letting those feelings get in the way of the work," he says. "I give you my word that I'll do my best to not let them get in the way anymore."

I want to tell him that his feelings are reciprocated—that I want to see him too. I want to tell Sonny not to give up on me and to just give me a little time and space to get this all worked out in my head, and that once I get my head back on straight, maybe we can work on having something together. Part of me wants to tell him all of that. But when I open my mouth, the words get stuck in my throat. The fear inside of me rises up and swallows them all.

"I appreciate that," is what falls out of my mouth.

A hit of disappointment crosses his face, but he nods, seeming to understand that I'm emotionally... stunted.

"When your team is back and you're finished with this case, I hope we can finish working on our op," he says. "I'd really like to get the animals who killed my people."

"I understand. And we'll get them. I promise you."

He hesitates, then says, "And maybe once we close that case out down there, we can go grab a drink so we can... talk."

"I agree... we probably do need to talk about things."

He looks uncertain but hopeful. And strangely enough, that's where I find myself right now. It's an unexpected feeling but not entirely unwelcome. I have no idea where those thoughts and feelings came from—maybe Dr. Azar and Astra's words are finally sinking in. But as I look into Sonny's crystalline blue eyes, I know they're true.

"I'm going to hold you to that," he says.

My lips curl upward. "It's a date."

CHAPTER EIGHT

Seattle PD, Homicide Division, Precinct W, Queen Anne District; Seattle, WA

After seeing Astra and the team off at the airport, I return to the Chapel. Opal is in her office with the door closed. She doesn't come out while I'm in the office, making the subtext clear: leave me alone. I make a mental note to have a sit down with her once this is all over. I need to clear the air and apologize for berating her in front of the team. The more time I've had to reflect on it, the worse I feel.

But that is something I'll have to do later. Right now, I've got bigger things to worry about. My only purpose in going back to the office is to brief Nina about what we're doing and to get the name of the detective assigned to Fish's case. This task takes her all of about thirty seconds to find—something I probably would have spent all day trying to figure out. When she tells me the name of the detective assigned to the case, I am less than thrilled.

Detective Scott Kramer is, by some accounts, a good cop. Most say he's smart, intuitive, and a dedicated, talented investigator. While all that may be true, my own experience with him, although limited, is that he's less than stellar. Suffice it to say, the handful of times I've dealt with Detective Kramer have left a lingering, sour taste in my mouth. I do know not everybody shares the golden boy image he's worked hard to cultivate. Some of the rank and file have said in confidence they think he's a glory hound who chases the spotlight. I've seen nothing that refutes that observation.

But if working with him helps me take down Fish's attacker, so be it. I'll have to swallow my opinion of him and focus on the work rather than on the personality of the person I have to deal with. We don't always like those we're stuck working with. I'm pretty sure it's a sentiment Opal would agree with right about now.

After badging my way through the front office, I make my way up to the third floor of the large, brick and glass structure that houses Seattle PD's precinct in the relatively posh Queen Anne District. I greet those I know with a smile, a nod, and a handshake. Although tensions between local and federal law enforcement do exist, I always try to be respectful of the men and women in uniform and the job they do.

My efforts have historically been unreciprocated by the fine folks of the Seattle PD—but whatever. I can't control what anybody else does. I can only control what I do and how I treat people, and I've always chosen to show respect. We're all on the same team and fighting the same fight. Even still, some people make it really hard to get along with them. Detective Kramer is one of those people.

I push through the doors that lead into the precinct's homicide bureau and am immediately greeted by Detective Josh Handler. He's a tall, portly man with a deep, booming voice and a ready smile. His humor tends toward the gallows variety, although that's to be expected of anybody who deals with death and the depths of human depravity on a daily basis. He's one of the good ones.

"Chief Wilder, good to see you," Handler says. "I can only assume you're haunting our hallowed halls to poach a case from one of my hard-working brethren."

I smile as I shake his hand. "Not poaching. Just offering some assistance."

"Dare I ask which case you're looking to offer your assistance with?"

"The Huan Zhao shooting."

"Ah. That one. That's going to be Kramer's case," he says, and I can't tell if the tone of distaste is for Fish or Kramer.

"Yeah, I heard he was on it. Anything I should know?"

He shrugs. "Nah. Just Kramer showboating again. You know how he is," he says. "An attack on a city official? Guaranteed headlines and TV interviews. Of course, he muscled his way onto the case. I have a feeling the only way you're getting anywhere near this case is if you manage to pry it out of his cold, dead hands."

"Yeah, when I heard he was assigned to the case I figured it would be a fight."

"You know he doesn't like sharing the spotlight."

"Not looking to," I reply. "More than happy to work in the background and let him take all the interviews he wants."

Handler purses his lips. "What's your interest in this case anyway? It's a local official. Doesn't seem like something the Bureau would normally be interested in."

"I'm just an inquisitive soul, Detective Handler."

His laughter rolls like thunder and echoes around the corridor. He shakes my hand again.

"Well, good luck getting a sniff of this case," he says.

"Appreciate it. Stay safe out there, Detective."

"Yeah, you too."

I turn and make my way through the bureau. It's busy and bustling, the murmur of voices and the ringing of phones filling the air around me. It's chaos. Frankly, I don't understand how people can work and be productive in such mayhem. I'm just not wired like that, I suppose. Detective Kramer is sitting at his desk in the far corner of the room, just beneath the window. He looks up from his computer, sees me coming, and I see his mustache twitch as his face darkens.

Unlike a lot of his peers, Kramer's desk and immediate work area is clean and orderly. I can respect that much about him at least. In his mid-forties, Kramer is six-two, toned, tan, and trim. The man is always stylishly dressed, well put together, and of course, camera ready. I'm not sure what his ultimate career goals are, whether he's looking to climb the ranks or what, but he carries himself with a confidence that says no matter what he sets his sights on, he will achieve it. A confidence bolstered when he was made one of the youngest homicide detectives in SPD history, earning his shield before he was thirty.

As I drop into the chair that sits in front of his desk, he leans back and runs a hand through chestnut-colored hair that's neatly styled with a light dusting of gray at the temples, which adds to his look of distinction. Kramer sits back and stares at me, his hazel eyes looking slightly curious but also slightly annoyed by my presence. With high cheekbones, a square jaw, and chiseled features, it wouldn't surprise me to see him on TV in some capacity at some point after he's built up enough cred working the streets.

"Sure, have a seat," he says.

"Thanks."

"I'd say it's lovely to see you, but I think we both know that would be a lie."

"Charming, as always."

"What do you want, Wilder?"

"What? I can't come by just to say hello?"

He frowns. "You? No. You always have an agenda."

"That seems mean."

"But always turns out to be true," he says. "So, let's not pretend we get along, skip all the niceties, and just fast forward to the part where you tell me why you're here."

"Fair enough," I respond. "The Huan Zhao shooting—"

"Let me stop you right there. It's my case, I'm not inviting you in on it, and you have no standing to take it from me."

"I'm not looking to take it from you."

"Then what do you want?"

"I just want to be looped in. I want to work on the case in the background."

He scoffs. "Thanks, but no thanks. This is my case."

"As I said, I understand that, and I'm not looking to take the spotlight away from you," I tell him. "I just want to help."

He stares at me in silence for a long moment as if he's trying to figure out what my angle is. I've been known as a thorn in the SPD's side for years now. Former Deputy Chief Ricardo Torres and I had a pretty heavy rift between us that quite literally came to blows, and even TJ Lee, who I genuinely like and have worked with on several occasions, has never exactly greeted me with open arms. Between the two of them, my reputation has sent quite a few ripples in the local law enforcement community. With Kramer, at least, I eventually came by my dislike for him honestly. The man is just disagreeable in so many different ways.

"What makes you think I need your help?" he finally asks.

"Because I have access to parts of the community you'll be investigating that you don't have. They aren't going to talk to you."

"I have contacts of my own."

A grin flickers across my lips. "Do you though?"

Filled with gangs, would-be mobsters, and more than a little distrust and suspicion of police, the residents of Chinatown are notoriously insular. They have a well-deserved reputation for not cooperating with the police. I know of more than a few criminal investigations that have died at the border of the Chinatown district simply because people there do not talk to cops.

"What's your angle here, Blake? Why are you so interested in pitching in here?"

"I've got some free time on my hands and just want to help. The attempted murder of a city official is a pretty big deal. I figured you could use a hand."

Kramer gives me a patronizing smile. "I think I'll be just fine on my own."

"I'm telling you, Kramer, you are not going to get anywhere."

"I appreciate you coming down," he says, his tone smug and smarmy. "And thank you for offering to help me out, but I've got this."

"Kramer, don't let your pride keep you from accepting my help. You know I've got resources you don't and—"

"Like I said, thanks for coming down."

"Kramer—"

"Since you found your way in, I assume you can find your way out?"

Frowning, I stare at him for a minute, the blood in my veins boiling with frustration and a tinge of anger. This is proving to be harder than I anticipated. Kramer is clearly enjoying being able to say no to me, and I have no leverage to force him to let me on the case.

I sigh. "Listen, I know we've had our differences in the past—"

"You can either find your own way out, or I'll have you escorted out," he says. "Apparently, unlike you, I have work to do."

It's taking everything in me to keep from reaching across the desk and slapping him silly. Gritting my teeth, I get to my feet and glower at him.

"You're going to run into brick walls in Chinatown. And when you do, you're going to call me," I tell him. "When you call, I'll do my best to keep from acting like you are right now."

He chuffs. "Goodbye, Wilder."

I turn and walk away, my hands balled into fists. I'm obviously going to need to go about this on my own. It's probably for the best since I honestly don't know that I could get through an entire case with Kramer without catching a charge for assaulting a police officer.

CHAPTER NINE

The Chapel, SNAP Team HQ, Industrial District; Seattle, WA

"How'd it go?" Nina asks.

"About as well as I expected," I reply.

"Shut you out, huh?"

"And he did it with a laugh."

"And you can't bully your way in?"

"I've got no standing," I tell her. "It's a local-slash-state crime. It's not federal, so unfortunately, I can't bully my way in."

Nina grins. "Anybody you can threaten or blackmail?"

"I'm working on that," I reply with a rueful chuckle.

Nina sits back in her chair. "Anything I can do to help facilitate you strong-arming somebody? I'm pretty good at finding blackmail material."

"That's disturbing. But could be useful. I'll let you know," I reply.

"I am at your beck and call, boss."

"I appreciate that. For now, we'll try to stay within the bounds of the law," I say. "We'll just have to run our own investigation. I can't believe the SPD has much more than we do at the moment, so not having their case notes might not be a world ender."

"What can I do?"

"I want you to dig up anything you can about the shooting. Take a peek at the dark web and see if there's any chatter about a hit on Fish," I say. "Also, look at the street cameras in front of Fish's building and on the streets around it. Hopefully, we'll find something we can use."

"Copy that," she replies. "I'm on it."

"Thanks, Nina."

Leaving her to do her thing, I walk to my office and drop into my chair. There's nothing I hate more than not having the least bit of control over a case. Unless Nina finds something we can latch onto or Kramer comes to his senses and invites me in, my options will be limited. I've got more access to Chinatown than Kramer because of my association with Fish, but most people will still be hesitant to talk to even me about his shooting out of fear of being targeted next for speaking with me in the first place. I need to find a way to crack through that wall of silence if I'm going to find out who pulled the trigger.

"Chief Wilder, do you have a minute?"

I raise my head to see Opal standing in the doorway, a frown on her lips and a determined gleam in her eye. She's got something to say.

"Yeah, please," I say. "Come in."

She closes the door behind her, then takes a seat in one of the chairs in front of my desk. Before she can say anything, I begin.

"First off, I need to say that I'm sorry," I tell her. "There are a lot of ways—better ways—I could have handled the situation in the bullpen yesterday. I shouldn't have undercut you in front of the team the way I did, and I apologize, Opal."

"I appreciate that, Chief. But it made me wonder if I'm the right fit for this job."

"I think you are," I tell her. "You have all the qualities I am looking for in a case manager."

She lowers her gaze for a moment as if collecting her thoughts, and I get the idea she was coming in here to resign but seems to be on the fence about it. Opal finally raises her eyes to mine.

"Chief, you wanted me to organize and prioritize your caseload. If I'm going to do this job, I need you to let me do it," she says.

"You're right. You're absolutely right," I tell her. "At the same time however, there will be times I need to divert the team to a different case. It likely isn't going to happen very often, but it will happen. Going forward, I promise to handle it much differently than I did yesterday. And again, I apologize. It was unprofessional of me."

She sits back in her chair and seems to ponder my words. Opal gives herself a small nod, then sits forward, elbows on her knees, hands clasped together. She's got questions.

"Chief, I'm not one to tell you who you can and can't associate with, but I've done a little bit of digging on this Fish character, and he seems shady. He seems—"

"Like a crime boss?"

A soft laugh drifts from her mouth. "Well, not to put too fine a point on it, but yes."

"Well, he was a crime boss once upon a time," I tell her. "But now, he's a respected businessman and a member of the city council."

"Went legit, did he?"

I nod. "He did."

"I don't understand your relationship with him. How can a Bureau Unit Chief be friends with a … criminal?" she asks.

"Fish started as an informant. He would feed me information that led to a lot of big-time arrests. He helped me take down a lot of bad people in Seattle's underworld. He helped me cut the heads off a lot of snakes."

Her expression turns skeptical. "I'm sure all those arrests were a tremendous benefit to his own business interests."

"They were. But you've been in law enforcement long enough to know that sometimes you make deals with the lesser of many evils to do a greater good."

She hesitates, then nods, accepting my words as truth. Opal is pragmatic enough to understand that sometimes, you have to dance with the devil if you want to clean up Hell.

"When I was working with Fish, gang violence in Chinatown was out of control. Multiple bodies a day were dropping. It was so bad, the SPD called us in to help. That's when I first met him," I tell her. "And yes, he was helping me make cases on his rivals and consolidating control over the neighborhood, but it was with a purpose. With Chinatown under his control, he brought stability. The violence tapered off, and the bodies stopped dropping. So yes, his help was self-serving, but it was for a greater good. It saved lives."

She stares at me with curious eyes. "But your relationship with him seems closer than handler and informant. You seem to genuinely care about him."

"Because I do. I got to know him while we were working together and got to know what kind of man he is. He's a good man. He's got a good heart. He is charitable and kind. Not many people know how many kids' educations he's paid for or the good work he's done for underprivileged and underserved people in the city. He genuinely loves this community, and he's only ever had the best of intentions. And he's done a lot for me personally. He's personally saved my life on multiple occasions. So, yes, over the years, I've become very fond of him. He's family to me."

She sits back in the chair and frowns. Opal is such a straight-edged, by-the-book kind of person that I can tell she's struggling with the idea of not just consorting with a known criminal but letting yourself grow so close to him that you'd refer to him as family. There aren't many people outside the team that know the true nature of my relationship with Fish. Most won't understand. Others might think it crosses some ethical boundary. It doesn't. I'm not providing him with any sort of unethical benefit or information, and I'm not investigating him for anything. And as of now, he's a law-abiding citizen.

I don't really like to advertise my relationship with Fish. I don't give anybody the details simply because it's not their business. Opal knows about the history, but I want to give her the context. She needs to understand the whole story. If she's going to be part of this team, I need to learn to trust her. And the only way to learn is by doing.

"I'm sorry. I'm just having trouble reconciling the idea of an FBI agent and a former crime boss being… family," she says.

"Nothing for you to be sorry about," I say. "I just want to give you the context of the full story, so you understand why this case is so personal to me."

"I… I can't say I fully understand how you're so comfortable being so close to somebody with such a checkered past."

"I don't know what to say to that," I reply. "All I can tell you is that Fish is a good guy who means a lot to me. And I am going to move heaven and earth to find out who did this to him. I understand your hesitance, so I'm not asking you to help me. This is my mission."

She's quiet for a long minute as she processes what I just said. What she needs to understand is that I don't need her permission or approval to have Fish in my life. She's either going to learn to accept it or not. But then her face softens, and the corners of her mouth curl upward. Slightly.

"Agent Russo wasn't kidding when she said you were an unorthodox unit," she says.

"We are. But this is one of the best units I've ever been part of," I reply. "A lot of people say it, but the people who fill that bullpen truly are family. And you have a chance to be part of that. If you want to be, that is."

She doesn't say anything for a moment, but her demeanor seems to be shifting. It's subtle and hesitant, but it's in that moment that I realize Opal has been looking to be part of something like this unit. To have a family.

That's something I can work with.

CHAPTER TEN

The Emerald Lounge, Downtown District; Seattle, WA

"Here you go, Chief," the waitress says as she sets a glass down in front of me.

"Thanks, Tamara."

"Everything okay?"

I nod. "Yeah. All good."

She frowns. "You sure? Kind of seems like you're carrying the weight of the world on your shoulders or something tonight."

Tamara is a great waitress. Warm. Friendly. Efficient. Observant. But the simple fact that she knows me well enough to be able to gauge my mood makes me think perhaps I come into the Emerald a little too often.

A small smile touches my lips. "It's just been a rough few days at the office."

"Ahh. That explains it."

I raise my glass. "Nothing some good scotch and better music can't cure."

"Then I'll make sure to keep the drinks coming."

"Please do."

"Hang in there, Chief. It's always darkest before the dawn."

"That's good advice," I say. "Thanks, Tamara."

She offers me a reassuring squeeze on the shoulder before she turns and bounces away. I lean back in my booth and listen to the quartet on stage playing a lively, upbeat number. It's good. Catchy. But it doesn't fit my mood at all. I take a swallow of my scotch, relishing the smooth trail that burns its way down my throat before splashing into my belly, warming me from the inside.

It's been a few days now, and I've gotten exactly nowhere with Fish's case. His condition hasn't changed, and his doctors are worried that it might not. Of course, that's not what they're saying. They're couching it all in positive affirmations, useless platitudes, and other professional niceties. But I've been around long enough that I can read between the lines. They're not overly optimistic about his recovery.

Stupidly, part of me feels like his recovery depends on me finding the person responsible for doing this to him. I know how utterly ridiculous that is, but it's flashed through my mind. Several times. I also know that my emotions about this case are keeping me from seeing it all clearly. I'm running into brick wall after brick wall, and not having my team here to help keep me on the straight and narrow isn't helping. I'm rudderless right now.

My hope is that Nina will be able to find something soon. She's been coming up empty, but she's taking that as a challenge and is working harder, doing everything she can to find something we can use—something that will point us in a direction—something that will get us off square freaking one. So far, it's been an exercise in futility and frustration. Leaning my head back against the padding of the booth, I close my eyes, letting the drink and the music work their magic on me.

But the spell is broken quickly when I feel somebody hovering beside my table. With an irritated sigh, I open my eyes to see Detective Scott Kramer standing there. Any magic the moment was imbued with comes crashing down with a resounding thud. Still, the fact that he's standing here isn't insignificant. I don't want to seem too eager to see him and fluff up his already-enormous ego.

"I was told you like to come here," he says.

"Detective," I reply. "I usually come here to get away from the office and all the problems that tend to go along with it."

A smirk curling his lips, Kramer slides into the booth across from me.

"Sure, have a seat," I say, recalling what he said to me when I showed up at his precinct.

Despite a lack of invitation and my obvious disinterest in sitting with him, Kramer signals the waitress for a drink. Tamara bustles over and takes his order. She seems to pick up on my irritation at the intruder, and when she returns with a whiskey sour for him, she sets a fresh glass of scotch down in front of me and casts sympathetic eyes my way.

"That's on the house, Chief," she says as she plucks Kramer's credit card from his fingers.

"Thanks, Tamara."

"What about me? I'm a cop too," Kramer asks, sounding offended.

"Sorry, but I don't know you."

She gives him a cheeky grin as she turns and bounds away, leaving him with a shocked expression on his face, as if he'd expected his badge or good looks to get him a freebie. I get the sense he usually gets what he wants, so it amuses me that Tamara shut him down. Grumbling to himself, Kramer settles in and takes a sip of his drink. We sit in silence for a couple of minutes, listening to the music. I figure he tracked me down, so he's got something to say, and it's not on me to fill the dead air with a pleasant chat.

"This music is not my thing," he says. "How can you listen to this garbage?"

"That observation right there tells me a lot about you, Detective Kramer."

"Yeah? Like what?"

"Like you've got absolutely zero taste in music," I reply. "It's a character flaw I assume extends to other parts of your life."

He harrumphs, annoyance on his face as he takes another sip. He's clearly unhappy about being here, which tells me my instincts were right and I'm doing all I can to keep the satisfied smirk off my lips since that's only going to irritate him further and won't help anybody—least of all, Fish. Kramer opens his mouth to speak, but his face twists and contorts like the act of forcing the words out of his mouth is causing him physical pain.

"So, it turns out you were right," he finally croaks.

That had to be painful for him. Kramer truly believes he's the smartest person in any room he walks into and isn't the sort of man who admits his wrong easily. So, watching him twist himself into knots as he spits out those words is immensely satisfying. I'm pretty positive I already know what he's referring to, but I'm feeling a little vindictive and want to twist the knife a little bit more just because I don't like Kramer and I'm petty like that.

"Oh yeah? What was I right about?" I ask.

His lips curl in distaste. Kramer knows I'm just being a jerk but also knows there's nothing he can do except take it if he hopes to get what he wants.

"You were right about me running into a brick wall in Chinatown," he grudgingly admits. "So, I've reconsidered your request to assist with the case."

Yeah, that's satisfying. "Oh? Did you now?"

His jaw flexes as he grits his teeth. "Are we really going to do this?"

"I've got nothing but time," I respond with a shrug.

He sighs and runs a hand across his face. "Fine. You were right; I was wrong. You're smart; I'm an idiot. You're good at this job; I'm incompetent," he growls, his voice dripping with sarcasm and disdain. "Happy now?"

I purse my lips as if thinking about it, then nod. "Yeah. I guess that'll do."

Kramer rolls his eyes and grits his teeth, his face etched with annoyance. I've got a strange feeling I'm not going to make his Christmas card list this year.

"So, what do you need from me?" I ask.

"I want you to speak with some of your contacts in Chinatown," he says. "I need to gather whatever intel about the shooting is floating around out there."

I take a sip of my drink, savoring this moment every bit as much as the scotch. I'm really enjoying watching Kramer squirm.

"All right. I'll talk to my contacts," I say.

"Great, then how about we meet tomorrow morning—"

"Hold up there, cowboy. These are my CIs, and it's my job to protect them," I tell him. "I'll talk to them and let you know what they say."

"No, I want to be there," he says. "I want to hear what they have to say firsthand."

I stare at him like he's lost his mind. "You're a cop. You know how the whole confidential informant thing works."

"This is my case."

"And those are my informants."

He grumbles under his breath and drains his glass, practically slamming it back down on the table. Like I said, he's obviously a man used to getting his way.

"What have you found so far?" I ask.

"Oh, you expect me to give you something when you haven't given me anything?"

And I thought I was petty. Struggling to keep from rolling my eyes, I take a drink to give myself a few seconds to settle down. Only when I think I can speak without pure disdain in my voice, do I raise my eyes again.

"Look, we're on the same side here. We want the same thing," I tell him. "That means we're going to have to work together. Which also means, we need to trust each other. When I tell you that I will tell you what my CIs tell me, word for word, I need you to trust that I will."

He glowers at me, still not happy with me not allowing him to be there when I talk to my informants. Kramer shakes his head. What I'm not telling him is that I've already got lines out to my CIs, and so far, they haven't sent a flare back. They're not talking right now. Knowing they're all in precarious positions—and talking to me would make that situation even more unsteady for them—I'm going to give them another day or so. After that, I'll push things along.

"Fine," is all he says.

"Now, your turn. What have you learned so far?"

"Honestly? Nothing," he says. "The people in Chinatown are stonewalling me. I'm no further than I was when you stopped by the precinct."

It's not what I was hoping to hear, but at the same time I'm not overly surprised by it either. I'm sure aside from the cultural reluctance to speak to the police, Kramer's swagger and ego made them even less willing to help him. He's the kind of guy who demands rather than asks. He believes in the iron fist and doesn't know how to properly utilize the velvet glove.

"All right. Well, let me speak to my CIs. Hopefully somebody will have something good to tell me that'll give us some direction," I tell him.

He runs the tip of his finger around the rim of his glass, his eyes fixed on mine. "Why are you so interested in this case?"

"Like I said, I've got some time on my hands, and an attack on a public official is intriguing."

"You know, some people say you have a relationship with the victim," he says. "I find that hard to believe since he's a crime lord, but your insistence on being part of this case is making me rethink that position."

"I don't have much use for gossip. You're welcome to believe what you want," I tell him. "But as far as I know, he's currently sitting on Seattle's city council and has a large number of legit business interests."

"Maybe now—"

"Like I said, I don't have much use for gossip."

"Uh-huh," he says slowly.

Kramer is going to believe what he wants to believe, and I am under no obligation to tell him anything about any relationship I have. But I am most definitely not going to disclose my relationship with Fish because I know him well enough already to know he will twist and distort things for his own ends, and I am not going to let him use my friendship against me like that. I deserve better than that… and so does Fish.

"Okay, I'll get back to you as soon as I have something," I tell him. "And I expect that you will do the same."

"You show me yours, I show you mine, huh?"

"Something like that."

He hesitates for a moment, a thoughtful expression on his face. "All right. I guess I'll look forward to hearing from you then."

"Good. Now, you can go and let me finish listening to this band in peace."

As if surprised by my dismissal, Kramer stares at me for a moment like he's not sure what to do with it. He's obviously not used to being given orders. But he recovers quickly and pastes that smarmy smirk on his face and shakes his head.

"All right. I'll talk to you soon, Blake."

"You will."

"Soon," he says as if trying to reassert control.

"Goodnight, Detective Kramer."

Still smirking and muttering under his breath, he turns and goes. Feeling pretty good about myself for winning the round, I signal to Tamara for a fresh scotch, then tune in to the music, suddenly enjoying it more than I had been.

CHAPTER ELEVEN

The Chapel, SNAP Team HQ, Industrial District; Seattle, WA

"YOU'RE SO PETTY," NINA SAYS AND GIGGLES.

"I am," I agree. "But it was just so satisfying watching him squirm as he asked for help."

I sit back in the chair at the conference table in the bullpen and tap my pen against the pad of paper in front of me.

"What is it?" Nina asks.

"It's just Kramer. I got the feeling he was working some angle."

"Based on everything you've told me about him, he probably was," she replies. "He's probably hoping you'll give up your CIs so he can get whatever he can out of them, then cut you out of the loop so he can claim all the glory for himself."

"Yeah, I figured that's probably what it is. I just don't like it. I also don't like how hard he was pressing me to give him my CIs. He's a cop. He knows how the game goes."

"He's in it for himself."

"All the more reason for me to keep the names of my informants to myself. He sees them as expendable and wouldn't lose a wink of sleep if he got them killed. It bothers me."

"Because you put more value on human life than he does."

I suppose that much is true. Perhaps that's why I'm still having difficulty getting past watching Garrett Arceneaux kill himself. He was a monster—there is no question about that—but his life still had value. He was failed by his parents, and in some ways, never had a chance. Seen from a certain angle, he too was a victim. Just like Kit was. Having given it a bit of thought, I can see now why Dr. Azar was so insistent on me being able to see the parallels between Arceneaux and my sister—something I've been willfully blinding myself to. It's something I didn't want to see.

Not that I think Kit is a monster. But I suppose there are plenty in this world who would argue otherwise. I can't fathom some of the things she's done. The things she was trained to do from a young age then forced to carry out. Like Garrett Arceneaux, she is a product of her environment. Like Garrett's father, this is who those people who took Kit built her to be. Unlike him, she didn't do the things she's done with any sense of pleasure. She did them to survive. She had no other choice.

And perhaps that is why I'm so compelled to overcompensate with her. Why I'm so overprotective and feel the need to be almost helicopter parent-esque in how I treat her. In many ways, she never had a chance either, and I guess I'm trying to be the parent she didn't have growing up. But I'm not protecting her. She's capable and can obviously do that on her own quite well. By hovering over her like I do, perhaps Dr. Azar is right and all I'm managing to do is drive her away from me.

I give myself a small shake. "Okay, we'll deal with Kramer when we have to. But I want to get ahead of him on this. Have you been able to find anything?"

"Not much," Nina admits. "But I did just get access to the street camera system, so I'll be going through that today."

"Good. That's a start."

"Why hasn't Kramer gone through the footage yet?"

"For all I know, he has and just doesn't see fit to share that information with us," I respond. "I don't imagine he's going to play fair with us."

"I just wish we knew what the motive was," Nina says. "I mean, I know Fish has a past and all, but he's doing good work for the city now. He's practically beloved."

"I'm not sure he's beloved by everybody. Some grudges run deep," I say. "I'm sure that whoever did this is somebody he crossed back in the day."

"Something gives me the feeling that's going to be a long list."

My lips twist wryly. "Longer than you can imagine."

"I think I might be able to help narrow it down some."

I turn to see Opal approaching us with a stack of files in her hands. She takes a seat at the table and begins to sort through the stack. She pauses, then raises her eyes to me.

"I've given it some thought, and I'm not going to pretend to understand your relationship with Mr. Zhao. I can see this man means a lot to you," she says softly. "And if I'm being completely transparent, I'm sure you can look through my history and say the same about some of the people in my life as well. I'm the last person who can judge you for it."

"I appreciate that, Opal," I say.

"And, having done some research, I can see he's very philanthropic and seems dedicated to doing good in the community. He seems to be working hard to make amends for his past," she says. "If there's one thing I believe in, it's second chances. God knows I've had my fair share of them."

"Haven't we all?" Nina chimes in.

Opal's lips curl gently. "Given the things he's been implicated in—"

"But never charged, let alone convicted of," I add.

"That's fair. But given his… checkered past, I can't say I'll ever feel warm and fuzzy toward the man. Still, he's doing a lot of good things that are helping a lot of people," she goes on. "That's something I can respect."

"I'm very glad to hear you say that."

She pauses, as if still trying to adjust to being "okay" with somebody whose past is as checkered as Fish's. I'll never say the man was a saint. Far from it. But the things he did were done for a greater purpose. He did a good job of shielding me from the terrible things he's done—or at least ordered to be done—meaning I can never directly tie him to anything. I think he knows if I'd been able to, I would have put cuffs on him myself—regardless of how fond I am of him—and took measures to protect him as well as our relationship.

But I'm not an idiot. I know some of the things he's done. I just can't prove any of them; therefore, I can't touch him for them. However, he did stop the rampant bloodshed. He brought peace and stability to an underworld that was out of control. I will never agree with his methodology, but there is no arguing with the results. And sometimes, as I well know, it's far better to dance with the devil you know than unleash the gates of hell and let all the demons out.

Aside from that, Fish is so much more than what he used to be. Like Opal, I believe in second chances. I believe in redemption. I kind of have to, given my sister's situation. But like Kit, Fish is using everything that was bad in him to do a greater good. To help people. To do some good in this world. If I'm not going to condemn Kit for her past, then I sure as hell can't condemn Fish for his.

"Okay, all that being said, I think I've narrowed a list of suspects down to half a dozen or so," Opal says and taps the folders on the table.

"How did you narrow that down?" I ask.

"I used to do crime analytics," she replies. "I studied all the major players in Chinatown over the past twenty years and believe I identified Fish's biggest rivals: all heads of powerful families in their own right, but subordinate to him, even now."

She said the last bit rather pointedly, as if confirming to me that she knows Fish still isn't entirely clean. I know he's not. But he's also not involved in the really criminal things he used to be and has more or less quashed all the protection rackets and extortion rings. I know there are still illegal gambling dens—hell, he owns one—but he's managed to choke off the drug runners, human traffickers, and gangs that used to call Chinatown home. He controls them all.

Fish's presence still looms large over the Seattle underworld. Given his position on the city council, he's just the figurehead of his family these days with men like Trevor operating the day-to-day business, following his directive to maintain the peace and order. Nobody is under any illusion about the illicit activity that still goes on in the underworld, but it's something everybody is willing to live with simply because Fish has brought structure to the chaos. Like I said, sometimes it's best to dance with the devil you know, and Seattle PD seems to feel the same way too.

"Anyway, I've identified these six as the most likely to benefit if Fish were out of the picture," Opal says. "Guang Xie, Feng Cao, Hua Meng, Shu Pei, Bai Shao, and Fei Duan. They all run their own organizations and are bound by Fish's laws in Chinatown, which I can't think they're too happy with. I think they've all got motive to want him gone."

"That makes sense," Nina says. "But why now? They've been living with these rules governing their organizations for years. What's the impetus to move on him now?"

"Trevor, Fish's right-hand man, may have given me the answer to that," I say. "He told me people think Fish has taken his eye off the ball with all his city council work. He believes they think the fact that he's gone legit means he's gone soft. Maybe that's why they moved now. Somebody thought they'd strike now and move up the ladder."

"Which means, if they suspect there's a power void, we might be in for some trouble," Opal says.

"Which also means we need to figure out who did this and put them in bracelets quickly," I say. "To that end, Nina, I need you to do a workup on those six names. Also, monitor any chatter online if you can and see if anybody's claiming credit or talking about next steps."

"I'm on it," she says.

"What can I do to help?" Opal says.

"Work with Nina. Review the footage she's pulling in," I say. "And let's put your analytical skills to use and see if you can help narrow down our suspect pool."

"Copy that," she replies.

"What are you going to do?" Nina asks.

"I'm going to go talk to my CIs, start beating the bushes and see what pops out."

"Watch your back out there," Opal says. "If there is a war brewing, given your proximity to Fish, you might be a target."

"Yeah, the thought crossed my mind," I reply.

Nina frowns. "I hadn't thought about that. Maybe you should take Kramer with you just so somebody's watching your back out there."

"I trust him to watch my back about as much as I'd trust a rattlesnake not to bite me," I tell her. "I'll be careful. I'll be fine."

"You better be," Nina insists.

I get to my feet and grab my things. Before I head out, I turn back to the table as Opal moves closer to Nina, then opens up her laptop. They're talking quietly together and shuffling the files back and forth, getting themselves organized for the task in front of them.

"Thanks for pitching in, Opal," I say.

She raises her head and shrugs. "Hey, I'm part of the team now, right? And one thing I believe is that teammates have each other's backs."

"Yes, you are," I say. "And yes, they do."

CHAPTER TWELVE

Bamboo Palace Restaurant, Chinatown-International District; Seattle, WA

Being one of the only white faces in the place, I draw plenty of eyes as I walk through the restaurant. I make my way across the floor, then slip through a door in the back wall and into the kitchen. A thousand different aromas hit me all at once, and my stomach rumbles, reminding me that I haven't had lunch yet. It's organized chaos back there with half a dozen men in white T-shirts, aprons, black pants, and bandanas tied around their foreheads pumping out a host of savory dishes that only make me hungrier.

Han Gao is sitting on an overturned milk crate in the far corner of the kitchen eating his lunch. When he spots me coming toward him, his eyes widen, and he stops chewing as an expression of near panic crosses his face. His eyes dart left and right—either trying to figure out if anybody is looking at him or for the nearest exit—I'm not sure. An expression of resignation settles over his face when I stop in front of him.

"Really, Han?" I ask. "A kitchen full of amazing-smelling food, and you're eating a burrito?"

He scoffs. "When you're stuck in this kitchen all day, every day, it loses its appeal."

"If you say so."

"What are you doing here?"

"You haven't been returning my calls," I say. "We need to talk."

He gets to his feet and sets his half-eaten burrito on a small table beside his makeshift stool, then angrily motions for me to follow him. We slip out a back door and into the alley behind the restaurant. He looks one way then the other, his fear palpable that we'll be spotted talking. He stands behind a large dumpster, obscuring himself from view, and shakes a cigarette out of his pack, then lights it.

Twenty-five years old, Han is a couple inches shorter than I am and slender with a wiry build. He's got a smooth, olive-colored complexion, dark, almond-shaped eyes, and dark hair that's tied back into a ponytail that falls to his shoulders. He's a good-looking kid. He's smart and could be doing a lot more with his life. But his name came up in a robbery ring I was investigating a while back, and rather than send him to prison for it, I flipped him. He's been working for me ever since and has been one of my most reliable sources… until these last few days anyway.

"Are you trying to get me killed, Blake? If anybody sees me talking to you—"

"Like anybody knows who I am."

"They don't have to know you to know you're a cop. I mean, just look at you. You might as well have a big sign around your neck that says, *I'm a cop*," he snaps.

That again. I sigh and shake my head. "If anybody asks, just tell them I'm your parole officer," I tell him. "It's practically true."

"Yeah, that's funny," he grumbles. "What do you want?"

"I want to know why you haven't been returning my calls."

"Because things are superhot in these streets right now, man," he replies. "After Fish got got, things are tense out here."

"He didn't get got," I tell him. "Fish is still alive."

"For now, maybe. But the way I hear it, he's on his way out."

His words are like a gut punch, and I have to fight off the dark tide of grief that rises within me. I don't want to think about that. Nor do I even want to put that out into the universe.

"Don't say that to me ever again," I say. "Fish is going to be fine."

"If you say so, Chief."

"I do."

"All right, all right. I didn't mean anything by it. Just relax."

I bite back the acidic reply on my tongue. I'm not mad at Han. He's just reacting to what's being put out there. It makes me think somebody's got a vested interest in putting word of Fish's demise on the streets. That also tells me that whoever wants that message out there also wants to make sure they get credit for it so their house is known as the new top dog.

Han takes a drag of his smoke. "What do you want?"

"I want to know who shot him."

"You and all his boys," he mutters.

"Han—"

"Okay, look, I'm sorry. I get you want to know who pulled the trigger, but I ain't tryin' to get involved in all that," he says. "You go poking around in that whole mess, and you're just asking somebody to put a bullet or twelve in you."

"You hear everything on the streets. Who's taking credit for it?"

"Nobody's taking credit for it," he says. "You think somebody wants to bring that kind of heat down on themselves?"

"Somebody wants to fill the power void."

"Sure. They all do. But right now, it's just wait and see," he says. "Fish's organization is still strong. Nobody's going to make a move until…"

"I don't buy that. Patience isn't in the DNA of these people."

"Maybe not. But nobody's going to claim they shot Fish if they didn't. That's just signing their own death warrant. These people may not be patient, but they ain't stupid either."

As much as I want to argue, what he's saying makes sense. If nobody is claiming credit for Fish's shooting, it's likely because Han is right: they probably don't want to bring the weight his organization can still bring on their own heads. But nature abhors a vacuum, and it will only be a matter of time before somebody gets over that fear and makes a move to solidify their ascension in the hierarchy of the underworld.

"Yeah, I can see you're starting to get it. It's only a matter of time before somebody steps up to the plate. More than one somebody will, if you ask me. That's why everything's so tense out here. Everybody's just sitting back and watching right now. This place is a freaking powder keg just waiting for somebody to light up," he says and takes a deep drag on his cigarette.

"It's going to be the Wild West out here."

"Nah. It's going to be a bloodbath. It's gonna be bad."

"All the more reason for me to get ahead of this. I need to stop things from exploding. And to do that, I need your help," I tell him.

He pulls a face. "Have you not heard a single word I've said? Everybody's just looking for a reason to start pulling the trigger."

"I heard you. But it doesn't change anything. I need intel. And you can go places and talk to people I can't go and can't talk to."

"Blake, I can't—"

"Han, you do this for me, and we're done," I say. "You do this, you get me some solid intel, and you and me will be square. I'll never darken your doorstep again."

He opens his mouth to reply, then closes it again as if he's thinking over what I just said. It's like the thought of being able to get off the leash I've got him on never crossed his mind. I can see the fear warring with the idea of freedom on his face.

"I do this … and we're square?" he asks.

"You'll never see my face again," I tell him. "I give you my word."

He runs a hand over his face, then takes another drag on his cigarette. Han is reluctant. He's terrified of poking his nose into the business of the families. At the same time, the possibility of finally getting off that hook and being free of me seems to be powerfully enticing to him. He blows out a thick plume of smoke and sighs. One of the other men from the kitchen leans out and motions to Han.

"Hey, kid, we need you in here," he shouts. "We got orders backing up."

"I'll be there in a second," Han says.

"Hurry up," the man calls.

Han turns to me. "All right, I'll do it. I'll dig around and see what I can find out."

"Good. Great."

"I'll touch base with you as soon as I hear something."

"Be careful, Han."

He scoffs. "Yeah. And if I end up with two in the back of my head, I'm not only going to blame you, I'm going to haunt you. Forever."

"Deal," I say. "Call me. Soon."

Without another word, he drops his cigarette and crushes it with his shoe, then turns and heads back inside. All right. The ball is rolling. If anybody can find out what happened and who did it, I'm confident it will be Han. I just hope I haven't sent him to his death by making him do this. Like he said a minute ago, now we just wait and see. And hope.

"Fingers crossed," I mutter to myself.

Rather than cut back through the restaurant, I walk down the alley, then out onto the street, heading for the parking garage where I left my car. The streets are congested with foot traffic. There are tons of tourists clogging the sidewalks, forcing me to weave my way through and around them all. Progress is slow, but I finally make it to the narrow side street that runs alongside the parking garage and am able to extricate myself from the mass of humanity.

Passing by dumpsters, trash cans, and a few people who've made the glorified alleyway their home, I keep my eyes moving, trying to see everywhere all at once. Ever since I ducked down this side street, I've had an itchy feeling that's got the hair on the back of my neck standing on end. I'm not one who's normally paranoid, but I trust my instincts. And my instincts are telling me something's off. It feels like I've got eyes on me, and it's not the homeless people.

I slip through the doorway and into the parking garage. It's packed with cars and plenty of people coming and going from Chinatown. Pushing my jacket back, I unsnap my holster as that itch on the back of my neck gets worse. My hand hovering near the butt of my weapon, I stop and turn in a circle, scanning the entire parking structure around me. A few people who are walking by gape at me, their faces blanching when they see my weapon.

"FBI," I say. "Get moving. Quickly."

They comply and practically sprint away, leaving me alone in this section of the garage. I stare at the host of cars all around me but don't see anybody moving among them. Still, that feeling of being watched persists. It grows stronger. Darting over to the staircase, I take two at a time as I dash to the third floor where I'm parked, listening closely for the sound of somebody pounding up the stairs behind me. When I make it to the third-floor landing, I stop and turn around. The staircase is silent.

My heart is racing, but I hold my breath and strain my ears, listening for the slightest sound of somebody furtively climbing the stairs. But I hear nothing. Nobody is following me. Feeling silly, I let out a breath of relief as the shot rings out, its booming report echoing through the parking garage. Sparks fly as the bullet glances off the concrete column beside me, the ping and whine of it filling my ears. A burst of pain—hot and searing—erupts in my cheek as a fragment of the pillar slices through my skin.

As blood cascades down my face, I pull my weapon and throw myself behind a car. Two more shots ring out, and I feel the impact of them punching into the car. Shouts of fear and confusion come from elsewhere in the garage as people react to the active shooter situation. It won't be long now before the air is filled with the shrill wail of sirens as the cops respond. Moving slowly and cautiously, I peek over the hood of the car I'm sheltering behind, searching desperately for the shooter, half expecting to hear the booming report of more shots being fire at me.

Nothing happens. No more shots are fired, and I don't see a shooter anywhere. My weapon out in front of me, I get to my feet and sweep left then right, my stomach clenched and my body taut. As I search the garage around me for the shooter, I hear sirens in the distance. They'll be here soon. Unfortunately, the shooter seems to have fled.

My weapon at the ready, I head in the direction I believed the shots came from and look around. I don't see any expended shell casings on the ground. The shooter either used a revolver or was savvy enough to police his brass, which tells me a little something about him. Frowning, I holster my weapon and get ready to deal with the locals.

"This is going to be a lot of fun," I mutter.

CHAPTER THIRTEEN

The Chapel, SNAP Team HQ, Industrial District; Seattle, WA

"ARE YOU ALL RIGHT?" OPAL ASKS, HER EYES WIDE.

"Yeah, I'm fine," I reply as I sit down at the conference table.

Nina and Opal are staring at the bandage on my cheek in horror like it's covering a gaping hole in my face or something. The detective handling the case in the garage told me they'd managed to dig a slug that had ricocheted off the pillar out of the fender of a nearby car. He told me they'd run it through the system, but he wasn't hopeful they'd find a match. They probably won't.

"Seriously, guys, it's just a cut. It's nothing," I tell them.

"A cut created by a bullet," Nina points out.

I chuckle. "It was caused by a piece of concrete—"

"Chipped off by a bullet that was shot. At you," Nina finishes.

"Well, the fact that I'm sitting here talking to you proves I'm fine."

"It looks like it was a close shave," Opal adds.

I pull a face because there's nothing I can say to that. It was a close shave. Two inches to the left, and we'd be having this conversation through a Ouija board. It's a little disturbing just how close I came to being killed in that parking garage, but it's not the first time, so it's easy to not get too bent out of shape about it.

"Any idea who might want to take a shot at you?" Opal asks.

"I think because most people in that world see me as Fish's girl Friday, it's probably the same group of people who took a shot at him."

"So, what you're saying is that it's a lengthy list," Nina says.

"That's exactly what I'm saying."

"Wonderful," Opal says.

"I did learn a couple of things," I say. "The fact that they used a revolver or policed their own brass tells me they're either familiar with forensics and evidentiary procedure, or they're a professional hitter. Although, the fact that I'm still alive argues against it being a pro."

"A professional hitter. That's comforting," Nina says.

"Like I said, he missed. That suggests he's not a pro," I reply. "All the same, I want you to keep combing the dark web chat rooms. See if anybody is out there gunning for Fish and me. If this is a pro, I'd like to know who's coming after me."

"Copy that, Boss," Nina says.

"How are we doing on the street camera footage?" I ask.

"Still processing," Opal replies. "We should have something a little more definitive either later today or tomorrow."

"Good. Okay. How about the analysis on Fish's rival bosses?"

"I'm still in the middle of that, but the early contender for me is Hua Meng," she replies. "The woman is ruthless. She's more ruthless than most of her male counterparts."

"That's a very male-dominated world. She'd have to be," I say.

"True, but she seems to take it to extreme levels," Opal replies.

"Fair enough. Why is she at the top of your pile?"

"I've found some information from about fifteen years ago. She and Fish had a particularly nasty conflict, and a lot of people ended up dead, including her nephew," she tells me. "Of the six rivals I'm analyzing, she is the only one who lost a family member in a conflict with Fish. And my understanding from what I've read is that when he finally made her bend the knee to him, the punishment he doled out for her going against him was pretty harsh."

"Yeah, that sounds like him."

"And still you back him," Opal says.

"It had to be," I reply. "You don't know what it was like before Fish took control of Chinatown. You don't know how much blood was spilled in those streets. Yeah, he was brutal when he brought everybody under his control, but he had to be. He couldn't give those monsters an inch of wiggle room, or it would start that cycle of violence all over again."

Opal frowns, still not thrilled with the idea of going to bat for somebody with Fish's history. I don't necessarily blame her for her feelings. But in this situation, there are a lot of nuances. To understand life in Chinatown and Seattle's underworld, the first thing you'd have to understand is that it's not black or white. There are many shades of gray.

"You're a statistics and analysis kind of woman, right?" I ask.

"I am."

"Look at crime statistics before Fish came to power and then after," I say. "Look at the rates of property crimes, murders, violent assaults, sexual assaults—look at them all."

"I understand your point that he's a stabilizing force. But the ends can't justify the means."

"Sometimes they do. It's one reason Seattle PD hasn't really gone out of their way to do anything about him—because he helps them, too, by quelling the chaos," I reply. "The underworld in Chinatown is a delicate ecosystem, and Fish is the one who gives it balance—who keeps things from ever growing wild and out of control. Whoever shot him is going to upset that delicate balance, which is why we need to scoop them up as quickly as we can. By doing that and restoring order, we can hopefully keep that ecosystem in check."

She opens her mouth to respond but then sits back and reconsiders. I can tell she's still not convinced about Fish. She probably never will be. But that's okay. She's not letting her personal feelings get in the way of doing the work. I think that speaks very well for her. It shows me she really is trying to be all in with this team, which is something I appreciate.

"Tell me more about Hua Meng," I say.

As if glad to be switching gears, Opal nods and consults her laptop. "Mama Meng, fifty-five years old, born in Chengdu. Known also as the Dragon Queen, she emigrated here when she was twelve. She was a good student, graduated from Brown, and now runs a network of massage parlors," she tells us. "In addition to the massage parlors, she dabbles in cocaine distribution as well. Although, it appears that she operates under the strict constraints Fish imposed on her."

"Dragon Queen," I say. "That's nice."

"A well-earned nickname, given her reputation. She is known as one of the most vicious and ruthless family heads in Chinatown."

"She's going to be fun to talk to."

"I'm kind of curious about these rules Fish imposed on these people. Do you know what they are?" Nina asks.

"I do," I tell her. "Fish put a cap on whatever vice they're selling. He only allowed them to deal so much product. More than that, they must all pay him a monthly fee for the privilege of being allowed to continue operating in Chinatown. A business licensing fee. he called it."

"And if they refuse to pay or don't follow his rules?" Opal asks.

"He gives them a chance to correct themselves, or he puts them out of business."

"You mean he kills them."

"Not at all. He doesn't have to do anything like that," I tell her. "His word carries so much weight that when he blackballs somebody, nobody will do business with them. Ever. He starves them out, and they will eventually fall back in line, or they'll just disappear—move on to another town and set up there. Like I keep telling you, he brought order to the chaos."

Before I can say anything more, my phone rings with an incoming video call from Lauren Church. Frowning, I get to my feet and start heading for my office.

"I need to take this," I call over my shoulder to them.

Once inside my office, I close the door behind me, then connect the call. Church's light brown eyes burn with an intensity, even through the phone, causing me to shift on my feet. There aren't many people who make me feel uncomfortable, but she is definitely one of them.

"Deputy Director—"

"Are you all right?" she cuts me off.

I'd ask her where she heard what happened, but it would be pointless. She wouldn't tell me. The fact that she knows this quickly after it happened only confirms just how well-connected she is. Her eyes and ears are everywhere.

"Bad news apparently travels fast."

"You're not new. You should know that by now, Blake," she says. "My question is, why didn't I hear this bad news from you?"

"Because I didn't feel there was anything worth sharing. I'm fine."

"You didn't think informing your direct superior that somebody tried to kill you was worth sharing?" she asks indignantly.

"Frankly, no. I didn't. Like I said, I'm fine," I tell her. "It's not the first time somebody's tried to shoot me. And it won't be the last. It's part of the job. I know and accept that and don't feel the need to come crying to you every time it happens."

The corners of her mouth flicker upward, but the amusement in her eyes quickly fades. This isn't just a social, how-are-you-doing call just to check up on my well-being. I can tell there's something heavy on Church's mind. And that sixth sense I have is tingling in the back of my mind, telling me I'm not going to like it.

"I would like to know why your team is in Cincinnati and you're there in Seattle," she says.

"I'm looking into the shooting of a city council member."

"Huan Zhao."

"That's right."

She looks at me for a moment, her lips pursed. "I'm told you have some kind of personal relationship with Mr. Zhao?"

"Yes, I do. He was a CI for me for a lot of years," I answer. "He helped me close a high number of very big cases."

I'm sure Church already knows all this, so I don't know why she's asking. It's not like I'm giving her new information. Perhaps she wants to know just how deep my relationship with Fish goes—which is something she may have heard rumors about, but very few people actually know. She might be testing me. This is her tune, after all, so all I can do is dance to it.

"Then, are you the best person to be looking into his shooting?" she asks.

"I am," I reply. "My relationship with him and all the players involved puts me in a unique position to be able to close this case."

"Do you have standing?"

"Detective Scott Kramer extended an invitation," I tell her. "We are collaborating."

She frowns and pauses for a moment. "Blake," she finally says. "My understanding is that Mr. Zhao is a major player in the Seattle underworld. How are you connected with him?"

"As I told you, he was my CI for a while," I reply smoothly and without missing a beat. "And I would point out to you that he has never been charged with, nor convicted, of a crime."

She gives me a withering look. "Don't do that, Blake. Don't parse words with me."

"Apologies, Deputy Director. I just thought you should have the facts," I say. "Regardless of his past, he is currently a sitting member of the city council and has a number of legitimate business and charitable interests. He's well respected in the city."

"His past is what I'm hung up on."

"We all have a past," I respond.

She frowns. "You're awfully protective of him."

"I'm protective of all my CIs. They put themselves in harm's way for me, and I feel like I owe them a lot. Mr. Zhao more than most."

"They put themselves in harm's way to avoid prison."

I shrug. "But they still put themselves in harm's way, so I feel responsible for them."

I'm walking a very fine line here. Nothing I've said is untrue. It's just not the full and complete truth as I know it. I'm doing my best to avoid lying to DD Church, but I'm definitely stretching the truth to the breaking point.

"Blake, I don't know that I'm comfortable with you being involved with this man," she says. "CI or not, he has a very sketchy, borderline criminal history."

"And he's now a member of the city council with a solid reputation and a respected businessman. We are all more than our pasts, Deputy Director."

She shakes her head. "Given his past, Blake... the optics are terrible."

"Respectfully, I think the optics would be a lot worse if we let the attempted assassination of a local politician go without doing our best to find the would-be killer."

"Why not let Detective Kramer run this case? Why involve yourself at all?"

"Because I can go places and talk to people Detective Kramer can't," I tell her frankly. "People in that world are distrustful of the police anyway. But given the way he goes about his job, they'll trust him even less. If I don't pitch in, this case will not be solved. What kind of message would that send to anybody with a grudge against their local politician?"

Church pauses and seems to be considering my words. Or perhaps more likely, considering the optics of action versus inaction as well as the potential political fallout. As fond of DD Church as I am, and as much as I believe she and I are aligned in most everything, she is a political animal, and she does have to consider the ramifications of things in ways I don't. Blowback from my actions will hit her differently. But I'm not going to let this go.

"Deputy Director, when we first talked about setting this team up, you said which cases I took would be at my discretion. You promised I would have autonomy in how I deployed my team without interference," I remind her. "I believe you gave me this command because you trust me—because you know I wouldn't do anything to make the Bureau look bad or, perhaps more importantly, tarnish your reputation."

She pauses for just a moment, then nods. "I believe all of that."

"Then all I'm asking is that you keep trusting me," I urge her. "There is nothing untoward happening right now. I'm simply trying to solve the attempted murder of somebody I feel responsible for. Somebody who has gone above and beyond to help me, even when it was to his own detriment. I feel I owe him at least that much."

She's quiet for a long moment, and neither her face nor her eyes give anything away. The woman has one of the best poker faces I've ever seen. But finally, her expression softens.

"All right, Blake. Do your thing," she says. "But I'm keeping an eye on you. I can see how invested you are in this case from three thousand miles away. But I don't want you losing perspective or objectivity either. If I feel that you have, I won't hesitate to pull you off this case."

"Thank you, Deputy Director."

"Keep me in the loop."

"I will."

"And do me a favor… try to not get shot."

I laugh softly. "I'll do my best."

CHAPTER FOURTEEN

Jade Pearl Billiards House, Chinatown-International District; Seattle, WA

Set in one of the older sections of Chinatown, the Jade Pearl is Fish's command center and the seat of his power. Although Fish himself is down in his office at city hall most days now, the day-to-day business of his organization is still conducted at the Pearl. It's where the other families come to pay their taxes and address any pressing issues. It's become kind of the unofficial capitol of Chinatown over the years.

The first floor of the building is a dingy but unassuming pool hall. Most of the young men sitting around playing are Fish's foot soldiers, tax collectors, and enforcers. Although, given the peace in the area, they don't do much enforcing these days. But Fish understands that having a standing army and keeping people employed is essential to retaining power and maintaining the peace, so he keeps them all on his payroll.

The second floor of the Pearl is where the magic happens. It's home to Fish's underground casino, filled with a host of different games of chance along with the office where he ran his empire. By this point, I'm such a known quantity around here that, although I garner many strange looks as I cross through the pool hall and then the casino, nobody stops or hassles me. The large man standing beside the door to Fish's office gives me a nod and opens it for me.

Fish's office is large and ornate, done in deep shades of red and dark woods, and a light hint of incense lingers in the air. The furniture is hand carved and elegant, infusing the atmosphere with a sense of sophistication and gentility. There's a certain gravitas that remains despite Fish not being here, which makes the office's current occupant seem woefully out of place.

"I thought I might find you here," I say as the door closes behind me.

"Even in times as trying as these are, the work must continue," he says.

Trevor Kondo is sitting behind Fish's oversized, ornately carved desk and looks up as I cross the office. I don't like him sitting there. It doesn't look or feel close to right or natural. It's kind of like watching a dog trying to ride a bicycle. Trevor's lips curl downward as I sit down in the chair before the desk, and he regards me with dark eyes filled with the disdain he feels for me.

Say what you will about the man—and I've said a lot—the one thing I can respect about him is that he doesn't sugarcoat the way he feels about me. I know where I stand with him. At least he's honest about it. And I would rather have somebody be blunt and truthful than hide their contempt behind a veneer of civility and falsity.

Trevor closes his laptop and sits back in Fish's chair. "I was not aware we had business together, Agent Wilder."

"We don't have business. Not together anyway."

"Then what are you doing here?"

"Hua Meng."

"What about her?"

"What can you tell me about her?"

Annoyance flashes across his features. "Probably not any more than you already know. You're always reminding me that you have tremendous resources at your disposal."

I cross one leg over the other and fold my hands atop my knee, ignoring his dig. I'm not here to be baited into an argument with him. My pettiness actually does have some limits.

"I have a feeling you've got a little more insight into the woman than I do," I reply.

He runs a hand through his hair. "What is this about?"

"This is about Fish's shooting."

"And you think Hua is behind it?" he asks, sounding amused.

"It's an avenue we're investigating, yes."

He scoffs. "Impossible."

"And why is that?"

"Because she does not have the spine," he tells me like it's obvious. "She pays her taxes faithfully and on time every month, has accepted her role, and never rocks the boat. She is content with the state of things. It would likely be a better use of your time and resources looking into some of the heads of some of the other families we have had problems with."

"Such as?"

"Pick one. Guang, Cao, Duan, Shao—they have all been very outspoken about their unhappiness with the state of things," he says. "I have told Fish many times we should do something to quiet their discontent, but he continues to refuse. Maybe if he had let me..."

His voice tapers off, but he doesn't need to finish that sentence for me to understand where he was going with that thought, and it's probably for the best he didn't finish it.

"So, everybody but Hua was outspoken about their dislike of Fish's rules?" I ask.

"Very much so."

"And Hua just silently accepted them?"

"That is what I said."

"Kind of makes her the last person you'd think would take a shot at Fish, huh?"

He opens his mouth to respond but pauses and swallows down whatever he was about to say. Trevor sits back and frowns, a thoughtful expression crossing his face as he looks away. He's silent for almost a full minute before turning back to me.

"I cannot see that. Not from her," he says. "I believe it was one of the others and have feelers out already—"

"Trevor, do not do anything stupid. You know Fish—"

"Fish is not here right now. And I cannot let what happened to him pass. We cannot afford to look weak. Not right now," he snaps. "Failure to act is simply going to embolden whoever did this. And we cannot let that happen. If we do, Fish will not have an organization to come back to."

"I'm telling you, let me do what I do. I will find the person responsible for this," I growl. "Stand down and let me work the case. Do not get involved, and do not get in my way. I don't want to have to arrest you."

Trevor is silent, his face dark and etched with anger. I doubt he's going to listen to me; he will continue on his path for vigilante justice. It only makes my need to get ahead of this—ahead of him—all the greater. I need to beat him to the punch.

"Anyway," I say. "I was told that her nephew was killed—"

"That was an unfortunate incident initiated by her nephew nearly two decades ago. If he had not come at Fish with a weapon, he would still be alive. His death is unfortunate, but it served a purpose," he cuts me off. "That's what finally got the Dragon Queen to fall into line. She finally realized the cost of defiance was simply too high."

"And you don't think she's harbored a grudge all these years?" I ask. "My understanding is that she's one of the most ruthless family heads in Chinatown and that violence is nothing to her. She doesn't strike me as somebody who's willing to forgive and forget."

"But like Fish, she also craves order over chaos."

"Does she?" I ask. "Or does she crave the sort of order *she* would bring?"

"She would not. I know her very well, and she would never try to kill Fish."

With every word he speaks, it reinforces my desire to speak with her all the more. It just seems obvious to me that somebody who flew under the radar and made a point of not rocking the boat would be at—or at least near—the top of a suspect list. That old saying about always keeping your eye on the quiet ones is an old saying for a reason.

"I'm surprised that you're so adamantly defending her," I say.

"I am not defending her. I just want you to find the person responsible as quickly as possible. I do not believe time spent investigating Hua is time spent wisely."

I shrug. "That's why I'm the investigator and you're not. If it makes you feel any better, I'm planning on speaking with all the other family heads, by the way. But I want to start with Hua Meng. So, please, tell me what you know about her."

He hesitates, and I can see he's thinking, possibly about what I said. Personally, I think Trevor dislikes me so much that he just automatically rejects whatever I say, almost like it's a reflex. It's ridiculous, but he acts like a sibling who resents me for the attention our parent gives me, thinking that he's entitled to all of it.

"Do you really believe that Hua could do something like this?" he asks reluctantly.

"I think it's very possible, yes," I tell him. "In my experience, the most outspoken tend to be all bark, little bite. It's those you'd least expect to be involved with something who end up being very involved. It's why I never rule anybody out of my suspect pool until I have a concrete reason to. And let's not forget she has ample reason to want to hurt Fish—the death of her nephew."

"As I said, that was a situation initiated by him—"

"It doesn't matter who started it. Logic tends to get thrown out the window when it comes to family," I cut him off.

He seems to consider my words. Trevor is always so sure of himself and thinks he has all the answers; the mere idea he could be wrong about Hua Meng is leaving a terrible taste in his mouth.

He's struggling with the possibility she could be the one who pulled the trigger. Struggling with the idea that he missed it—that he should have seen her coming but didn't. But most of all, he seems to be grappling with his emotions knowing his main job is to protect Fish, and he failed to do so.

"She is ruthless… that is true. But I have only ever witnessed that side of her in relation to those who work for her. She has never shown that sort of aggression toward Fish. And let us not forget: it has been almost twenty years," he says.

"Some people hide their emotions well and bide their time. It could very well be that this anger has been simmering inside of her all this time and she chose to strike now, when—as you put it—Fish has taken his eye off the ball and is being perceived as weak… which I completely disagree with, by the way. But if others feel as you do, then maybe she thought it was time to strike."

He's silent for another minute, and I can see the wheels in his head turning as he seems to be considering everything I've just said and having an internal debate. As if he's settled the debate in his mind, Trevor nods to himself, then finally raises his gaze to me.

"Hua operates out of a flower shop called Eastern Blooms," he says. "You can find her there almost every day."

"Not at her massage parlors?"

He shakes his head. "She keeps a buffer between the parlors and herself for obvious reasons. Julie Ching is her most loyal and trusted soldier. She oversees the parlors. But it is my understanding that Hua runs her other business interests out of the flower shop."

"If that's true, that seems reckless," I reply. "Drug distribution charges tend to carry stiffer penalties than prostitution charges."

"She does not trust anybody completely. Certainly not enough to let anybody oversee that aspect of her business other than her," he replies. "It is all about control."

I nod. "That makes sense. So, in her flower shop."

He nods. "In her flower shop."

"Can you tell me if you or Fish have received any other credible threats recently?"

"It is not like we document them," he replies. "But no, we haven't had any threats I would consider particularly troubling."

"So, things are peaceful and pleasant in Chinatown?"

He purses his lips. "For the most part, yes."

I study his eyes, searching them for some hint of deception. But I see none. He is either very good at controlling and masking his emotions, or he's telling me the truth. I want to believe it's the latter. I want to believe that we are on the same page and want the same thing, which is to find the person responsible for Fish's condition.

But I don't trust Trevor any more than I trust Detective Kramer. Both men always have their own angles and agendas that they're playing. And although he seems to be outwardly helpful, I have no doubt that Trevor is racing for the answers, hoping to get ahead of me so he can handle Fish's shooter the way he wants to… not the way the law requires me to. It reminds me that I'm on a clock—one that's ticking louder with every passing second.

"All right, thank you, Trevor," I say as I get to my feet. "Please give me a call if you hear anything that might be useful."

"Of course," he replies smoothly.

Yeah, right.

CHAPTER FIFTEEN

Brunson Professional Building, Downtown District; Seattle, WA

I TURN ONTO THE STREET THAT WILL TAKE ME BACK TO THE office when my phone rings. I glance at my phone sitting in the bracket on the dash and see the call is coming from an unknown number. Turning the music down, I answer.

"Blake Wilder," I say.

"Agent Wilder?" the man's voice comes through the car's speakers.

"Yes?"

"Good afternoon, this is Roy Odell," he says like I should know who he is.

I pause for a moment, but he doesn't continue. "And you are?"

"Oh. Apologies, I thought you would know me," he says. "I am Mr. Zhao's attorney."

"Ahh," I say. "Right."

Fish had mentioned his attorney's name to me a while back, but I'd put it out of my mind since I saw no reason to retain that bit of information.

"What can I do for you, Mr. Odell?" I ask.

"We need to have a conversation, Agent Wilder."

"About?"

"This isn't something we can discuss on the phone," he says. "Can you come to my office?"

With the attempt on my life fresh in my mind, meeting with somebody I don't know just doesn't seem like the smartest thing I can do right now.

"Yeah, I'm not sure that's a good idea—"

"Oh, right. Apologies," he cuts me off. "Mr. Zhao instructed me to give you a word to let you know this is on the up and up. Patchwork."

I pull to the side of the road and turn on my hazards. A long time ago, Fish gave me a code word he said would be given so that I knew whoever was calling me had legitimately been sent by him. At the time Fish set up this little system, I'd thought he was being paranoid. But he had insisted it was important, so I told him I'd remember the code word. I honestly never expected to have somebody give it to me. Of course, I never expected that somebody would try to kill him either.

It seems like he had anticipated and prepared for things that hadn't even been on my radar—things that probably should have been on my radar. In that way, I understand exactly how Trevor is feeling. In a way, I feel like I failed Fish too.

"Where are you, Mr. Odell?"

"The Brunson building. It's on—"

"I know where the Brunson is."

"My office is on the sixteenth floor," he says. "Odell and White."

"I'll be there in twenty."

"See you soon."

I disconnect the call and sit back for a moment, listening to the cars racing by me as I try to quell the torrent of emotions surging through me. I don't want to believe that Fish is going to die. But the fact that his lawyer is contacting me at Fish's direction suggests that Mr. Odell thinks there's a strong possibility of it happening. It's a thought that fractures my heart.

"Pull it together, Blake," I mutter.

Odell is obviously calling me for a reason. It tells me that Fish wanted me to know something. I want to believe Fish had the foresight to put together something pointing me to the likeliest suspect in the case of his untimely demise. Maybe he had proof of it. Maybe he had something that would lead me to his would-be killer. I have no idea what Odell has for me, but I have a strong feeling it's going to be important to the case.

I give brief thought to calling Kramer and having him meet me there. If it's important to the case, he should probably be involved. But I quickly reject the idea. Whatever it is and whatever Odell has to say, it will very likely reveal the nature of my relationship with Fish, and that's information about me I don't want Kramer having. If it's relevant to the case, I'll fill him in later, when I can control whatever information is revealed.

Getting my head back in the game, I turn around and head back to the downtown district, my mind still spinning as I try to figure out what this is all about.

I step off the elevator and into the large, plush lobby of the Odell and White Law Office. The lobby is sleek, modern, and clean. Four chairs line the wall to my right beneath artistic photographs of Washington's rugged landscape, and the wall to the left is adorned with photos of Odell, his named partner,

Jamison White, and their four senior partners beneath them. Everything about the lobby exudes competence and efficiency.

Across from the elevator a pretty and professional-looking twenty-something brunette sits behind a long, waist high desk. She offers me a cordial smile.

"Good afternoon," she says.

I approach and give her a nod. "I'm here to see Mr. Odell. My name is Blake Wilder."

"Of course," she says and gets to her feet. "If you'd follow me, please."

I'm sure I would break my ankles in the heels she's wearing, but she manages to glide gracefully through the office as she leads me down a long hall that ends at a large wooden door. She raps once then opens it.

"Ms. Wilder is here to see you, Mr. Odell," she says.

"Thank you, Claudia."

The woman gives me a nod and ushers me inside, closing the door behind me. A man is already crossing the office floor, his hand extended and a warm smile on his face. An inch or so taller than me, Roy Odell is a lean, trim man in a well-tailored, designer three-piece suit, charcoal gray with pinstripes, a white shirt beneath a dark gray vest, and a violet tie. His jacket hangs on the rack tucked discreetly in a corner near the door. His silver hair is cut short and neatly styled, and his dark eyes are quickly sizing me up.

"Agent Wilder," he says. "Pleasure to meet you."

"Please, call me Blake."

"Only if you call me Roy."

"Deal."

"Please, have a seat."

He escorts me to one of the two large, comfortable chairs in front of a desk that appears to have been hand-carved from a large piece of driftwood that was shaped, shellacked, and mounted on a black steel frame. It seems out of place with the rest of the furniture in his spacious office, which is light wood and modern in design. It makes me think that piece of wood has some sort of significance to him. His diplomas hang on the wall to the right of his desk along with photographs of what I assume is his family.

Odell sits down behind his desk, the glass wall behind him offering a gorgeous view of the city beyond as well as Mt. Ranier and the Cascades in the distance. The man has obviously done well for himself. Given that he works for Fish, I have to assume he only takes on high-dollar clients. It would also stand to reason that, given Fish's background, Odell doesn't mind operating in the legally, if not morally, gray areas of society.

He leans back in his chair and studies me for a moment. "I'm sure you're wondering what this is all about."

"It's crossed my mind, yes."

The smile on his face fades and is replaced by a more sober expression as he sits forward, clasping his hands together on the desk in front of him.

"Fish has been my client for a long time," he says. "He was with me when I was running my office out of a dumpy, one-room setup above a restaurant in Chinatown. He's loyal. And that's one of the things I appreciate about him the most. That kind of loyalty is rare these days."

"You seem to have done pretty well for yourself since then."

He nods. "In large part because Fish has steered clients my way. A very different kind of client than I was working with in that shabby old office. If I'm being honest, he helped get me out of my old ambulance chasing ways and into something better—not just more lucrative, but doing work that's better for my soul."

"And what kind of law do you practice, Roy?"

"I'm sure you won't be surprised to know criminal defense and some personal injury cases were my bread and butter back then," he tells me. "But since those early days, I've gotten into corporate law. I also handle probate, contracts, things like that. I do still handle a few criminal defense cases now and then, if they're compelling, but I'm a little rusty at it. I've found that it's kind of like riding a bike, and I still enjoy it despite it being a very different set of skills."

I stare at him, waiting for him to get to the point of this meeting. As if reading my mind, or perhaps just correctly interpreting the expression on my face, he chuckles to himself.

"Apologies. I sometimes ramble on and on," he tells me. "Anyway, I heard about Fish. A most distressing situation. Most distressing."

"It is."

"I'm sorry, Blake. I don't know the intricacies of your relationship, but you very obviously mean the world to him, and I can only assume those feelings are reciprocated."

I hesitate for a moment, unsure what to say since I don't know this man. But if Fish trusts him enough that he was comfortable giving him our code word and revealing the details of our relationship, I suppose I can too.

I nod. "They are."

His eyes fill with sadness, and it's not hard for me to see how much Fish means to him too. He's more than just a client to the lawyer. He's a friend.

"Well, in the event that something ever happened to him, Fish had some papers drawn up that he wanted me to execute—"

"Let me stop you right there. If you're talking about a will, Fish is still alive," I say. "And I'm certain he's going to recover. This is not only premature, it's unnecessary."

"I want to believe that too. But this is my job, Blake. I have to do this," he says. "Fish was getting a living trust set up, and one of the components is giving you power of attorney. He designated you as the one who will make his health care decisions in the case of incapacitation, which… which is where we're at right now. As much as we both don't want to consider it, he is incapacitated and needs you to make his medical decisions."

"What medical decisions are there to make? He's still alive—"

"I think you know what decisions need to be made. He was very clear about not wanting to be hooked to machines to support his life."

My stomach turns over on itself, and my heart leaps into my throat. When I first took Odell's call, this is not what I thought this would be about. I did not see this coming. And this is not a responsibility I want.

"I'm not capable of making these decisions," I tell him honestly. "I'm too emotionally invested and can't think clearly."

"Regardless, he trusted you to make these decisions. He signed papers to that effect."

I shake my head, fighting back the waves of emotion battering my soul. "I can't do this. I really cannot do this."

"There's more," Odell says. "Given that he has no children of his own and no heir, he has also instructed me to draw up papers that name you his sole beneficiary. In the event that Fish… that he does not make it, you are set to inherit everything."

"Everything?"

"Everything."

I rake my fingers through my hair, disbelief washing through me as my stomach churns and a greasy, nauseous feeling rises within me. This rabbit hole I'm being sucked into is getting even deeper. This can't be happening. This seriously cannot be happening right now.

"Roy, you and Fish obviously go back a while, and I'm not naïve enough to think you don't know what sort of business he used to be into… is still into, even if it's marginally so these days."

"I do know. I know everything," he says. "I might even know more than you. But that is by design. His greatest desire was to protect you."

"Can you stop talking like he's already gone? He's not."

"Of course. Apologies."

"Anyway, being that you know what he's into, he can't believe I am going to take over his empire. He can't believe I'm going to—"

"Let me put your mind at ease. His intention is not for you to ascend to the top of his organization. Far from it," he tells me. "But he wants you to have every one of his holdings—his buildings, his portfolio, bank accounts—the works. He's simply leaving you all his earthly wealth and possessions. They will all be yours. As for his organization, he said that is going to have to sort itself out. And yes, he knows the chaos that preceded him will return, but he said there is simply nobody he trusts to take over his affairs."

"Nobody he trusts?" I ask. "What about Trevor?"

"That is the one thing you will not be getting," he says. "Control of the Jade Pearl Billiards Hall will be given to Trevor. Fish said it will be up to him to make his own way."

I sit back in my chair, my head spinning and my vision wavering. None of this makes sense to me, and I don't know what I'm supposed to do with it. With any of it.

"Why would he do this?" I ask.

"Isn't it obvious?" Odell replies. "He loves you, Blake. He thinks of you as a daughter."

A choked sob bursts from my mouth, and I can't hold back the tears that overwhelm me. I lower my head and scrub away the tears, struggling to assert control over myself. It takes a few minutes, but I finally manage to calm myself down enough to function. As I sniff back the tears, I raise my head again. Odell is looking at me with an expression of pure sympathy and kindness.

"I understand this is overwhelming and perhaps more than a little daunting. But wishing something didn't happen doesn't make it so," he says firmly. "Fish has been shot, and we need to accept the possibility that he may not recover. And decisions must be made... decisions he trusted *you* to make. Please don't let him down."

Odell pulls a sheet of paper out of the folder in front of him and slides it across the desk toward me. I pick it up, and even though I can see the words, I might as well be looking at something written in Cantonese for all the sense they're making to me right now.

"What's this?" I ask.

"We're going to start with this. This is the sheet granting you power of attorney," he says. "I need you to sign this, Blake. More importantly, Fish needs you to sign this."

Fresh tears well in my eyes as he hands me a pen. It feels like it weighs a thousand pounds as I hold it in my hand. Feeling as lost as I did the day I came home to find my parents' dead bodies on the floor in our home, I shake my head and look to Odell.

"It's okay," Odell says gently. "This is what Fish wants."

Gritting my teeth, I swallow down the twin fists of fear and grief that are gripping my heart and squeezing so hard, I feel like I can't breathe. But I manage to scrawl my name on the lines Odell highlighted with red, sticky arrows. When I sign the last one, I drop the pen and push them all away from me as fast as I can.

"Good. That's really good," he says.

"It doesn't feel good."

He looks at me, his lips twisted wryly. "No. Nothing about this feels good. You're right."

"So, what now?"

"Now, I'll give you copies of these papers; you will want to show them to his doctors, talk with them, and assess the situation," he says. "After that, I think you'll know what to do."

"I don't think I'm strong enough to do it."

"Nonsense," he replies. "Fish told me you're the strongest person he's ever known."

I wince as Odell's words send another stitch through my heart, and I find myself in a battle to keep a fresh wave of tears from falling… a fight I know I'm going to lose.

"That's enough for today," he says. "We'll get together at a later date and talk about the next steps and what's to come."

"What's to come is Fish waking up from his coma and recovering," I tell him.

His eyes are gentle, and his smile is soft. I can see he wants to believe the same thing, but I can see the skepticism in his face. I also know he's bound by pragmatism and the rules of his profession to honor the wishes of his client.

"I hope so too," he finally says. "I really do."

CHAPTER SIXTEEN

The Chapel, SNAP Team HQ, Industrial District; Seattle, WA

"WOW. EVERYTHING?" NINA ASKS.

"Everything—except the Jade Pearl," I say. "That's being left to Trevor, which I suppose means he's leaving his organization to him as well. I can't say I'm thrilled with that idea."

"Why is that?" Opal asks.

"Because Trevor doesn't have the temperament. He believes in peace through force. His big idea to solve Fish's shooting was to go and kill the heads of the other families, no questions asked," I reply. "He wanted to send a message."

"When he would have simply ignited a war," Nina says.

"Exactly," I say. "And whenever Fish does finally go, which I am hoping is many years from now, with Trevor in charge, I fear Chinatown is in for a lot of carnage."

"He's going to bring back the bad old days," Nina grouses.

"I guarantee it," I respond. "Diplomacy is not a word he's familiar with."

Opal is quiet but has a thoughtful look on her face. Perhaps she's reconsidering her view of Fish, seeing for the first time that things could—and would—most definitely be worse with somebody else at the top of the food chain. She clears her throat and turns to me, and I can see in her eyes that she isn't ready to have that conversation yet.

"So, he gave you power of attorney," she says. "I guess that means you have to make the final decisions about his medical care."

"I do," I reply somberly.

"That is a tough ask," Nina says. "I wouldn't want that kind of power."

"I don't either."

"It shows how much he trusts you," Opal says.

"He's shown me that in a thousand other ways."

She shakes her head. "This is next level trust. This is literally the power of life and death. I know you don't want this power, but it's a testament to his feelings for you."

"I guess so. Anyway, I'm not making any decisions one way or the other today. We've got bigger things to worry about," I say. "Speaking of which, where are we with the footage?"

"We were able to find the footage of the shooting," Nina says slowly.

"All right. Good work," I reply. "Put it up on the main screen please."

Nina and Opal exchange a glance, and in that moment of silent communication between them, I already know what their concern is.

"It's all right," I tell them. "This is the job. And I knew I was going to have to see some unpleasant things when I took this case. I'm fine. Let's see it."

The screen at the foot of the table flashes to life, and Nina calls up a black and white image that's a bit grainy. It's not the best footage, but it's not the worst we've seen either.

"What are we looking at?" I ask.

"This is from a street cam about a block from Fish's building," Nina replies.

"What about footage from his building?"

"The cameras don't have an angle on the street," she says.

"They're more concerned with seeing who's coming through the front door than what happens on the street beyond it," Opal adds.

"Okay, let it roll."

A few seconds go by, and we're seeing nothing but the empty street. But then Fish's black Escalade comes into view. It slows as it approaches his building, then stops at the curb in front of the covered walk that leads into it. The driver jumps out and races around to the other side, opening the back door for him. Fish climbs out and presses something into the man's hand, obviously a tip. There's no audio, but we can see him saying something to the driver that makes them both laugh.

Fish pats the man on the shoulder, then waves as he goes around and gets behind the wheel and drives off. We watch as Fish pulls his phone out of his pocket, seeming to be reacting to a call, then presses the phone to his ear. In the distance, a pair of headlights appears, drawing slowly and inexorably toward Fish.

"Look up," I whisper. "Look up."

But he doesn't look up. This script has already been written and the movie already filmed. He continues talking on his phone, gesturing wildly and seeming to be growing more agitated. The black SUV pulls up alongside him, and somebody leans through the passenger side window holding a long gun. The shooter must have said something because Fish finally looks up, and I watch in horror as the muzzle of the weapon flashes. Fish twitches and jerks as the rounds tear through him. He crumples to the ground, and the SUV speeds off.

A thick, dark wave of emotion washes over me, and I struggle to keep it in check. Now is not the time for that. Now is the time to get my head in the game and work the case. This is our first solid lead, and I need to keep my mind clear enough to take advantage of it.

"Can we get the plate on that SUV?" I ask.

"Negative," Opal replies. "The camera quality isn't good enough to pick it up."

"Nina, scroll back," I say.

She does, running the footage back to just before the SUV pulled up alongside Fish. Tapping a key, she lets it play. A brutal stitch in my heart, I watch as the man leans through the window again, the gun in his hand and pointed at Fish.

"Okay, stop," I say.

Nina hits a key and stops the footage, the shooter perfectly framed. Getting up from my chair, I walk closer to the screen and stare at the image for a minute.

"Can you blow this up?" I ask.

"I can, but it's going to pixelate the image more than it already is," she tells me.

"That's okay. Just blow it up."

"You got it."

She blows up the image and, just like she'd said, the image is pixelated and distorted. But I'm not looking to make out the shooter's features. I just wanted to confirm that I was seeing what I thought I saw on the first run through.

"He's got a balaclava on," I say. "No matter how good the picture, we wouldn't have been able to see his face anyway."

"What kind of weapon is that?" Opal asks.

"Looks like it could be an AR-15. Maybe an M4," I reply. "I'll have to look at the medical report to see what caliber bullet they pulled out of him."

"Pretty heavy-duty stuff," Nina says.

"Unfortunately also pretty common these days," I reply. "Anybody can get their hands on these things."

"Which means we probably have a snowball's chance in hell of tracking the weapon from the point of sale," Opal says.

"I think it's adorable you think they bought it legally," Nina says.

"I think the snowball has a better chance than we do of tracking that weapon," I tell her. "But if we can recover it, we can hopefully get a ballistics match, which will help us secure a conviction on the back end."

I turn away from the screen, unable to look at Fish's broken form any longer. I hear Nina tapping at her keys and know she's taking the footage down out of respect. Turning around, I give her a thankful nod. She gives me a gentle smile in return, then lowers her head and starts working on something else.

"So, what's our next step?" Opal asks.

"I'm going to go see Kramer and update him on what we have—which isn't much," I reply. "But I at least want him to feel like I'm keeping him in the loop."

"That's kind of you."

"I do my best."

"And after that?"

"I'm not sure just yet," I respond. "But that SUV is the key. We've got to find a way to track that vehicle down."

"I think I can help with that," Nina says slowly.

"What do you have?" I ask.

"Give me just one minute," she says and keeps working.

"Take your time."

As she continues working, my mind unwantedly flashes back to the image of Fish being shot. I knew this case was going to be emotional the moment I took it. I knew it was going to be difficult the minute I saw him in that bed hooked up to that battery of machines. But seeing the event that led to that—seeing him actually being gunned down—somehow made it all the more real, which in turn made it even more emotional and even more difficult. I wasn't ready to see it. I needed to see it, but I wasn't ready, so I'm grateful for the brief respite as Nina works on whatever she's working on to gather myself.

Nina turns, a grin on her face, practically bouncing in her seat. "I think we've got him."

"Talk to me."

"I followed the SUV on traffic cams, and a couple of blocks from Fish's building," she says excitedly, "he passed through an intersection with a camera and plate reader."

She tapped a few keys, and the image of the intersection came up. The camera is much clearer than the street cam near Fish's building, and it gives us a clean shot of the SUV… and its occupants. Unfortunately for us, the driver and passenger both are still wearing their balaclavas, so we can't see their faces. But the image of the plate is pristine. Opal is already firing away at her keyboard the moment it comes into focus.

"The SUV belongs to Henry Ma. Thirty-seven years old and single, Ma owns a dry-cleaning business and lives in the Lower Queen Anne District," Opal reads off her computer screen.

"Does Mr. Ma have a record?" I ask.

Her eyes bounce back and forth as she reads her screen. "Not that I can find. As far as I can tell, he's clean as a whistle," she says, then turns to me. "But really, what are the odds somebody who took a shot at a city official is stupid enough to use his own car?"

"Criminals, by and large, are stupid," Nina says. "Blake loves to say that."

"Because it's true," I respond. "But I take your point, Opal. However, if he's clean as a whistle, it's possible he's not very well versed in avoiding detection. The only thing stupider than a criminal is somebody who's not used to committing crimes trying to commit a crime."

Opal nods. "Or it means he's smart enough to cover his tracks. Like you said, that shooter of yours policed his cartridges. For all we know, he could be a seasoned pro."

"Well, sounds like I need to have a conversation with Henry Ma to see if he's stupid or not," I say. "Really good work, guys."

Opal shifts in her seat and seems uncertain. Our training tells us that we should never go solo and should always bring backup with us when going into any unknown situation. Especially when this could likely be the guy who already took a shot at me once. She seems to be teetering on the verge of offering to go with me. Knowing her reluctance to be in the field after what she experienced, I let her off the hook.

"You two keep digging into the footage," I say. "Comb it backward and forward. Find me anything else you can."

"Copy that," they say in unison.

Opal's expression is relieved—and guilty.

CHAPTER SEVENTEEN

Residence of Henry Ma, Lower Queen Anne District; Seattle, WA

"FBI?"

"That's right," I reply. "I'm Unit Chief Wilder. And you are Henry Ma?"

He nods, his eyes still fixed on my badge, horror etched upon his face. He licks his thin lips, then swallows hard, seeming to be attempting to gather himself. Ma is a small man: five-five or five-six at most and lean. His coal-black hair is cut short, and dark, almond-shaped eyes are hidden behind a pair of wire-rimmed glasses. He's got a smooth, olive-colored complexion, and a bit of a baby face that makes him look twelve instead of thirty-seven.

"Uh, yeah. I'm Henry. What's this about?"

"Can we speak inside, Mr. Ma?"

He looks behind him, then turns back to me, his expression confused. But he shrugs, then opens the door and steps aside.

"Sure. I guess," he says.

I walk into the small bungalow-style home, which is clean and tidy. Framed photos of his parents hang on the wall above a small table that holds candles, incense, and bowls of fruit. Ma leads me into the living room, gesturing to the chair that sits perpendicular to the sofa, and offers me a seat. A cup of coffee sits on the table, tendrils of steam curling off the surface, and the anchors on the local TV station are muted. Everything about this place is normal. It's as plain and unassuming as the soft-spoken man himself.

On the surface, he seems like a mild-mannered—perhaps even milquetoast—kind of guy. The khakis and plain blue polo shirt only serve to reinforce that image. I can't explain why, but I get the sense there's more to him than that. There's no one thing about him that I can point to and say, yes, that's what it is. Over the years, I've learned that most everybody has something deeper—perhaps darker—lurking below the surface. You just have to dig for it.

I have no idea what I'm going to find when I dig into Ma, but I feel like there's something there. He's just too... normal. Plain. The sort of guy you'd forget five minutes after meeting him, and I kind of feel like that's by design. His ordinariness almost feels like an artifice. There is just a vibe I feel, a sense in the pit of my stomach, that tells me there's more to Henry Ma than meets the eye. What that is, however, I don't know.

"So, what is this about, Agent Wilder?"

"Huan Zhao," I say. "Do you know him?"

A thoughtful look on his face, Ma takes a moment and seems to be thinking.

"No, I don't know that name," he says. "I'm sorry."

"You're sure?"

"It doesn't ring any bells, no. I'm sorry."

"Huh. That's interesting."

"Why is that?"

"What would you say if I told you that we have your vehicle on camera at the scene of a shooting?" I ask. "More, we have footage of a man with your physical build pulling the trigger?"

That last bit is obviously an embellishment, but he doesn't know that. I'm just hoping he unintentionally gives something away as I watch his reaction closely. But much to my disappointment, his face remains completely passive. Expressionless.

"I would say there is some sort of grave misunderstanding," he says. "I do not own a gun, and I most certainly would never shoot somebody. Especially somebody I don't know."

"Are you sure about that, Mr. Ma?"

"I'm positive," he replies smoothly. "But, now that you mention it, I do recall reading about a recent shooting in the paper. He's a city councilman, right?"

"Yes. That's correct."

Neither his eyes nor his face gives anything away. If he's lying, he's doing a tremendous job of hiding it from me. He looks and sounds sincere. Even still, there's something about this guy that's got me on edge. I don't know what it is, but I sense something else about him, lurking just beneath the surface. It's like seeing a shadow on the other side of an opaque piece of glass… I can make out the form and shape but can't see anything with any clarity. All I know is that my gut is telling me something about this guy is off.

Ma leans forward and rests his forearms on his thighs, his hands clasped together. "In fact, I can prove to you that I was not behind the wheel of my car the night Mr. Zhao was shot."

"And how can you do that?"

"Give me just a moment," he says.

Ma gets up and heads out of the living room. An uneasy feeling steals over me so I get to my feet and unsnap my holster, standing casually, but with my hand hovering near my weapon. I hear Ma shuffling through what sounds like papers in the other room, and a moment later, he comes back into the room and stops, putting his hands up.

"Easy," he says and waves the paper he's holding. "I was just getting this."

"What is it?"

"A police report."

Letting my jacket fall closed, I walk over and take the paper from his hand and quickly scan the text. And as I read what's been printed, I feel like an idiot.

"My SUV was stolen about a week ago. That's the police report I filed," he says. "So, it's not possible for me to have been in the car the night that man was shot."

Well, damn. He's right. There is no way he could have been the shooter because he didn't have his car. My gut isn't perfect, but it's rarely this far off. It doesn't change my belief that there's something more about this man, but the window into his soul has grown even more opaque. I don't understand it, but there is something about this man I don't trust. In the face of this police report it's irrational, but I know, deep down on a primal level, this man isn't who he says he is.

"As you can see, the SUV isn't even in my possession, Agent Wilder."

"I can see that," I say and hand the document back to him. "How did it come to be stolen?"

He pulls a face. "The same way every other car that gets stolen is stolen, I suppose."

"Where was it when it was taken?"

"In my driveway," he replies. "I went to bed and woke up the next morning to find it gone."

"And you didn't leave it unlocked or…"

"No, Agent Wilder," he says testily. "I locked and set the alarm the same as I do every single night when I get home."

"And you never heard your alarm—"

"No, I didn't hear my alarm go off," he says. "Whoever took it must have found a way to disable my alarm before it could wake me."

"And, do you have any idea who took it?"

"Is that a serious question?"

It's not. Not really. That stolen car report put me so far back on my heels that right now, I'm just throwing anything and everything against the wall, hoping something sticks. I have nothing but this series of inane questions that do nothing but irritate him and frustrate me with the hope that he says something to trip himself up.

"Is there anything else, Agent Wilder?" Ma asks. "I really do need to get on with my day."

"And you say you've never heard of Huan Zhao before?"

"How many times must I answer that question? The answer will not change," he snaps. "No, I do not know him."

I sigh and quickly search my brain, looking for something I can throw out there that might trip him up… something that might implicate him. Try as I might, I come up empty. I have absolutely nothing. I'm just having a hard time reconciling my gut feeling about Ma with the big platter of nothing sitting right in front of me. He's not just the mild-mannered dry-cleaning man. He's something more than that. I know it. But my gut isn't proof of anything.

I fish a card out of my pocket and hand it to him. "Thank you for your time, Mr. Ma. If you think of anything, please give me a call."

"Sure."

I walk out of his house and back out to my car knowing I'm never going to hear from the man. My every instinct is telling me something about that guy is off. His car being stolen and then used in Fish's shooting just seems too convenient to me. Of course, there is that annoyingly rational voice in the back of my mind telling me I might just be trying to force a square peg into a round hole out of desperation to find the person who did this. It's a voice that seems to be growing louder and won't let me ignore it.

"Oh, shut up," I mutter as I climb into my car.

CHAPTER EIGHTEEN

Seattle PD, Homicide Division, Precinct W, Queen Anne District; Seattle, WA

"Hey," he says.

"Hey."

"Have a seat."

"Thanks," I reply and drop into the chair in front of his desk.

Before I had even gotten down the street from Ma's house, Detective Kramer called and wanted to meet. He said he wanted to go over what we have and update each other on the case. The last thing I wanted to do today was spend even a single second with him, but I need to keep up the illusion that I'm playing nice. I also figured it might be a good idea to get a peek at what he might be hiding from me, and so, I made my way to the precinct.

"I just wanted to check in with you," he says. "See where you're at. Show you where I'm at. You know, pretend we're working the same case."

My lips twist wryly. Clearly, he and I are on the same page about things. I figure I can pull back the curtain a bit and give him a show—especially since I honestly don't have a lot.

"All right, well, we got street cam footage of the shooting," I start.

"I had our techs check, and they didn't find anything," he says.

"I guess your techs didn't look very hard."

"Where did you get the footage?"

"From the city's street cam system," I say like it's the most obvious thing in the world—because it probably should be. "I'll make sure Nina sends you a copy of the footage."

"I'd appreciate that. What does it show?"

"The quality of the footage is poor, so unfortunately, not much," I tell him. "But she was able to tap into a plate reader camera at an intersection the car passed through a couple of blocks away. We got the name of the vehicle's owner—"

"That's fantastic."

"It's not. I spoke with him this morning—"

"You went and spoke to him without me?" he says indignantly. "I thought we were supposed to be working this case together? Or at least, making it appear that we are."

I have to fight to keep from rolling my eyes. He's fine with my team doing the grunt work behind the scenes, but wants to be there, front and center, when there's a potential case-breaking event in the works and cameras might be present. Typical.

"Honestly, I didn't think it was going anywhere. How stupid would a bad guy have to be to use his own car in a drive by shooting?" I say, throwing what Opal had said at him. "I was just checking off a box. And it was a dead end, just like I figured it would be."

He leans back in his chair, his lips pursed and a sour look on his face. "In the future, since this is still my case, I would appreciate it if you let me know before unilaterally making moves like that by yourself."

I snap him a mocking salute. "Aye, aye, Captain."

"What else do you have?" he asks. "Why do you think this guy is a dead end?"

"Because the SUV was stolen," I reply. "He showed me the police report. The vehicle wasn't in his possession at the time of the shooting."

"Huh."

"Yeah."

"All right, I showed you mine. Time to show me yours," I say. "What do you have?"

"An idea."

"An idea?"

He nods. "Up for a field trip?"

Not really. But he's piqued my curiosity. "Sure."

"You drive."

We've spent most of the day buzzing around town, traveling from one shop to the next. Admittedly, it hasn't been as terrible as I thought spending a day with Kramer might be, but it hasn't exactly been sunshine and roses either. We pull to a stop in the parking lot of the last place on our list—Junker's Wrecking Yard.

"Last chance," I say.

"Don't remind me," he grumbles.

We get out of my SUV and head across the parking lot. A bell chimes as we walk into an office that smells like motor oil and gasoline and is filled with the sound of country music. A tall, grizzled man with a blue ball cap over his scraggly gray hair, deep set blue eyes, and three days' worth of growth on his cheeks and chin, looks up at us from his position at the desk. When his eyes fall on Kramer, a sour expression crosses his face.

"And here I was, having a nice day," he grumbles.

"I see your reputation precedes you," I whisper.

Kramer shoots me a dark look and frowns, then turns back to the man in the blue cap.

"What do you want, Kramer?"

"I want to know what you're chopping up out back," he replies. "You happen to have a black SUV back there? What was it… a Yukon?"

I nod. "It's a black Yukon."

The man sighs. "We really doing this?"

"What are the rules, Jack?"

The man's sour look curdles even more as he spits a gob of brown tobacco juice into a bucket beside his desk. I do my best to keep from vomiting.

"Fine. Let's go," he says.

As we walk, Kramer turns to me. "Jack here runs one of the more prestigious chop shops in town. I look the other way and pretend to not know about it in exchange for information when I require it. Like now."

"I see," I reply.

Developing CIs is important to our work. To do that, we sometimes have to make deals with criminals. In the grand scheme of things, running a chop shop is still illegal, but is probably low on the list of criminal offenses, and can sometimes yield valuable intel. I'm actually impressed that Kramer was able to rope this guy in as an asset. I honestly didn't think he had the finesse or people skills necessary for that kind of work.

Jack leads us through his labyrinth of a salvage yard, the stench of oil, dirt, and gasoline growing thicker the deeper we get into the yard. We pass a dozen or so different people who are pulling pieces off wrecked out cars they need for their own. He leads us to an outbuilding that sits unobtrusively near the back, then uses a key to unlock the padlock that hangs from the chain on the door. Jack pulls it open, then gestures for us to step inside. I follow Kramer through and step into a large, open garage.

On the floor are half a dozen different cars. These aren't wrecked. Despite being in various stages of deconstruction, they're all in good condition—obviously stolen.

"Over here," Jack says.

We follow him to the far side of the building where a tarp covers a large SUV. He grabs the corner and yanks it off, revealing a black Yukon. Kramer turns to me.

"This was brought in a couple of nights ago. Ain't had a chance to get to work on her yet. It was on the schedule tomorrow," Jack says.

"Brought in by whom?" I ask.

"By persons unknown," he replies.

"Right," I say.

"Is this it?" Kramer asks.

I pull my notebook out and quickly flip through the pages. Jack sighs and shakes his head as a wry smile crosses his face, then he spits another gob of tobacco juice on the floor.

"That's disgusting, by the way," I say.

"Lady, I'm about thirty years older than you, and even I know how to use my phone for all this kind of stuff," he says, his voice deep and gravelly.

"Seriously?" Kramer asks. "You do realize this is the twenty-first century, right? We've got these handy little computers in our pockets—"

"Shut up. Both of you. You guys do your things your way, and I'll do my things my way," I cut him off, drawing a chuckle from him.

I find the page with the plate number I'd jotted down back at the Chapel and compare it to the plate on the Yukon sitting in front of us. It's a match.

"This is it," I say.

"Excellent," Kramer says.

I turn to Jack. "You're going to need to take this off your schedule. It's coming with us."

"Now, wait a minute," he starts to protest.

"Those persons unknown used this Yukon in an attempted murder before they brought it into you," I tell him. "There may be valuable forensic evidence inside, so we're taking this. Unless you want to get into a conversation about your business and how you came to be in possession of this Yukon, we can certainly do that."

His face blanches. "Attempted murder? Now, I didn't know anything about that."

"Relax," I tell him. "I know how this game works, and we're not here to bust you."

"As long as you don't give us a hard time about it," Kramer adds.

Jack shakes his head and scowls, clearly not happy about giving up the Yukon and being out the money he paid for it, but knowing he's not in a position to argue. Kramer turns to me.

"All right," he says. "I'll have this taken to the SPD garage—"

"I'd rather have it taken to the FBI lab—"

"Out of the question. My case, my car, my garage," he says.

My scowl matches Jack's as I find myself in the same position he's in. Like him, I'm in no position to argue because this is Kramer's case, and he can revoke his invitation at any point.

"Fine," I say. "But I want to be kept in the loop the whole way. If you find a used tissue, I want to know about it."

"Fair."

"And if there is any potential for DNA evidence, I want that sent to our labs since we've got the better toys," I tell him.

He hesitates for a moment, then nods. "Fine."

"All right. I guess we have ourselves a deal then."

"We do," Kramer says.

"Yeah, you got a deal. I'm happy for you. But I'm the one footin' the bill and gettin' screwed in this whole thing," Jack grouses.

"Smile, Jack," Kramer says. "At least we're letting you stay in business."

I laugh and, for the briefest of moments, find myself actually liking Scott Kramer.

CHAPTER NINETEEN

Mountainview Medical Center, Downtown District; Seattle, WA

I step into Fish's dimly lit room, my eyes first falling on his still form beneath the sheet in his bed. I'm instantly hit by a wave of emotion. The room is quiet, the air tinged with the acrid smell of antiseptics and death. But when I realize Trevor is sitting in a chair in a shadowy corner of the room, that emotion building within me instantly evaporates and my body grows taut, as if the mere sight of him throws me into self-defense mode.

His fingertips pressed together, Trevor sits with his legs crossed, his dark eyes glinting in the dim ambient light. He says nothing. He just sits there, staring at me.

"If you're auditioning for the role of creepy supervillain, you nailed it," I say.

The corner of his mouth twitches, but he says nothing. He drops his hands into his lap and lets his gaze fall to the floor. The air crackles with tension, and the mutual dislike between us has never been more evident than it is right now. Trevor finally raises his head. His eyes are narrowed to slits and hard. Although he seems to be battling to control his emotions and keep his face neutral, it's impossible to miss the anger burning in his eyes.

"The doctors say there's been no change in his condition," he says.

"I can see that."

"Decisions will need to be made," he says. "And my understanding is that you are the person who has been appointed to make them."

His voice is hard and bitter, and he glares at me like he finds it offensive that Fish would have trusted me enough to make any decision on his behalf, let alone his medical decisions. As much as I want to tell him to go screw himself, there's some small part of me that understands. Trevor was raised like he was Fish's son. He's the only father figure Trevor has ever really known, which is something he and I have in common.

But rather than come together through that shared bond in our time of shared grief, Trevor has gone the other way and built a wall between us that's even higher and thicker. It's obvious that his resentment of me has never been greater.

"Why?" Trevor asks. "Why did Fish give you power of attorney?"

"I have absolutely no idea. It's something I've asked myself a thousand times already."

He frowns. "I will never understand why he was so partial to you. All you've ever done is cause problems for him."

For years, I have tried to play nice and keep the peace with Trevor. I've done my best to ignore every jab, every snarky comment, and every bit of vitriol he hurled at me. I'm done with it. Maybe it's because I'm standing here looking at somebody I care about hovering on the edge of death and I'm the one who has to decide whether to push him over or not, but my patience with Trevor has run out. I'm done with him.

I round on Trevor, my face burning, and my veins filled with fire. "Your immaturity is very likely why Fish didn't trust you to make decisions for him. You behave like such a spoiled, entitled little brat, he doesn't believe you have the capacity to do the right or smart thing."

Trevor is on his feet in a heartbeat, his face twisted with rage. "Who in the hell do you think you are to speak to me that way? I was with Fish long before you came into his life. I have helped him build his empire. I have done everything for him, and you have done nothing but weaken him."

"Everything but grow up and learn to be a decent human being," I counter. "You never understood what Fish wanted—what he *truly* wanted. All you want is power, Trevor, when all Fish wanted was peace and to put meaning to his life. That's the difference between the two of us. I understood that about him."

Trevor's face darkens and his lips curl back over his teeth. He looks like he desperately wants to take a swing at me, and part of me wishes he would. I'm not really a big fan of violence, but the idea of whooping Trevor and putting him in his place is appealing as hell right now. It won't solve a thing… but it might make me feel better for a little while.

Trevor closes his eyes and draws a deep breath, then holds it and seems to be silently counting. As he lets it out, his dark eyes open again, and some of the ferocity I saw just a moment ago seems to have ebbed. He pauses and composes himself.

"This bickering resolves nothing," he says, his voice low and calm. "Regardless of whatever exists between us, decisions must be made. We need to do the right thing by Fish… *you* need to do the right thing by him."

"Trevor—"

"You know I'm right, Blake. You know he did not want to live this way," he says and gestures to the machines. "If this can even be called living."

"I'm not ready to give up on him yet."

Trevor's jaw flexes. "Letting him linger on like this isn't going to bring your real parents back. Do the right thing by him. Fish chose you to make these decisions for him, so reward his faith in you, and do what he wanted you to do."

His words strike such a deep, painful chord inside me that it leaves me breathless and speechless. Before I can recover, Trevor heads for the door but pauses with his hand on the knob.

"Have you ever stopped to consider that Fish being in that bed, hooked up to all those machines, is *your* fault?" he asks without turning around.

"How do you figure?"

"Knowing what you do and the sort of people in his life, are you really naïve enough to imagine there would be no consequences to him for being so close to a Fed?" Trevor asks. "Did you really presume your presence in his life would not cause anger among some of those people? Especially given the fact that you pressured him into helping you take some people down?"

"I didn't pressure—"

"If I had to guess, I would say somebody took exception to you being in his life and punished him for it," Trevor says. "As far as I'm concerned, you are as responsible for him being in that bed as the person who pulled the trigger."

He glances over his shoulder and stares at me with sheer disdain on his face before turning and walking out of the hospital room, leaving me sputtering and unable to formulate a coherent reply. It's only when the door clicks shut behind him that a response forms on my lips. But uttering a four-letter reply to a door just doesn't have the same impact as being able to say it to his face.

I do my best to dispel the impotent rage burning inside of me as I pull a chair to Fish's bedside and sit down. Taking his hand in mine, I sit with him in silence for a few minutes. In that quiet, Trevor's words echo through my mind. Is he right? Is my hesitance to take Fish off life support related to my still unresolved feelings about my parents? Is there something in me that believes by keeping Fish alive, I'm trying to compensate for their deaths?

"I'm not sure what to do," I whisper, my voice quavering. "I'm certain this isn't what you want, but I don't want to give up on you either… not when I still have hope that you'll come back."

The only response is the beep and hiss of the machines that are keeping him alive. I hate to admit that Trevor is right about anything. The man doesn't have the first clue who I am. And he certainly doesn't understand the things I've endured in my life. But is it possible he knows enough that he can see what I'm doing even if I can't? Am I so obvious and transparent to somebody I despise, but remain completely opaque to myself?

Deep in my gut, I'm sure Trevor is right. Fish doesn't want to live this way. He's also right that this isn't living. But my heart won't let me do what I'm sure is the right thing. It hits me then that I never realized just how much Fish means to me—not until this moment, as I hold the power of his life, or his death, in my hands.

"Why did you do this to me?" I ask. "Why would you ask me to do this?"

As I hold on to his hand and lower my head, alone in that room, I finally let the tears flow.

CHAPTER TWENTY

Eastern Blooms, Chinatown-International District; Seattle, WA

"IF ALL THOSE DRUGS ARE IN THIS SHOP, WHY ARE WE tiptoeing around it?" Kramer asks. "Why don't we bust her for what she's got, then lean hard on her?"

I look at Kramer, doing my best to keep from rolling my eyes. "They did teach you about probable cause at the police academy, right? We can't just bust in there and search the place until we find something we can use. We'd need a warrant for that. And we don't have anything close to probable cause for a warrant. A judge would laugh us out of his chambers."

He grunts. "Then what are we even doing here?"

"I want to size the woman up," I tell him. "Maybe if we rattle her cage hard enough, we can get her to slip up. If she's even involved, that is."

It's going to take a few days for SPD to finish processing the SUV, so I decided to use that time productively. Since he showed me trust by letting me tag along to see Jack, his informant, I figured I can extend an olive branch by letting him join me as I question Fish's biggest rivals. It's easier to seem magnanimous since Hua Meng isn't one of my CIs. Besides, having some backup when questioning some of the most ruthless people in the city isn't a bad idea.

"So, we're just fishing," Kramer says.

"Hope you brought your pole."

The bell over the door rings as we step into the cool air of the shop. The wall to our left is one large refrigeration unit filled with buckets of loose flowers as well as pre-arranged bouquets, all vividly colorful, behind the sliding glass doors. Several tables and stands are set up on the floor of the shop, displaying the different accessories—balloons, stuffed animals, etc.—that can be included with your arrangement. The air is… fragrant. The aroma of so many different flowers saturating the shop is almost cloying. Soft string and flute music plays, and despite the nearly overwhelming floral aroma, there is a sense of peace and calm in the store.

A woman in her mid-fifties carrying a broom steps through a doorway behind the counter on the far side of the shop. She's small, no more than five-three and thin, almost pixie-like, with a smooth, olive-colored complexion. Her short black hair is flecked with gray, and she has gentle lines at the corners of her obsidian-colored eyes. In blue jeans and a dark blue button-down shirt with short sleeves, she's casual and, to me, doesn't look like the head of a brutal crime family.

"Welcome in, how can I help you?" she asks.

We badge the woman as I make the introductions. "This is Detective Kramer of the SPD. I'm Unit Chief Wilder, with the FBI."

Her face is completely neutral, and if she's surprised to have a pair of cops in her shop, she gives no hint of it. If anything, she looks completely unimpressed.

"As I asked a moment ago," she finally says, her voice soft and lightly dusted with an accent, "how can I help you?"

"Hua Meng?" I ask.

"Yes. Although, I suspect you already have my name and photo in your files," she says. "It's nice to meet you Agent Wilder. You are something of a ... legend."

"Legend?" Kramer asks.

Meng looks at him. "A great many people who made trouble in Chinatown are currently in prison because of her efforts."

Kramer grunts, steps away, and starts walking through all the displays, seeming to be taking it all in. He's not being subtle about what he's doing. He's looking for any sign of criminal activity he can use as probable cause to conduct a search. It's a waste of time. Does he really imagine a crime boss like Hua Meng, who's been operating in Chinatown for decades, is going to be stupid enough to leave a bag of coke lying around in plain sight?

Frankly, I'm glad he's not hovering over us, just in case Ms. Meng mentions my relationship with Fish. It's not information I want Kramer to have, and I realize that bringing him along to this meeting might have been an oversight on my part. I didn't really consider all the possible ramifications. But he doesn't seem to be paying attention to us.

"What do you want, Agent Wilder?"

"I want to talk to you about Fish."

She nods. "I assumed you were here to discuss that. However, let me save you some trouble. I had nothing to do with it."

"That's fine," I reply. "I still have to ask some questions."

Meng stares at me for a moment, seeming to be wrestling with something in her mind. She gives herself a brief nod, as if she's come to a decision.

"Fish has always said you are fair. He trusts you," she says. "Can I trust you, Agent Wilder?"

"You can."

"Are we completely off the record?"

She's quiet a moment as she studies me. Meng is taking my measure and trying to decide whether she hears sincerity in my voice or not. I hesitate. I probably shouldn't go completely off the record with her, but I understand why she wants to be. I'm sure she's got a ton of incriminating evidence. But that evidence could be used to incriminate her as well, hence the request to be off the record with it all. It's smart. If I don't agree, she won't talk. If I do, I can't use anything we find against her. Meng is clever—an attribute that has served her well for many years.

But at this point, I've got to take what I can get. I nod.

"Then ask your questions," she says.

"I understand you, unlike some of your counterparts, had no problem following the rules Fish put in place," I say.

"That is correct."

"How is it that the others had a problem with the rules, but you didn't?"

"Because my counterparts are intemperate fools."

"Care to elaborate?"

She sighs and begins to sweep the floor around us. "Times have changed, and there is a new generation that has risen. Fei Duan and I are the only original family heads left," she says. "The new heads of the other families—they're young, hotheaded. Foolish. To them, strength, power, and respect can be had through violence."

"And that isn't your philosophy as well? My understanding is that you are one of the most ruthless heads in the city. I hear they call you the Dragon Queen because of the things you've done, for God's sake—"

"I've done what I had to do to stay in control of my family," she cuts me off hotly. "To ensure this new breed doesn't infect my family with their cancer. My acts are necessary and for a purpose. They are never gratuitous. I am not, by nature, a violent person, Agent Wilder."

"But sometimes, some people just need to be killed, huh?"

A brief grin flickers across her thin lips. "Your words, not mine," she says. "As for being fine with Fish's rules, that is because

I respect the man and what he has done very deeply. Would I like more profit? Of course. But I do well enough, and not having to wade through blood or dodge bullets every day is worth it. Peace and order in the streets allow us all to prosper. That is something this younger generation does not understand. They are—"

"Intemperate."

"Yes," Meng says with a smile. "However, that is why I do not begrudge Fish for his rules. He has always treated me with respect and provides a service to this whole community. And that is why I wish no ill upon him. The alternative is… distasteful. It is frightening to consider, if I am being honest."

It's strange to hear somebody with a reputation for ruthlessness express fear of anything. Kramer wanders back to where we're standing and eyeballs the woman. She gives him an icy stare, her lips turning downward. He turns to me.

"So? She give you anything?" he asks.

"I have nothing to give you," Meng replies.

He turns his gaze to her. "What if we went into the back room and found all your drugs? Would you have anything to give us then?"

"Kramer," I hiss.

Meng looks at him with an amused glimmer in her eye. "Do not mistake me for an ignorant woman. I am well aware of my rights, Detective. Do you have a warrant to search my place of business?"

He remains silent and shifts on his feet as the cocksure expression on his face slips.

"I assume not," she said. "Since you do not have a warrant, I am certain you must be aware that anything you find—and I am not admitting there is anything to find—cannot be used in any sort of legal proceeding against me."

Kramer's expression sours. He's clearly underestimated the woman, and I have to stop myself from laughing. She put him in his place better than I could have. Kramer is flustered. He simply turns and walks out of the shop, muttering under his breath the entire way. When he's gone, I turn back to Meng, who looks rather pleased with herself.

"I apologize for him," I say. "His people skills need some work."

"I am used to dealing with police who assume they can gain somebody's compliance by bluffing and bullying," she replies.

"So, if you were to hazard a guess, who might have been responsible for Fish's shooting?" I ask. "Which of the other families—"

"If I were to hazard a guess, it was not one of the families who shot Fish. The kids are foolish, but in my opinion, none of them have the strength or spine yet to mount an attack on him. None of them would want the sort of backlash that would follow if they were to take that shot and miss," she says.

"No?"

She shakes her head. "Not yet. There will come a time when somebody feels strong enough to take their chances, but it won't be for some time yet," she explains. "Fish may not have as large of a footprint in Chinatown as he once did, but his presence and, more importantly, his organization remain. He has gone legitimate, but make no mistake, Agent Wilder. Huan Zhao is a product of this life, and if he survives his wounds, there will be a reckoning. Everybody knows that, and right now, everybody is holding their breath, waiting to see what happens. There is genuine fear on the streets."

I pause and let her words sink in. I am certain Fish has evolved beyond that. Yes, he's a product of these streets and this life, but he's more than that now. Perhaps I'm being naïve, but I don't want to imagine that if he does survive his wounds, that he will regress and seek retribution. He is better than that. What she said about it not being one of the Chinatown families, however, is echoing in my mind.

"Not one of the families," I say. "Then… who?"

"I cannot say. But in this new life he has created for himself, Fish has made many more new rivals, and likely, many more new enemies as well. This new life of his is, in some ways, fraught with even more peril than his life before. Out there, he doesn't have the same sort of protection he enjoyed here in Chinatown."

She makes a good point. I have been so laser focused on the enemies he's made here, in this life in the underworld, simply because it made sense. Criminals do criminal things. But Meng isn't wrong about potential enemies and rivals in his new life. It's not necessarily the high-stakes world of DC politics, but even local and city politics can be cutthroat and can get downright nasty.

Having their power and control challenged has made many a person lose their mind and do the unthinkable. And if there is one thing Fish has never been shy about doing, it's challenging a person's power and control. He's a natural boat rocker.

"Thank you, Ms. Meng," I say. "I appreciate your time."

She gives me a slight nod. "Good luck, Agent Wilder."

I walk out of the flower shop and find Kramer leaning against the car, his arms folded over his chest, his displeasure written all over his face.

"What was that?" he asks.

"You walked into that all on your own," I say. "You underestimated her, and she made you look like a chump. That's on you."

He sneers but doesn't argue further. "Get anything out of her?"

"Yeah," I say. "We might be looking at the wrong nest of vipers."

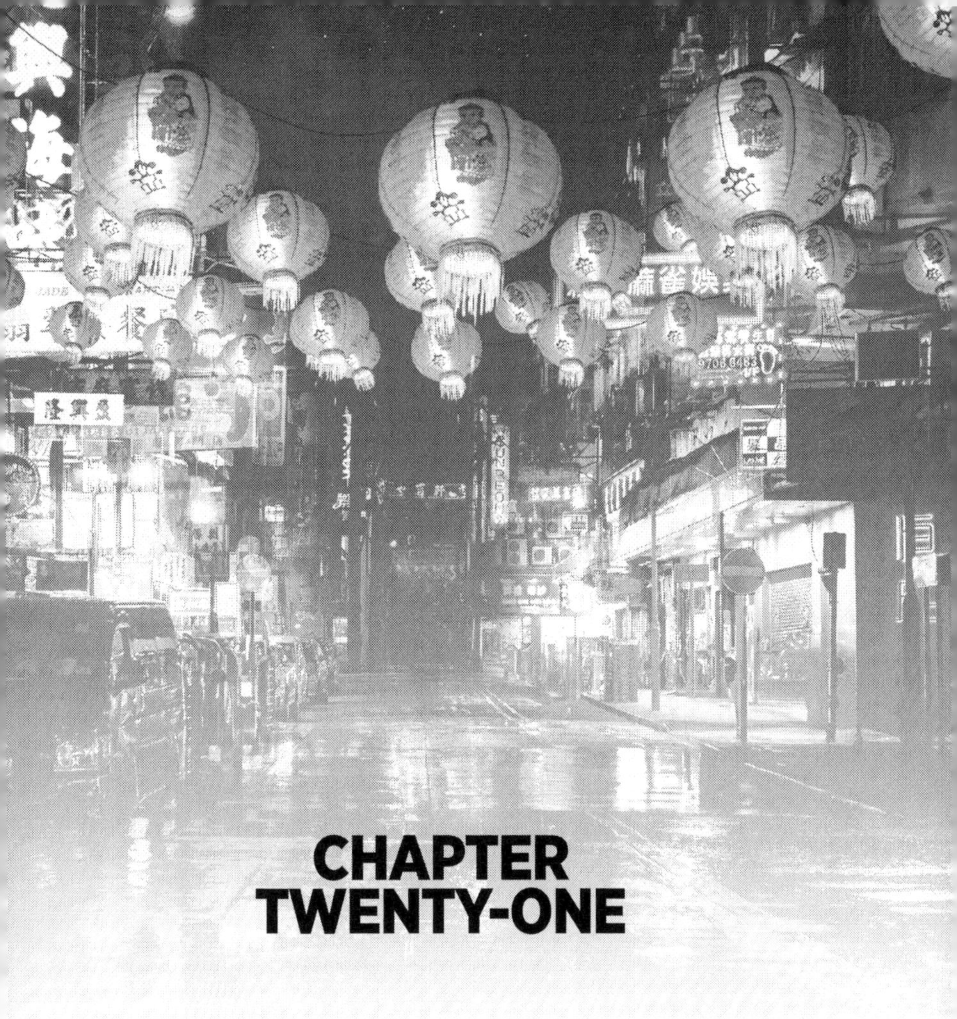

CHAPTER TWENTY-ONE

City Hall, Downtown District; Seattle, WA

After our meeting with the Dragon Queen, Kramer said he needed to get back to the precinct, which was just peachy with me. I want to do this part alone anyway since I'm playing a hunch. I take the elevator up to the fourth floor where the city council's offices are located, then step out of the car and into the lobby. I make my way down the hall and find Fish's office.

The door is cracked, so I push it open and find a young woman sitting behind the desk. She looks up as I walk in. With chestnut-colored hair that's cut short, hazel eyes, and a smooth, fair complexion, she looks somewhat young—probably mid-to-late twenties. She's dressed smartly in a charcoal pantsuit with a white blouse beneath the blazer and has a professional bearing.

It strikes me as I walk in that I've never visited Fish in his office before. The anteroom is quiet and very generic, with the same dark blue carpeting that's out in the hall, off-white paint on the walls, several chairs that don't look too inviting, and black and white photos of the city on the walls. Several plants stand in the corners, and his assistant's desk looks like something from IKEA. Standard governmental issue.

"Oh, I'm sorry, Councilman Zhao is not in," she says.

I flip open my badge. "Unit Chief Blake Wilder, FBI."

She gives me a wan smile. "I'm Melinda Ackerman. I'm Councilman Zhao's assistant," she says. "He's spoken of you. You're the one person he said never needed an appointment to see him."

"Is that so?" I say with a feeling of fondness.

"It is," she replies as her expression sobers. "Are you looking into what happened to Mr. Zhao as well?"

"I am."

"I'm glad it's you," she says. "Mr. Zhao told me you are the finest investigator he's ever known. If anybody can find the monster who did this, I'm sure it's you. I have a much better feeling about you than the other guy, and my grandma always said when I got a feeling about people, it was usually right."

"The other guy?"

"Yeah, Detective Kramer. He was here the other day asking about threats too. I didn't get a good vibe off him. It was like he was just checking boxes and didn't exactly seem... invested in finding Mr. Zhao's shooter, if that makes sense. He came in, glanced at these files and asked a few questions that just felt... generic. I mean, he didn't even write anything down. He was in and out of here in less than ten minutes."

I'm not sure whether to be glad that Kramer is doing a little legwork on his own or irritated that he didn't mention it to me. Of course, I haven't kept him apprised of all my movements either, so I suppose I can't be too upset. Besides, it doesn't sound like he actually did any sort of in-depth investigation.

"I appreciate your confidence in me, Melinda, but this case is very complex," I say. "It would be best to manage your expectations."

"Sure, yeah. Of course," she replies.

Her face clouds over with emotion, and as her cheeks flush, I can tell she's struggling to keep the tears from falling.

"You two were close," I say.

She nods. "He was the kindest man," she says, her voice thick. "One time, my car broke down, and I didn't have the money to get it fixed. When Mr. Zhao found out I was taking the bus, he rented me a car and then had mine fixed. He said it was just to make sure I was to work on time, but I know it's because he's a good man."

"That sounds like him."

"Yeah," she says softly. "He always does nice things like that. He really is the kindest, most considerate man I've ever met. It's why I can't understand why somebody would do this."

"That's what we're trying to figure out."

"Is there some way I can help?"

"There is," I say. "You work hand in hand with him? You see and hear pretty much everything that's happening in and around this office?"

She nods. "I do."

"Good. The first thing I want to ask about then are threats he might have received from the public," I say. "I assume he's received some?"

"He liked to say he wouldn't be doing his job if some people didn't get upset with him."

"Do any in particular stand out?"

She chuckles. "A few. We've gotten some really colorful ones," she tells me. "We print them out and keep them in a file. Most are harmless—just people blowing off steam. But it's good to have a record just in case."

"Of course. That's a good practice," I respond. "May I see them?"

Melinda gets to her feet. "Follow me."

She goes to the door to the right of her desk and opens it, stepping inside and turning on the light as I follow her in. Fish's office is as generic as the anteroom. Everything is subdued and understated, which is about the polar opposite of Fish, who is as flamboyant as they come. Everything about the man, from his clothes to his personality, is designed to draw attention to himself. He's got the spirit of a showman and an energy that's infectious. It's probably one of the things I like most about him since I'm not that way in the least. I admire his ability to put himself out there the way he does—something I've never been comfortable doing.

As generic as the office is, no doubt kept that way to put on a professional appearance, he still managed to put his own stamp on the place. I recognize some of the paintings on the walls as having come from his office down at the Jade Pearl, same as the large stone Foo Dog that sits in the corner. On top of his desk are some small figurines that had once sat atop his desk at the Pearl. When I see the framed picture on his desk of the two of us, my heart lurches, and I have to swallow down the lump in my throat.

The wall above the credenza behind his desk is filled with photographs of Fish with city dignitaries and a few celebrities, but most are of him with the children he works with. His smile is wide and warm, and it's not hard to see how much he loves what he does. Fish is most always in a good mood, and you'll usually find him laughing with somebody. He knows how to make the best of things. But the pictures of him and the children show just how genuinely happy it makes him to champion them… to make sure they are well cared for and provided for.

That's just who he is. Whether it's underprivileged kids in the city, an assistant who needs her car fixed, or a federal agent who needs a safe place to call home, Fish is always there, always happy to step in and make sure people have what they need. It's a side of the man I wish people like Church and even Opal would see and embrace. Of course, it's impossible to not acknowledge the things he's done in the past. I just wish he would get as much credit for the good he does in this world as the scrutiny and judgment he receives.

Melinda walks over to a tall filing cabinet and opens the second drawer. She pulls two thick files out, then carries them over and sets them down on Fish's desk with a solid thud.

"Wow," I say. "I guess by his standard, he's doing his job really well."

"This is just the last six months," she says. "After that, we box them up and keep them down in the storage room. But I keep everything backed up on digital files. He can be a bit old-fashioned in his way of doing things sometimes."

"Sounds like him," I say, not telling her I can absolutely relate. "You have these all stored digitally?"

She nods. "I do."

"Then would you mind if I take these?" I ask. "I'd like to have my team analyze them, then run the names of the senders."

"By all means."

"Terrific. Thank you."

"Of course. If it helps find who did this to Mr. Zhao, I'll give you whatever you need."

"I appreciate that, Melinda."

"Is there anything else I can get for you?"

"Actually, there is," I say.

Administrative assistants tend to be walking fountains of information. They're often unseen and unnoticed by the movers and shakers, but they see and hear everything. And more importantly, for my purposes, they tend to talk to one another. It's that way in most any office, be it the FBI field offices, the hallowed halls of Congress, or city hall. There is always somebody listening. The paper threats in my hand are a valuable lead that we'll run down, but the hunch I'm playing is that Melinda is going to have heard the scuttlebutt I'm actually after.

"How can I help?" she asks.

"Did Mr. Zhao have problems with any other members of the council? Or anybody in city hall, actually," I say. "Did he have any particular rivalries or clash with anybody?"

Melinda purses her full lips and looks out the window for a moment, considering my words. She finally turns back to me.

"I mean, he's gotten into it with almost everybody on the council at one point or another," she says. "Mr. Zhao is nothing if not passionate in his beliefs."

"That's very true. But was there anybody he got particularly heated with?"

"Well, I mean, he and Councilman Drummond had some pretty good clashes," she says. "Drummond said we shouldn't be spending as much on children's programs as Councilman Zhao does. It kind of set him off."

"Yeah, that definitely would. Does Councilman Drummond strike you as a man who carries a grudge? Somebody who might—"

"Oh, no. Not him. He's very kind and compassionate. But like Mr. Zhao, he's very passionate about his positions. They've clashed, but I haven't ever heard of any genuine bad blood between them. They respect each other."

"What about anybody he might have had bad blood with?" I ask. "You're in a position to hear the word around city hall."

"People gossip. I like to listen," she says with a mischievous smirk. "But I don't usually traffic in rumors. It's mostly just to help Mr. Zhao. It helps him when he knows what other people are talking about."

"Of course. I like to listen to people talk too," I say conspiratorially.

"Well, this is just people talking, but I did once hear Councilman Fitcher get so upset with Mr. Zhao that he said he was going to kill him. I mean, it's just bluster. Things get heated and people say stupid things. I never took it to mean he'd kill Mr. Zhao literally. You know what I mean?"

"I do."

It probably is just fiery rhetoric, but it gives me something to check out. It's worth finding out if Councilman Fitcher was so upset that he decided to make good on his threat.

"That's great, Melinda. I really appreciate you talking with me today," I say. "And I will make sure to get these files back to you as soon as I can."

"No rush. Like I said, I've got them all backed up digitally."

"Terrific. And if there is anything else you can think of, or anything you might recall, please give me a buzz," I say and hand her a card.

"I'll do that," she says. "And please, find out who did this. Mr. Zhao may not be everybody's cup of tea, but he's a good man. And he didn't deserve what happened to him."

"I agree with you. And I promise you, I'll do my very best."

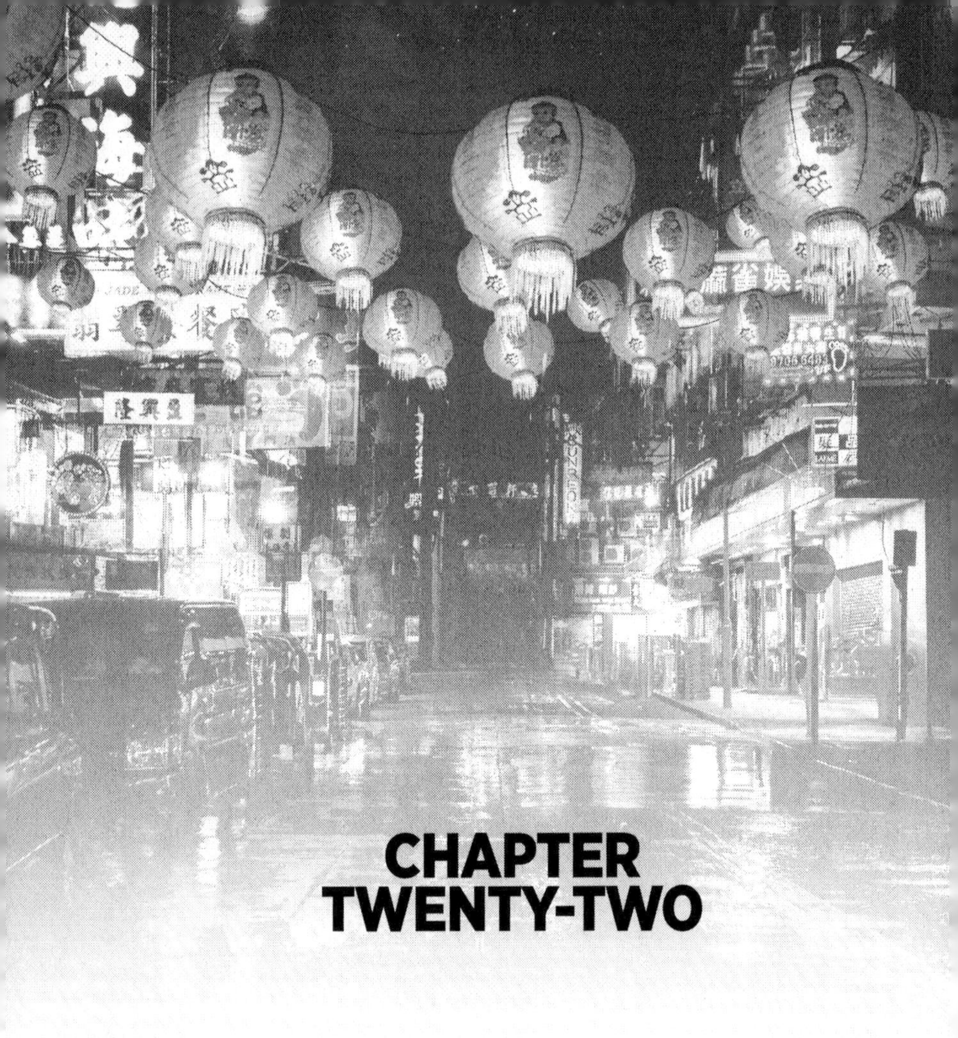

CHAPTER TWENTY-TWO

City Hall, Downtown District; Seattle, WA

FIGURING THERE'S NO TIME LIKE THE PRESENT, MY FIRST stop after leaving Fish's office is down the hall to the office of Councilman Harrison Drummond. Melinda said he respected Fish, but I'm not leaving a single stone unturned in the search for the one who tried to kill him. If they clashed, he's on my list of persons of interest until I have a reason to remove him. Guilty until proven innocent, I suppose. It's not the proper way to view people, but at this point, I don't really care. As long as I don't do anything to violate their rights, what's in my head doesn't matter.

I step into the anteroom to find Drummond's assistant sitting behind her desk. Her nameplate reads Jennifer Reidel, and she's a thirty-something platinum blonde with light blue eyes, a trim figure, and a professional smile that holds all the warmth of Antarctica.

"May I help you?" she asks in a tone that suggests she'd rather do anything but help me.

"Unit Chief Wilder," I say, offering her my badge. "I'd like to speak with Councilman Drumond please."

"Sorry, Councilman Drummond isn't in—"

The words had just barely cleared her lips when the door to her right opens and a man I take to be Councilman Drummond thanks to the nameplate affixed to the wall steps out.

"Jen, can you—"

He swallows the rest of his sentence when he sees me standing there with my badge still in hand. Jennifer grimaces. Dressed in blue slacks, surprisingly inexpensive shoes, a dress shirt that looks like it came off the rack, and a sensible light blue tie, Drummond is neither a cutting-edge fashionista nor exceptionally flamboyant. He's sensible and obviously doesn't spend a ton of cash on his wardrobe. That's something I can respect about him.

"FBI," he says. "You must be here about Huan?"

"I am."

"Please, please, come in," he says. "Jen, please hold my calls."

She turns her eyes up to me and shrugs. "Sorry, it's my job."

"Don't sweat it."

I follow Drummond into his office, and he shuts the door behind us. He motions for me to take a seat in one of the chairs in front of his desk while he drops into the chair behind it. His office is exactly like Fish's. Same deep blue carpeting, same industrial factory furniture, same eggshell white paint on the walls. The only differences are the personal flourishes. It's probably a matter of practicality since there aren't many lifers in the city council, and keeping the same basic model in every office saves the city a ton of money when the seats turn over.

Drummond proudly displays his undergraduate degree from the University of Washington and Masters from Washington State along with framed photos of his family, a beautiful blonde woman and their two young children. He's not much older than me but already has the perfect nuclear family. Their photographed wholesomeness will be perfect for his campaign posters and ads when he eventually runs for a higher office, which I would bet my entire pension on. He just has the look of a climber to me.

Drummond gets settled and turns his gaze to me, his expression sober. "What happened to Huan is terrible. It's just awful."

"It is."

He clears his throat and leans forward. "So, how can I help you, Agent..."

"Wilder," I respond. "Unit Chief Blake Wilder."

"Very good, Chief Wilder. How can I help you?"

"I wanted to ask you about your relationship with Mr. Zhao. I've been told that the two of you had some memorable clashes."

He blows out a silent laugh. "I've had clashes with everybody on the council. I've even had clashes with the mayor. I wouldn't consider any of them exceptionally memorable."

"No?"

"Not really. Politics is a rough and tumble business, Chief Wilder. If you don't fight for what you're most passionate about, you may as well just hang a sign around your neck that says 'doormat,'" he tells me. "I fight for what I'm passionate about and for my constituents. That's the nature of the game we play here. I won't apologize for that, nor will I change the way I do business."

"Fair enough. But how was your relationship with Mr. Zhao outside of chambers?"

"It was fine. I respect Huan very much. He's an intelligent, driven, and passionate man who also fights for his causes and his constituents. He and I agree on more than we disagree on and are on the same side more often than we're not."

"I was told the two of you didn't get along," I tell him, stretching what Melinda told me.

"I have no idea who told you that, but it's simply not true. In fact, he's been to my home a number of times. My children are very fond of him. So is my wife," he says with a rueful chuckle. "In fact, she says I should try being more like him."

"How so?"

"He's always even-tempered and never seems to get upset about much," Drummond replies. "The only time I've ever heard him raise his voice is when he and I went at it about funding some programs for children in the city. I argued the money would be better spent on first responders. He disagreed. Vehemently. But I respect that about him. He stands his ground and is not afraid to fight for what he wants."

"And how did you resolve your differences?"

"We agreed that both programs are important, so we found a compromise. We worked together and found a way forward," he replies, his tone wistful and tinged with sadness. "That's one of the best things about him. He's always willing to find a way to compromise and looks for ways that everybody can win."

"That sounds like the way he operates."

He nods. "I like that about him. He refuses to back down once he's dug in, but he also doesn't have to be the winner. He recognizes that we're all in this together."

Drummond leans back in his chair and runs a hand over his face. He gazes out the window, his expression thoughtful and his eyes filled with sadness. He genuinely seems to like Fish—seems to be authentic in his reactions and emotions surrounding his shooting.

"I hate that this happened to a good man like Huan. All he's trying to do is make this world a better place. We may not agree on how we get there all the time, but he genuinely wants to leave the world in better shape than he found it. It's a rare quality these days," Drummond says.

"Councilman Drummond, is there anybody who doesn't hold him in the same kind of regard you seem to?"

"I honestly don't think any one of my colleagues would try to kill one of our own," he says. "But if you're looking for somebody who didn't like Huan, you're going to want to look at Paul Fitcher. Those two were like oil and water. Or perhaps oil and fire is the better metaphor. They were on opposite sides of most every issue, and unlike Huan, Paul is not one to compromise. Honestly, he's one of the most difficult people to deal with around here."

"Have you had personal run-ins with him?"

"Oh yeah. More than I can count," he replies with a rueful chuckle. "Paul is the hardest of the hardliners, and anybody who's even slightly to the left of his positions gets labeled a bleeding heart. He's not a bad guy necessarily, and he's certainly entrenched in his positions and won't budge. He's not a compromiser, but he's not a killer."

"Why does he dislike Mr. Zhao so intensely?"

"He's not shy about saying Huan doesn't belong on the council," he says. "I mean, look, we've all heard the rumors about Huan's past. About the sort of man he used to be and the things he's been accused of. I have no idea if any of it's true—none of us do—but Paul is taking it all as gospel. He says Huan is a criminal who should be in prison, not helping decide the fate of this city."

"What about you? What do you say?"

Drummond shrugs. "I've heard the stories, but to the best of my knowledge, you can't convict a man based on rumor. What I can tell you with absolute certainty is that since he's been on the council, he's been nothing but upstanding and professional," he says. "Now, is there some truth to the rumors? Who knows. There's a lot of smoke for there not to be some fire. But I judge somebody based on how they treat their fellow man, and Huan has never been anything but an upstanding gentleman here in City Hall. So, he's all good with me."

I pull my notebook out and jot down a couple of notes, specifically questions I want to ask Paul Fitcher when I get a chance to sit down with him. In my experience, those with the loudest bark are seldom the ones who bite, but that's not always the case. Knowing he doesn't like Fish means I at least need to have a conversation with him. As I said, no stone unturned. But I would honestly be surprised if this Fitcher character is my guy.

"Last question, Councilman Drummond, and forgive me ahead of time—"

"I was home the night he was shot," he says. "And no need to apologize. I understand you have a job to do, and this is standard protocol."

"It is. So, you probably understand I need to ask if there is anybody who can back that up?"

"Just my wife and children," he replies. "It was spaghetti night."

"Spaghetti night, huh?"

"The kids love it, and my wife's sauce is spectacular."

It's so wholesome. I'm sure it will make its way into his eventual campaign for Congress or whatever office he aspires to. I can almost see the ads now.

"All right, that's going to do it for now then," I say as I get to my feet. "I appreciate you taking the time out to talk to me."

"Of course. If there's anything I can do, just give me a call. I want to see the animal who did this brought to justice."

"So do I," I respond. "Thanks again for your time."

I make my way out of his office then down the hall to find Councilman Fitcher's office. I step into the anteroom and am greeted by his assistant, a thirty-something brunette who seems to have a sunnier disposition than Jennifer.

"Councilman Fitcher is expecting you, Chief Wilder," she says.

I stare at her, dumbfounded for a moment, drawing a laugh from the woman.

"Word gets around these halls pretty quick," she informs me. "We don't get FBI agents in these parts too often. Councilman Fitcher said it was only a matter of time before you came by and so, he cleared his schedule for you."

"Oh. Well… thank you," I say.

"Please, go right in."

Feeling like I'm back on my heels already, I walk into the councilman's office to find him on a call. He raises a finger to indicate he needs a minute. Fitcher is a tall, broad man with a deep, gruff voice. He's bald up top, he has a neatly trimmed beard that's dark brown and flecked with gray, and his dark, wide-set eyes never seem to stop moving. He's in a dark suit that's a nicer cut than Drummond's but far from lavish. His jacket hangs on the back of his chair, the top two buttons on his vest are undone, his shirt sleeves are rolled up to the elbow, and he's wearing a blood-red tie.

Fitcher's office is exactly the same design and color as Fish's and Drummond's, and like them, his personal stamp is all over the place. He displays degrees, family photos, and plenty of mementos from various hunts he's gone on. One wall is lined with taxidermic animal heads, and below them hangs a large hunting rifle. A pair of antique pistols are in a glass case on a bookshelf in the corner as well as photos of him on what appears to be a safari in Africa. He's a clear advocate of the Second Amendment and sport hunting. To each their own.

He disconnects the call and drops his cell onto his desk, then offers me a nod. "Chief Wilder. Pleasure to meet you."

"You too, Councilman Fitcher. And I appreciate you squeezing me in."

"Just call me Paul. And you're welcome. I want to get to the bottom of this, same as you."

"Very well," I reply. "I suppose it's best if we just jump into things."

"I always appreciate directness."

"Good. I understand you aren't particularly fond of Councilman Zhao."

"Can't stand the man," he replies. "You want my honest opinion? He doesn't belong in office. The man is a criminal."

"You are aware he was never tried or convicted—"

He waves me off. "An unindicted criminal is a criminal all the same," he says. "As I'm sure you've gathered, I'm a pretty strict law-and-order guy. I've heard all the stories about the man they call Fish, and truth be told, I think there's truth in every single one of them. In fact, I'll go you one better. I've got a lot of friends within the Seattle PD, and they've told me that back in the day, Zhao was an informant for the Feds, and they helped wipe out his competition—enabled him to become Chinatown's big boss. What do you think of that?"

I think his sources are pretty good. Thankfully, they don't seem to be good enough that he knows Fish was working as *my* informant. I decide to keep that information close to the vest. Being as pro-law and order as he seems to be, I can't imagine how bad this man might have flipped out on me had he known I enabled Fish to become Chinatown's "big boss."

"When you work in law enforcement, and any cop will tell you this, you sometimes have to work with unsavory people to effect positive change for the most people," I tell him.

"I'm surprised to hear you say that," he says, his tone dripping with judgment. "Being a Unit Chief in the FBI, I'd have figured you to be as anti-criminal as I am."

"Make no mistake, I am anti-criminal. But I've also been doing this job long enough to know that accomplishing the greater good sometimes means you've got to work with all sorts of characters," I say diplomatically. "But we're getting a bit off topic here. Right now, I want to ask you about Mr. Zhao."

His face contorts in distaste. "Yeah, well, I'm sorry he got shot and hope he recovers, but I'm not going to lose any sleep or shed any tears over it."

I physically sit back in my seat like he just smacked me, and for a couple of moments, I'm rendered speechless. That is not the sort of answer I was expecting.

"Wow," I finally say. "That was… blunt."

"Like I told you, I value directness," he says. "It's no secret that I don't like the man, and I'm not the sort who plays political word games. I tell it like it is."

"Clearly."

"Now, that being said, just because I don't like the man doesn't mean I wished him any harm," he says pointedly. "Nor does it mean I did anything to him—or facilitated anything that happened to him."

So much for my carefully crafted interrogation techniques. No laying verbal traps for him to walk into. His bluntness cut straight through it all and got right to the heart of the matter. It's actually kind of impressive, but could, of course, be designed to be that way. One way some criminals try to avoid detection is by being overly honest or helpful right from the start.

However, the sense I get about the man is that what we see is what we get with him. The man is who he is, and he makes no apologies for it. His personality is brash and abrasive. But I get the sense that he has a loud bark but doesn't bite hard. At least, not in the way that ends with gunfire anyway. He relies on intimidation and his ability to bully people into compliance.

"Councilman Fitcher, can you tell me where you were the night Mr. Zhao was shot?" I ask.

"I was at a fundraiser dinner," he says. "I'm getting ready to announce the launch of my campaign for Congress. I was there from about six until after midnight. And before you ask, there are a few hundred people who can testify to that. There's also plenty of video. You can check my website and my social media feeds."

I jot down some notes mostly to give myself a minute to ponder my next question only to find that I don't have one. He's told me everything I need for the moment. Now it's a matter of verifying the information. But, I don't have any reason to assume it will turn out to be false. Fitcher may be blunt and possibly narrow-minded, but he strikes me as honest. I have a feeling that quality in him may be compromised once he enters the halls of Congress. Honesty is something, in my opinion, that rarely survives the DC experience.

"Okay, well, thank you for your time, Councilman. I appreciate your honesty," I say.

"Anytime," he replies. "And just so you don't go around saying I'm a bad guy, I do hope he recovers from his wounds. What happened to him is terrible and shouldn't be tolerated. The animal who did this should be thrown into a cage."

I can practically hear the "but" coming as I get to my feet and give him a minute.

"But the way I see it, you lay down with dogs, you're going to get fleas," he says obviously unable to stop himself. "But I hope he recovers."

And there it is. "Well, I'm sure he'll be heartened by your thoughts and prayers."

"Good luck, Chief Wilder."

"Have a nice day, Councilman."

CHAPTER TWENTY-THREE

The Chapel, SNAP Team HQ, Industrial District; Seattle, WA

"Well, Fitcher wasn't lying," Nina says and points to the computer monitor.

She taps a key, and a video from the fundraiser Fitcher claimed to be at the night of Fish's shooting begins to play. In a well-tailored, light-gray, three-piece suit and navy blue tie, Fitcher stands at the podium going on about his plans once he is elected to Congress. He's blunt and direct, of course, holding nothing back and speaking about weighty current events in a tone that makes it hard to miss his disgust. His outrage and plain manner of speaking is what seems to be fashionable in politicians these days.

"Check out the time stamp," Nina says. "Lower left-hand corner."

I look to where Nina is directing my attention and see what she's talking about. "Any way the time stamp was altered?"

"Call me paranoid, but that was my first thought too," Nina replies. "You must be rubbing off on me or something."

Opal grimaces. "Is paranoia a common thing around here?"

I shrug. "You'd be surprised. A little paranoia can be a good and useful thing."

"It's true," Nina adds. "We've seen way stranger things than this."

"Huh. Well, you all have a different way of doing things than I'm accustomed to," Opal says.

I remind myself again that Opal's background isn't in the sort of investigations we do. She's mostly been on the administrative side of things and hasn't actually been in the trenches like we have in a long time. But she was a field agent for a while, so it will just take her a bit to get her bearings and put that hat on again. She's really shown me some solid potential during this investigation, so I'm optimistic she'll get there.

"You'll get used to it," I respond.

"Anyway, sorry for the tangent, but to answer your question, I checked and no. The video is legit. All of them are," Nina tells me.

"Which means we can strike Fitcher off the suspect list," Opal says.

"We can move him to the back burner, but not take him off entirely," I respond. "Just because he didn't pull the trigger himself—which I didn't think he did anyway—doesn't mean he didn't facilitate the shooting. I realize it's pretty out there of a theory, but I don't want to leave any stone unturned."

"Fair enough. How are we going to go about proving—or disproving—that then?"

"Nina, take a peek at Fitcher's financials. I want to see if he's moved around any large sums of money recently," I say. "Also, look for any offshore accounts he may have that he can pull from since he's probably too smart to use his regular accounts."

"I'm on it."

"What's your read on Fitcher?" Opal asks. "Do you think he's our guy?"

"Honestly? I don't. But until we have something to definitively clear him, we need to keep looking at him. He's got a known antagonistic relationship with Fish and plenty of motive to want him dead," I respond. "Also, Nina, I want you to do a deep dive on Councilman Harrison Drummond. Give me everything you dig up on him."

"Didn't you say he was a nice guy?" Opal asks.

"I did. He was very helpful and forthcoming. I can't tell you the number of times the helpful and forthcoming person turns out to be our suspect," I tell her. "Oh, and he's also got an alibi that's unverifiable. Spaghetti night just isn't going to cut it for me, so I'd like to know if he's got any dark, dirty secrets he's hiding from us."

"All right then," Opal says with a chuckle.

"Anybody else in City Hall you want me to dig into?" Nina asks.

"Just those two for now," I answer. "Nobody else I talked to set off any bells in my head. We'll get to them, but they're low priority right now."

Nina's fingers fly over the keys as she sets to work. It's going to take her a little time to get the information on Drummond I asked for, but I'm anxious and start tapping my foot on the floor beneath the table.

"You realize that's not going to make this go any faster, right?" Nina asks with a sly grin.

A rueful expression crosses my face. "Sorry," I say, then turn to Opal who is scanning the files of threats I brought back from Fish's office. "So, you grew up in Florida?"

She nods. "Born and raised in the Tampa area—"

"BA in Criminology from Florida State and a Masters in the same from Miami," I recite from memory. "Didn't want to get away for school?"

"I liked being close to my family."

"Your middle name is Faiza? Is that… Persian?"

"Egyptian. My mother was Egyptian, my father was from Orlando. They met while he was stationed overseas," she says. "Faiza is my grandmother's name."

"And what about your parents?" I say.

"Passed away a while ago."

"I'm very sorry."

"Thank you. Like I said, it was a while ago," she replies. "After they passed, I didn't feel the need to stay in Florida. It just didn't feel like home anymore. That's when I joined the Bureau, and I guess the rest is history."

I had all that already just from reading her personnel file, but reading about something isn't the same as hearing somebody talk about it. I can tell by the thickness in her voice that her parents' deaths, a while ago or not, still weigh heavily on her. She was obviously close to them and still misses them every day. That's something I can relate to and is a bit of common ground between us.

"All right," Nina starts. "This is obviously just a quick and dirty background, but Drummond is squeaky clean. About the only thing I can find on him is an unpaid parking ticket from about seven years ago—although he eventually did pay the fine. His marriage seems solid, there's no hint of discord, and there's nothing unseemly with his kids. By all appearances, he's about as boring and normal as Opal."

"Hey," Opal objects, then laughs.

"Obviously, I'm going to dig deeper, and if there's something to be found, I'll sniff it out," Nina tells me. "But this seems like a dead end."

"Just like you thought," Opal adds.

"Just because he seems pretty normal doesn't mean he actually is. Politicians, like everybody else, have skeletons in their closets. Probably even more than normal people," I say. "Keep digging please. On Drummond and Fitcher."

Nina and Opal trade a look.

"Are you sure, boss? I know we want to do our diligence, but I can't imagine that a sitting city council member would call out a hit on a rival—"

I hold up a hand. "I know. Just indulge me on this. We don't have many other credible leads at the moment, and I don't want to move on from this angle until we can be sure."

Nina lets out a breath. "Okay."

She returns her attention to her keyboard, but barely lasts ten seconds before whipping her head back around with a devilish grin. "Oh, hey, your boyfriend is at the main gate."

I snap my head to the monitors, expecting to see Sonny at the gate, but it's not. It's Kramer. I frown and turn to Nina who is trying to stifle the giggle that's written all over her face. The shrill sound of the buzzer echoes through the bullpen.

"Don't make me slap you into the middle of next week," I grouse.

"Pretty sure that's an HR violation," Opal states.

"You're going to learn soon enough that Blake is a walking, talking HR violation," Nina says.

"That's … not untrue," I say. "Go ahead and buzz him in."

Nina taps a key, and the gate starts to roll open. Kramer drives through as I get to my feet then walk to the door and hold it open since he doesn't have the code to let himself in—and I'm not going to give it to him. I watch as he parks and climbs out of his unmarked Charger. He leans back in and grabs his messenger bag, then heads toward me.

"Hey," he says.

"Hey. Come on in."

He follows me in, and I see him looking around, nodding in approval. "Nice digs. It's a hell of a lot better than our squad room."

"Detective Scott Kramer, this is Agent Opal Rivers and technical analyst Nina Alvarado," I say, making the introductions.

"Pleasure," he says as he takes a seat at the conference table and sets his messenger bag down in front of him. "It this your whole team?"

I shake my head. "The rest of the team is in Ohio working a child abduction case."

"And you're not with them?"

"Our function is to work as many cases as we can," I tell him. "To do that, we sometimes have to split our resources."

He nods. "Doing double the good, huh?"

"Something like that. We're something of a pilot program," I say. "If the SNAP Team is a success, we'll start putting together more teams around the country and do even more good."

"I like it," he says. "So, what did you get up to today? I sent you a text earlier—"

"Yeah, sorry, I've been tied up all day. I was interviewing people down at City Hall."

"I could have saved you the time since I already did that."

"So I heard," I respond. "But I had the time, and it was good for me to have the conversations anyway."

"Yeah? Learn anything?"

"To be determined," I say and motion to the files sitting in front of Opal. "Right now, we're analyzing all the threats Mr. Zhao received to see if there are any viable leads in there."

"I already did that and there's not much in there. Certainly nothing worth chasing," he says.

I want to ask him how he'd know, given that he barely glanced at the files according to Melinda, but I hold my tongue. Now is not the time to get into a pissing match with Kramer. Not when we seem to be getting along and working in tandem for the first time since we made our tentative truce.

"Well, we're going to analyze the correspondence if for no other reason than for my own edification anyway," I say.

He shrugs. "Waste of time but have at it."

"Thanks," I say, and if he notices the sarcasm in my tone, he ignores it. "And what brings you to our humble abode today, Detective? Is this about the SUV we found at the scrap yard?"

"It is indeed."

"Good. Enlighten me."

"The techs tore it down to the studs," he says. "The vehicle was wiped clean. There wasn't a fingerprint, fiber, or hair to be found. The idiots who stole it did a terrific job of cleaning the whole thing and managed to avoid leaving a single trace of themselves anywhere. They did such a good job of it, they erased any trace of the actual owner of the SUV. It was as clean as if it had just rolled off the showroom floor."

"Damn. Then we have nothing," I say.

"Now, I didn't say that," he replies with a wolfish smile.

Kramer reaches into his messenger bag and pulls out a plastic evidence bag and holds it up proudly for me to see.

"What's that?" I ask.

"It is a ticket for a parking garage," he replies.

"And… did you want me to guess which parking garage the ticket is from?"

"That would be fun, but we don't have that kind of time," he replies. "No, this ticket is from the parking garage down at City Hall."

"And where did you find it?"

"It was under the seat. Whoever cleaned the ride missed it," he says.

"You're kidding me."

He shakes the bag at me. "Does this look like a joke to you?"

I take the bag from him and look at the ticket inside. It is indeed a ticket from the parking garage and is dated a few days before Fish was shot. Something about it is troubling me. I can't say exactly what it is right now, but something feels… off.

"Care to take a ride back down to City Hall with me? See if we can put a face to this ticket?" Kramer asks.

Red flags are waving in my head, but I could be jumping at shadows and seeing ghosts that aren't really there. Contrary to what I told Opal a little earlier, although paranoia can be helpful, it can also be detrimental and cause you to see conspiracies where none exist. This could very well be one of those times.

"Yeah," I tell him. "I'm in. Let's go see what we see."

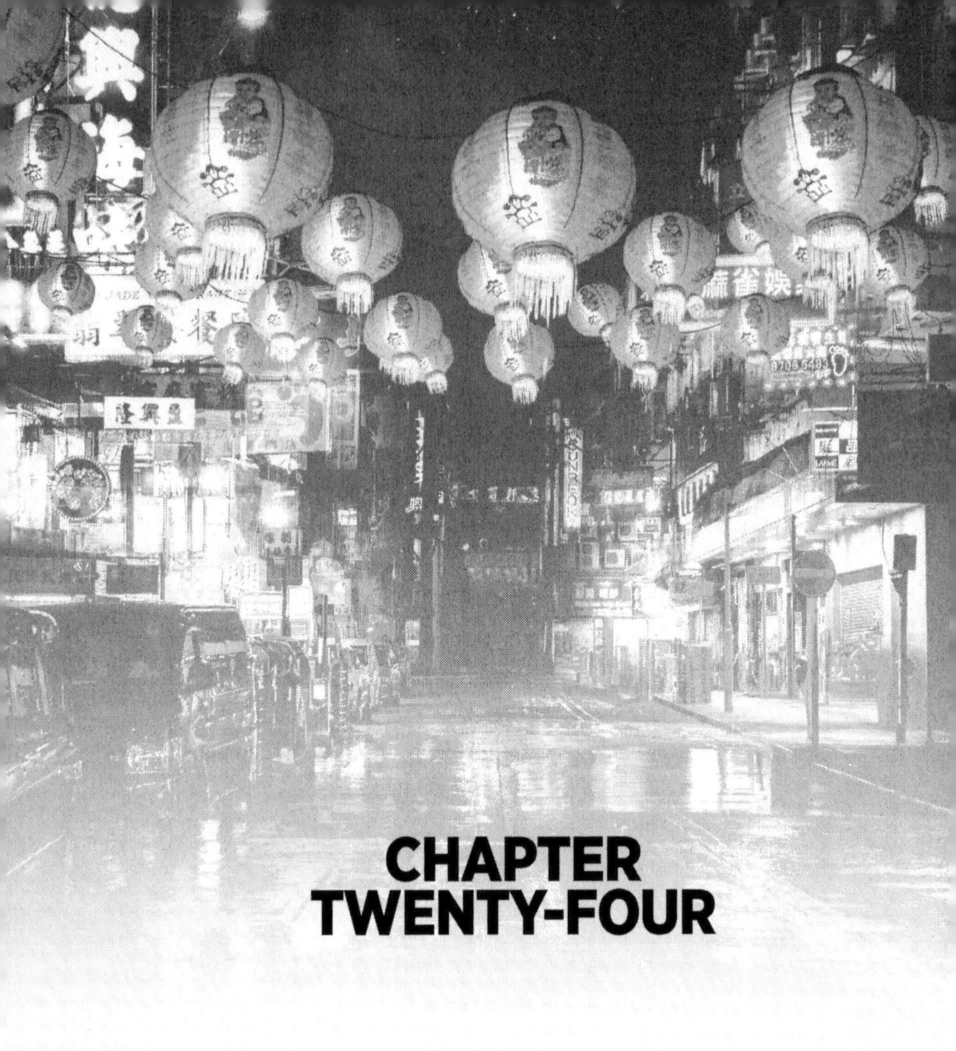

CHAPTER TWENTY-FOUR

City Hall Main Security Office, Downtown District; Seattle, WA

I CLIMB OUT OF MY SUV AND WAIT FOR KRAMER TO GET OUT of his car. He's on a call. I'd insisted on driving separately, telling him I need to get to a meeting when we're done here. When he finally disconnects his call, Kramer gets out of his car and walks over to me with a smug expression on his face like he just solved the entire case.

"Ready to find our shooter?" he asks.

"I've been ready," I reply. "I'm just not sure we're going to find him here."

He scoffs. "Don't be a Debbie Downer. Of course we will."

"I think you're making that parking stub do a lot of work here."

"It was in the shooter's vehicle," he replies testily.

"And I think we need to figure out how it got there."

He sighs heavily. "Because the shooter dropped it in there. Obviously."

"Kramer, I—"

"Are you coming with me or not?"

Without waiting for me to reply, he turns and heads into the building, muttering under his breath as he goes, clearly unhappy about me raining on his parade. For me, there are just too many questions surrounding that parking stub to hail it as the smoking gun that Kramer claims it is. It just seems too convenient for my liking. When I'm working a case, if there's one thing I have a hard time trusting, it's something that falls into our laps so easily.

But stranger things have happened, so I follow Kramer through the doors and into the main floor of the building. He's got a longer stride than I do, so I have to hustle to catch up to him. I finally do as he turns down the stairwell to the basement, where the main security office is located. Kramer reaches out to knock on the door, then stops and turns to me, a curious but irritated expression on his face.

"Are you always this much of a pessimist?" he asks.

"Realist. And this ticket is just too easy."

"Come on, Blake. You've been in this game long enough. Sometimes, we get lucky. And sometimes, criminals are really stupid."

There's not much I can say to that simply because I've said it myself countless times. And he's not wrong. Sometimes we do get lucky. But I don't think we're dealing with a stupid criminal, and Kramer may be putting all his eggs in this basket, but I'm not counting them until they hatch.

"All right, this is your show," I tell him. "I'm just along for the ride."

He pulls a face. "I know you don't expect me to buy your sudden team player attitude. But you are right about one thing. This is my show."

I bite back the acidic reply sitting on the tip of my tongue and do my best to give him a pleasant smile. I'm sure it falls far short of pleasant, but whatever. He smirks, then turns and knocks on the door to the security office, holding his shield up to the camera. A moment later, a buzzer sounds followed by a hard click as the lock disengages. Kramer grabs the door handle and pulls it open, then steps aside and lets me go in ahead of him.

A young man sitting at a desk in front of a bank of a dozen monitors stands up and turns to us. He's about my height with short, black hair and dark eyes. He's trim with a strong jawline and looks as if he works out regularly. The gray uniform shirt has a company badge over the left breast pocket and a silver, rectangular name tag that reads, "Parsons" over the right breast pocket.

"Detective Kramer, SPD, and this is Chief Blake Wilder, FBI," Kramer announces us.

"Keith Parsons, security guard," he says with a nervous chuckle. "And yeah, I've seen you on TV before, Detective. Like, a lot. You only work the big, important cases, so I assume you're here about Councilman Zhao's shooting?"

"Yeah," Kramer mutters with a frown.

He doesn't say anything more, which is surprising, given how much he seems to enjoy hearing himself speak. He probably just doesn't want to give me any more ammunition to use against him since I've already accused him of being a camera-seeking glory hound. I'm amused.

"I want to be a cop too," Parsons says. "I'm going to apply to the academy."

"Is that so?" Kramer asks.

"Yep. I think I've got a shot," he replies. "I want to be out there in the streets doing some real good work like you."

Kramer gives him a smile that doesn't quite reach his eyes. "Well, help us out and perhaps… I can help you out with that."

"Yeah?"

"Possibly so, yeah," Kramer says noncommittally.

I want to step in and tell him it's pretty unethical for him to dangle help with Parsons's academy application to entice him to help us, but I opt to remain silent. He's in charge of this circus, as he so pointedly reminded me out in the hallway.

"Yeah, so anyway, how can I help you?" Parsons asks.

Kramer reaches into his bag and pulls out the parking ticket, still encased in plastic, and holds it up for Parsons to see. The security guard squints as he studies the ticket for a moment, then looks to Kramer with an expression that says he has no idea what he wants. I lean against the back wall and fold my arms over my chest, letting Kramer take the lead on this. After all, he's the one calling the shots.

"You monitor the gate in and out of the parking garage, yeah?" Kramer asks.

Parsons nods. "We do."

"And you can match up the time stamp on this ticket with the footage from the cameras on the gate at the parking garage?"

"Uh, yeah. I think so. Sure," Parsons tell us. "This ticket is from staff parking structure. Visitors use the lot on the other side of the campus where I'm sure you parked."

"Good. Then I need you to hop on your computer there and show me the footage from the time stamp on this ticket."

Parsons glances at me with an uncertain look on his face before returning his gaze to Kramer. "Don't you need a warrant or something for that?"

"No, I don't need a warrant for this," Kramer says irritably.

"I'm not sure. I should—yeah—I should probably call my supervisor."

"You can do that," Kramer cuts him off. "But we're looking into an attempted murder, and every minute you waste is another minute you're giving the shooter to get away. Now, if you're going to be a cop, you're going to have to make tough decisions on the fly. How quickly you make good decisions is literally a matter of life and death. This is one of those moments, Keith. Are you going to rise to the occasion and help us catch a killer? Or are you going to wilt under the pressure? What kind of cop do you want to be? This is where you start figuring that out."

I have to admit, he's pretty good. That's about one of the most inspirationally manipulative speeches I've ever heard. I almost want to applaud it. And judging by the expression on Parsons's face, Kramer's words are having the intended impact.

"I—I want to be a good cop. One who gets things done," Parsons says.

"Then you need to act quickly. Decisively. You can't wait for somebody to tell you what to do. You need to take that bull by the horns, son."

Parsons nods as he drinks down all the Kool-Aid Kramer is serving up. The detective claps him on the shoulder and looks the wannabe cop in the eye.

"I was certain I saw something special in you, Keith. The minute I saw you, I was sure you've got what it takes to be good police."

"Y—you did?"

"You bet."

Fired up and filled with the confidence Kramer pumped straight into his veins, Parsons sits down at the terminal on his desk and starts to work the keyboard. He calls up the view of the gate in the parking garage on the monitor in front of him, then turns to Kramer.

"Okay, let me see that ticket," Parsons says.

Kramer hands him the plastic bag, and the guard takes a few minutes to study the printing on the ticket. Once he finds whatever he was looking for, he turns back to his computer and starts to plug the information in. The view on the monitor changes and presumably calls up the footage from the time listed on the ticket Kramer gave him.

"This is the footage from the time stamp on the ticket," Parsons says.

The footage is sharp and in color, which is a nice change of pace from the film we usually get. I watch as a silver Audi rolls up to the gate. The angle of the camera changes to show us the face of the person reaching toward the machine to grab a ticket. And when I see the man's face, I have absolutely no reaction to it. I'm neither surprised nor unsurprised when I see him—probably because I'm skeptical of this whole line of evidence anyway.

"That's our guy," Kramer says triumphantly. "That's our shooter."

Parsons turns to him, his face twisted with disbelief. "Councilman Drummond?" Parsons asks, his voice matching his expression. "You're kidding, right?"

"I am not," Kramer replies.

"Come on, man," Parsons says. "Drummond is so... boring. He's like this dorky dad kind of guy. No way he's mixed up in Councilman Zhao's shooting."

"Keith, one thing you're going to learn as a cop is that you can never tell who's mixed up in what just by looking at them. I've arrested quite a few soccer moms for murdering their husbands—women you would have never thought would do something so heinous," he says.

While Kramer is right about never knowing who is capable of murder or other terrible crimes, I'm going to call BS on his quite-a-few-soccer-moms claim. He's fluffing up his resume to impress the kid. I'm tempted to call him on it but bite it back. There's no point. I can already see where this is going, and I need to figure out a way to derail this train before it really gets rolling.

"You need to keep an open mind, Keith," Kramer says, happy to be holding court with somebody who quite obviously admires him. "We all have monsters inside us, and we're all capable of doing terrible things. Even a guy who seems as normal as Drummond."

"Yeah. That makes sense," Parsons says.

"Isn't that right, Chief Wilder?" Kramer adds.

"Sure. Whatever you say," I respond. "This is your show, after all."

Kramer's lips press together tightly, clearly not pleased by my disinterest, so he turns back to Parsons to get his ego stroked a little more. I listen to them having a little chest thumping, back slapping, egotistical, bordering on chauvinistic, cop-bro talk. All I can do is stand there and try to keep my lunch down. Eventually—and thankfully—Kramer wraps it up.

"So, can you give me a couple of stills of that image of Drummond? Make sure you get the time stamp on the photo," Kramer says. "I also want a digital video file as well."

"Yeah, you got it, Detective."

"And be sure to back up this footage. I don't want it disappearing if somebody decides to accidentally wipe the server. Things sometimes get a little screwy when you're investigating high-profile people," he adds conspiratorially.

Parsons nods. "I will. People say stuff like that is all conspiracy theory, but how many of those have we seen lately that have turned out to be true?"

"Amen, brother," Kramer says.

Parsons jumps to it, doing what Kramer asked him to do, working hard to impress the detective. I almost feel sorry for the kid, to be honest. There is zero percent chance that Kramer actually does what he said he'd do and helps Parsons get into the academy. I am one hundred percent sure, however, that he will forget who the security guard even is the second we step out of this office and into the hallway beyond the door. The way he's using this kid is kind of sad.

Parsons gives Kramer what he asked for, and the detective claps him on the shoulder. "You're a good man. I'm sure you're going to make a good cop."

"And you'll put in a good word for me with the academy?"

"Absolutely. One hundred percent."

"Thank you, Detective Kramer," Parsons says with a tone of hero worship in his voice.

Kramer tips me a wink. "Let's roll."

I follow him out of the security office and into the hallway, and we head, unsurprisingly, for the elevator. Kramer pushes the button, then turns to me.

"We've got our guy. I can feel it," he says.

"I don't think we do."

"This again," he says, rolling his eyes. "You saw him on that footage as clear as I did. How can you just dismiss him as a suspect?"

"I'm not dismissing him. I'm just not as sure that he's our guy as you are," I respond. "He and Zhao are friends. I mean, what's his motive?"

Kramer shrugs. "I have no idea. Maybe he didn't like the tie he was wearing. Or maybe they butted heads over some ordinance they were trying to pass."

"And you think that's enough for him to kill the man?" I point out.

"Motives aren't always cut and dried like that: ultimately, they're immaterial. All that matters is evidence we can see and touch. And right now, we have a ticket connected to Drummond and his face on camera—"

"We don't have his face on camera at the scene."

"No, but we have his parking ticket."

"Which is inconclusive. At best."

"Yeah, well, it's good enough for me to warrant a conversation. Unless you have some overwhelming objection to me talking to him?"

I don't. Given the preponderance of the evidence we have in hand right now, we should, at the very least, have a conversation with Drummond. But this whole situation smells fishy to me. Since I can't put my finger on it, however, I can't really say much.

"No objection," I say.

"That's wonderful. Thank you so much," he says, his voice dripping with sarcasm.

We climb into the car, and he punches the button a little too hard. The doors close, and I try to unravel the knot in my brain as the elevator starts to ascend.

CHAPTER TWENTY-FIVE

Councilman Drummond's Office, City Hall, Downtown District; Seattle, WA

"I'M SORRY, COUNCILMAN DRUMMOND IS ON A CALL," Melinda objects.

Kramer shrugs. "He's going to have to call them back. We need to speak with him. Now."

I cast an apologetic glance at the assistant whose face is red with consternation. Kramer came blowing in like a hurricane, demanding to see Drummond and barking orders at her, completely flustering the woman. But she pulls herself together and stands up straighter, casting a firm, narrow-eyed gaze at the blustering detective.

"Do you have a warrant, Detective?"

He frowns and seems to deflate just a touch, some of the wind taken out of his sails with what I assume is his usual MO of steamrolling his way over everybody until he gets what he wants. It makes me like Melinda even more.

"That's what I thought," Melinda says. "Therefore, just like everybody else who comes through those doors, if you want to speak with Councilman Drummond, you'll have to make an appointment."

Kramer's face reddens, and his jaw clenches as he grits his teeth. He's not a man used to hearing the word no, nor does he seem to like it much. Wanting to get this over with to see what we really have, or don't have, I step forward.

"Melinda, I'm sure Councilman Drummond is busy, and I'm sorry to interrupt, but this is important. Is there any chance we can sneak in to speak with him? We just need five minutes," I ask.

The assistant's frosty glare warms a bit when she turns her gaze to me. "Let me go in and see if he's got a few minutes, Chief."

"Thank you. I really appreciate it."

"Of course."

Melinda turns and walks into Drummond's office, softly closing the door behind her. Kramer turns to me, a sour expression on his face.

"Sometimes, you catch more flies with honey than vinegar," I say, shrugging.

"Whatever," he grumbles.

A minute later, Melinda comes back out and holds the door open. "Councilman Drummond can give you five minutes, Chief."

"I really appreciate that. Thank you," I say.

"You're very welcome."

She doesn't look at or even acknowledge Kramer, taking her pettiness up a couple more levels, making me like her even more. She's so relatable. I give her arm a gentle squeeze as I walk into Drummond's office with Kramer on my heels. She closes the door, leaving us with the Councilman who's sitting behind his desk, his eyes filled with worry.

"Chief Wilder, Detective Kramer," he says. "What can I do for you?"

Kramer steps in front of me and drops the evidence bag with the parking stub onto Drummond's desk. The Councilman picks it up and studies it for a moment before setting it back down with a confused expression on his face.

"And what is this?" Drummond asks.

"We were hoping you could tell us," Kramer says.

He shrugs. "It looks like a ticket from the parking garage."

As I did in the security office, I lean against the wall beside the door and slip my hands into my pockets, letting Kramer run the show. I watch closely, though, studying Drummond as he answers the detective's questions. I don't claim to have the answers to everything, and it's entirely possible that Kramer is right and that Drummond is our guy. I'm not convinced though. And if Kramer is as blunt and direct as I expect him to be as he questions the Councilman, I think Drummond's reactions and body language will be very telling. I sometimes learn more by sitting back and watching than I do when I question them directly.

Kramer drops into the chair in front of Drummond's desk and crosses his legs as he leans back, staring at the Councilman in silence for a long moment. Drummond shifts in his chair, uneasiness crossing his face. He glances at me, and I give him a small shrug, but say nothing.

"That's right," Kramer says. "It's a ticket from the parking garage."

"All right. Should that mean something to me?"

"We matched that parking ticket to you, Councilman," Kramer says.

"Okay. If you say so. What is this about?"

"What would you say if I told you this ticket was found in the vehicle that Councilman Zhao was shot from?" Kramer asks.

Drummond opens his mouth as if he's about to respond but closes it again with an audible click of his teeth when the meaning behind Kramer's question seems to sink in. He blanches, but his eyes narrow as he clenches his jaw.

"Then I would say somebody's playing games here, and you are way off track, Detective," Drummond says through gritted teeth.

"Am I though?"

"Yes. You are," Drummond replies. "If you think I had anything to do with Huan's shooting, you are laughably wrong."

"Isn't it true the two of you clashed on a number of things? I have people who say you two fought like cats and dogs—"

"As I explained to Chief Wilder, yes, we clashed on political issues. That's the nature of what we do. Outside those chambers, Huan and I are friends."

"Yeah, I've heard you say that," Kramer says. "But I've also heard that you're pretty upset about Zhao blocking a bill you wanted to pass for one of your pet projects."

Drummond runs a hand across his face and shakes his head. He lowers his gaze, seeming to be trying to control the emotions I can see bubbling just below the surface. When he seems to have himself in check, he raises his head again.

"As I just told you, that is the nature of what we do. I've blocked as many of Huan's bills as he's blocked mine," Drummond says, his voice low and tight. "Just because we don't always agree politically doesn't mean we can't be friends. We respect one another."

"Yeah, so you say," Kramer replies. "Although, if that's true, can you explain how this parking ticket—*your* parking ticket—wound up in the shooter's vehicle?"

"I can't," he says honestly. "But if you found it in the shooter's car, the only thing that makes sense is that somebody stole it and planted it in the vehicle."

"And where might they have stolen it from?"

"From my car. Obviously," Drummond snaps. "We scan the ticket when we leave, and I always forget to take them out, so somebody obviously saw that, broke into my car, took it, and planted it in this other vehicle. Somebody is obviously trying to frame me."

"And why would somebody do that, Councilman Drummond? Why would somebody go to all that effort to frame you?"

"I have no idea," Drummond practically screeches. "To throw you off their scent by making you shift your focus to me? How in the hell am I supposed to know?"

Kramer sits back and stares at the flustered, red-faced Drummond for a long moment, using the silence to ratchet up the pressure. It seems to be working because the councilman is shifting in his seat like he's sitting on a hot grill. He glances over at me, seeming to be silently pleading with me to stop this spectacle, but all I can do is give him another small shrug. I have no authority here.

"Have you heard of Occam's Razor, Councilman?" Kramer asks.

"Of course."

"See, I'm a big believer in the theory that the most obvious answer is usually the right one. So, when I find a parking ticket belonging to someone in the vehicle somebody was shot from... I see a pretty direct line to the answer."

"That's a very simplistic worldview, Detective."

"How so?"

"Because that sort of simplistic, narrow thinking can—and does—often lead you to false conclusions," Drummond says. "Nothing in life is as simple as you seem to want it to be. I did not shoot Huan Zhao. I had absolutely no reason to. Like I keep telling you, he is my friend."

"Yeah, you do keep telling me that," Kramer says. "Do you own any guns?"

"No, I don't. I abhor firearms, and I've always been very public about that. You're welcome to come search my house for any if you wish. I won't even make you get a warrant to do it," he replies, his tone hard. "If you think I shot Huan over a political disagreement because you found a parking ticket in a car, you are as stupid as you are lazy."

Kramer chuckles. "Councilman—"

"No. I think we're done here. I'm done with this ridiculous fishing expedition," he cuts Kramer off. "If you have any more questions, you can contact my attorney. I trust you can see yourself out. Good day, Detective."

Kramer remains in his seat, his expression dark and his eyes burning with anger. He'd obviously expected the councilman to be a pushover and, I guess, confess to everything and throw himself on Kramer's mercy. But he's obviously got a little more spine than people credit him with. I'm proud of him.

"Councilman—"

"I've invoked my right to an attorney, Detective. If you have anything more to say to me, contact her. Otherwise, we're done. Good day."

I hold the door open as Kramer stalks out, walking as angrily as he looks. Before I follow him through, I turn to Drummond.

"Sorry about that," I say.

"Don't worry about it. This isn't the first time I've dealt with Detective Kramer," he replies.

I give him a polite nod, then close the door behind me as I go. The walk back out to the parking lot is quiet as Kramer continues to stew. His face is pinched, his jaw tight, and when we get to our cars, he turns and glowers at me like this is somehow all my fault.

"A little help in there would have been nice," he growls.

"Hey, it was your show. I was just along for the ride," I respond, delighted to throw his words back in his face.

"Yeah, well, that guy is hiding something."

"I didn't get that read on him at all."

"He lawyered up pretty quick. In my experience, people who lawyer up that fast usually do so because they're hiding something."

"Kramer, you were accusing him of being involved with the shooting of his friend. What did you expect him to do?"

He plants his fists on his hips and looks around the parking lot for a moment, his face twisted with anger. If this were a cartoon, he'd have steam pouring from his ears. The thought forces me to stifle a giggle since I doubt Kramer would appreciate me having a laugh at his expense.

"I've got enough to take to the DA. Yeah. I'm going to take this to the DA and see if he can get an indictment," Kramer says.

"You don't have nearly enough," I reply. "You don't want to do this."

"Yeah. I think I do."

"Kramer, don't let your desire to get your face on the news with some splashy arrest drive this decision. We don't have enough—"

"This is about justice," he says, his voice hard.

"That's not what it looks like from where I'm standing."

He opens his mouth to no doubt deliver some scathing retort, but before he can, my phone rings. I pull it out of my pocket and see it's from Opal. Thankful for the reprieve, I connect the call and press the phone to my ear.

"Hey," I say. "What's up?"

"We've got a problem," she replies.

CHAPTER TWENTY-SIX

Eastern Blooms, Chinatown-International District; Seattle, WA

THE SECOND I WALK THROUGH THE DOOR, I'M HIT BY THE acrid stench of gunpowder that continues to linger in the air. A throng of suited detectives and uniformed cops filter in and out of the flower shop, dutifully checking off all the boxes as they run through an investigation I have a feeling will be little more than pro forma. Murders in Chinatown have never been a high priority on the SPD's to-do list. I've known too many cops who see the murders involving known crime bosses as a case of the trash taking itself out.

I walk through the store, weaving around the crime scene techs who are marking off the myriad of bullet holes in the walls—along with the blood and shell casings on the floor—and photographing everything. The glass cases are all blown out, leaving the floor of the shop covered in shards of glass that twinkle in the light and flowers and plants that have been shredded. And amid all the wreckage, Hua Meng lies on her back in a thick, crimson pool on the floor just behind the front counter, her eyes wide open and fixed on something in the next world.

Meng's body has been ravaged by bullets, and a nine-millimeter pistol lies on the ground near her outstretched hand. The attack on her shop looks so sudden and so vicious, I'd be surprised if she managed to get a shot off. I walk into the back of the shop, and like the front, it's utterly destroyed. The walls are torn apart by bullets, and everything made of glass is shattered and lies on the floor. Through the open door on the far wall, I see a staircase. I pass a pair of techs who give me a nod as I start down.

"It's grim down there," one says.

"It usually is," I reply.

There are several pools of dark, thick blood on the floor of the large, windowless room. Four bodies are in a line, face down on the concrete with their hands bound behind their backs. A tech is kneeling next to the bodies, photographing them. A layer of fine, white powder, almost like dust, coats the three stainless steel tables that line the center of the room. Boxes that have been torn open and emptied are scattered all over the floor, and a variety of drug-related paraphernalia is strewn all over. This is obviously where Meng's product was packaged.

"Lined up and shot execution style," the tech says.

"Yeah, I can see that."

"Cold blooded stuff."

I point. "Those look like .223 shells on the ground to me."

The tech nods. "They do."

"I have a feeling once you run the ballistics, they're going to match the bullets pulled out of Councilman Zhao," I say.

"And the bullets pulled out of Guang Xie and Feng Cao," the tech says dryly.

"Excuse me?"

"Cao and Xie were both hit earlier today," he tells me. "The scenes were just as bloody as this one. Seems like somebody's sending a message."

"Yeah. Seems like it."

The murders of Xie and Cao is news to me. The instant he tells me, though, combined with this bloody, violent scene, I have a gut feeling about who's behind this. And I have a feeling I already understand the message he's trying to send.

"That powder on the table is likely going to test positive as cocaine," the tech says. "Looks like a textbook drug hit to me."

"That's what it looks like," I say.

"Probably because that's what it is."

I cringe when I hear Kramer behind me. There are cameras out front, so of course, he's here. I don't even know why I'm surprised. Kramer stands beside me and surveys the room around us. I can practically see him salivating over the press coverage this will get.

"Meng is the third family head to catch some bullets today," Kramer says. "Looks like somebody's cleaning house and consolidating their power."

"And I'm sure you have a theory on who that is."

"I do."

"Enlighten me."

He scoffs. "Isn't it obvious?"

"Clearly not to me."

He grins. "This is Drummond's handiwork. He started off by trying to kill Zhao. Then he moved to eliminating Xie and Cao. And now Meng—and he stole her drugs."

I turn to Kramer. "You have got to be kidding me."

"Do I look like I'm kidding?"

"No, you don't," I respond. "And I have to tell you, I find that pretty disturbing."

Kramer steps forward and looks down at the bodies on the ground, silent for a couple of minutes. I can practically see him trying to fit all the pieces together in his mind as he tries to cobble them into a coherent narrative. He seems to be trying to make the facts fit his story rather than letting the facts reveal the story. He's looking for a win, something big to add to his resume—and of course, the headlines that go with it. To do it, he's fixated on Drummond because of that parking stub, which I admit is problematic, but hardly tells the entire tale.

"Are you really telling me you think Harrison Drummond, Mr. Wholesome, the all-American, spaghetti-night guy, is setting himself up to be the next big boss in Chinatown?" I ask incredulously.

"I've seen stranger things happen," he says. "And I'm sure you have too."

"And you're basing this all on that parking ticket."

"It's the only real concrete piece of evidence—"

"That could have been planted in the shooter's SUV. We can't say with any certainty," I argue. "There's no way to prove it remained in Drummond's custody the whole time."

"We've also got the bullets—like you said, the bullets we pull out of these four poor schmucks is likely going to match the slugs we pulled out of Zhao."

"And can you put the weapon in Drummond's hands? The man who doesn't like guns?" I ask. "In fact, do you have any other proof of his involvement at all?"

"Not yet. But I will."

Kramer slips his hands into his pockets and stares at me, his displeasure with me more than apparent. It's as if he expects me to just sign off on all his cockamamie theories. If that's what he thinks, the man clearly has no idea who I am.

"I have to say, I'm pretty surprised, Blake. And pretty disappointed," he says.

"Yeah? About what?"

He shrugs. "I've just heard you're a champion for out-of-the-box thinking."

"There's a difference between out of the box thinking and absolute looney-tunes thinking," I tell him. "You're running with a theory you have absolutely no evidence to back up—"

"Like I said, I will. Don't you worry about that."

"I have to worry about that because if we're going to build a case, it's got to be on a rock-solid foundation, and right now, the foundation is about as shaky as Jello. You still haven't been able to come up with a coherent motive."

"Power. Money. Greed. You know as well as I do that those are the most basic reasons for murder," he replies. "It's possible that Drummond, likely through his association with Zhao, got a taste of that life and wanted it all for himself."

I gape at him for a moment, waiting for the punch line. It doesn't come.

"You have to admit," Kramer continues, "masquerading as a weak-kneed, spaghetti-eating, beta-male would be a pretty good cover for a new crime boss, right?"

"That's just… preposterous."

"Is it though?"

"Yeah, I think it is. You have no actual evidence to back up any of this. Look, this is not the way I work my cases. We need—"

Kramer holds a finger up to stop me. "Let me stop you right there. Thank you for your help on this case, Chief Wilder. But I think I'm going to be all right on my own from here on out."

"Detective—"

"We're done, Blake. I'll take it from here. You have a nice day," he says. "Officers, can you escort Chief Wilder off my scene?"

The two patrolmen step forward and give me an apologetic expression but do their jobs. They follow me up the stairs, through the shop, and under the tape line, then stand there to keep the gawkers out and make sure I leave the scene. Gritting my teeth, I head back to get my car, anxious to get back to the Chapel. The clock is ticking, and if I don't get some answers—some real answers—Kramer is going to railroad an innocent man.

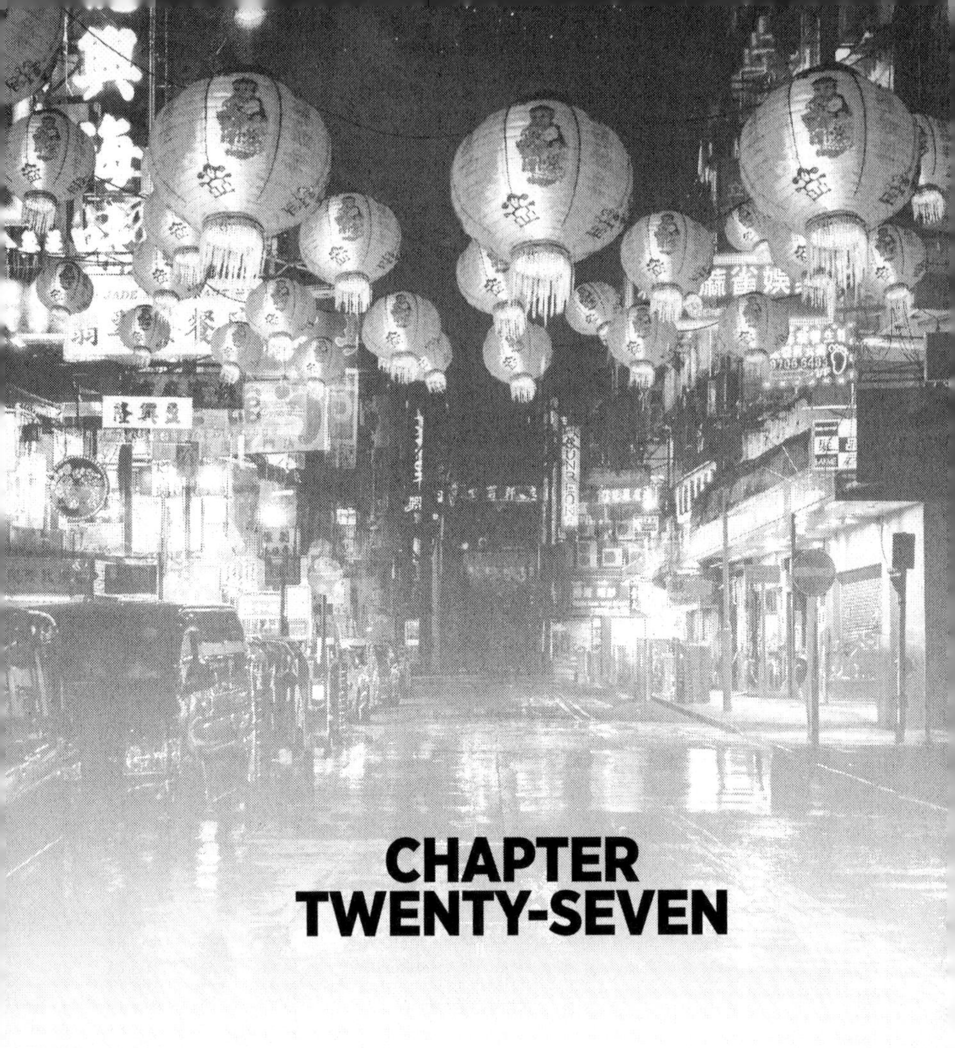

CHAPTER TWENTY-SEVEN

The Chapel, SNAP Team HQ, Industrial District; Seattle, WA

“OKAY, JUST TO PLAY DEVIL’S ADVOCATE HERE, BUT are we sure Drummond isn’t our guy?” Opal asks. “I mean, being this white-bread kind of guy would be a good cover, and there is the matter of the parking stub. I hate to say it, but Kramer has a few good points.”

“He does. And I’m not necessarily crossing Drummond off the list,” I agree. “I just want to be able to say definitively, one way or the other, whether he needs to be included or excluded.”

Nina shifts in her seat and swivels to face me. "Not to be a wet blanket or anything, but given that he revoked his request for help, are we even supposed to be working this case anymore?"

"Probably not. But I'm not going to stop looking into it because I think Kramer is headed down the wrong path. I want Fish's shooter found, not the most convenient person," I answer. "Kramer is after headlines. He wants to see his name in lights. And I'm not going to let him put the wrong person in a cell while Fish's real shooter is still out there walking around."

"What about DD Church?" Opal asks. "If we keep digging, Kramer is very likely going to file a complaint with her."

"If he wants to file a complaint against me, let him. But it's not going to hold much weight if we can lock up the actual shooter," I say. "I'll deal with Church if it comes to that."

"Better to ask for forgiveness than for permission, huh?" Nina asks.

"Exactly," I answer. "That being said, if either one of you doesn't want to be involved with this, I understand. You'll get no pressure from me to—"

"Oh, I've never been one who follows all the rules," Nina says. "I'm in."

Opal shrugs. "Don't ask me why I'm doing this, because I think it's nuts to go against the rules and regs, but I'll do whatever I can to help too."

"That's the spirit," Nina says. "See? She's becoming one of us already."

"I'm not sure if that's a net positive or negative just yet," Opal says with a sly grin. "But what I can say for sure is that if I were ever in trouble, I'd want somebody fighting to help me like you guys are doing. The least I can do is try to be the kind of person I'd want in my corner."

"So, let's get started then," Nina says. "How do we go about figuring out if Drummond should be included or excluded from the suspect list?"

"By confirming his impossible-to-confirm alibi," I answer.

"Oh. Great. Piece of cake," Nina chirps.

"And do you have any direction on how we go about doing that?" Opal asks.

"I'm open to ideas," I reply.

Nina and Opal exchange glances, their blank faces telling me they had none. It seems to be going around. Sitting back in my chair, I think for a minute, trying to come up with something.

"Well, when all else fails, go back to basics," I say.

"What do you have in mind?" Nina asks.

"Nina, I want you to track his phone and the GPS in his car the night of Fish's shooting," I say. "I want to know where he was."

"I can get those, sure, but it's easy enough to beat if he left his car and phone at home," Nina says. "He could just as easily have used a burner and a car that's not registered to him."

"True. But let's just get that information anyway. We'll worry about burner phones and ghost cars later if we need to."

"Copy that."

"How about us?" Opal asks.

"We are going to go through the Council's agenda, meeting by meeting, and see if there is anything especially contentious they were working on. Specifically, I want to know if they were dealing with anything worth killing somebody over. Opal, you watch the video feeds of the council meetings, and I'll sift through the transcripts."

"On it," she replies.

For the next few hours, the three of us work on our assigned tasks. I pore through what reports are available on the other Chinatown shootings, then move on to the last couple years' worth of transcripts the council is required to post online. It is about the driest, most boring stuff I think I've ever read. If this is what being a government official is really like, I'm glad I have absolutely no desire to ever go into it. I might actually die of boredom. Frankly, I'm not sure how the council members manage to keep themselves awake and alive.

I glance up at Opal, who is watching her computer screen with rapt attention. She looks like she's watching some gripping thriller instead of the video version of what I just weathered—like it's the most interesting thing she's ever seen. It underscores just how different we are. It also makes me glad we've got her on the administrative side of our little operation since it is obviously her element. I just want to be out on the streets and don't want to be bothered with that side of things.

"Anything interesting, Opal?"

"This is all just fascinating," she says. "I've heard people say you should never see how the sausage is made, but I'm enjoying this."

"And I thought I was a nerd," Nina deadpans.

"You are a nerd. Just a different flavor of nerd," I tell her.

"That's probably fair," she replies.

Opal chuckles, then turns to me. "There were a couple of clashes between Mr. Zhao and some of the other members, mostly over appropriation of funds, but nothing I'd say was especially heated. Certainly nothing I'd say was likely to end in murder. It just seemed to me to be passionate, opinionated people standing firm in their convictions."

"Personally, I think passionate people who stand firm in their convictions are very capable of trying to murder somebody. I see it on *Dateline* all the time," Nina says.

Opal shrugs, seeming to concede the point. But I hear what she's saying. Local ordinances and appropriations aren't exactly the high-stakes game you see on a federal level. But is it enough to want to kill somebody over? I just don't know.

"For what it's worth, Drummond strikes me as passionate, but not violent," Opal says. "He's very well-spoken and firm, but from what I've seen, he's willing to compromise. He uses his words and works with his colleagues. He doesn't seem like the sort of guy who'd try to get his way at the end of a gun."

It confirms my initial read on the man, which is good, I guess. But it's far from being evidence. I have no doubt that Kramer has people in the DA's office that he's friendly with and can get them to bring charges solely on his word and reputation. And they might very well be able to gain a conviction based on circumstantial evidence. I've seen convictions happen on flimsy cases and even flimsier evidence more times than I care to admit. Which is why we desperately need to find something to either bolster the case or debunk it entirely.

"Honestly, I don't see any political reason for Mr. Zhao's shooting," Opal summarizes. "Nothing I've seen is high stakes enough for that."

"That was my take too."

"Which brings us back to square one. We've got no motive," Nina says.

"Hey, boss, is this a good time to talk about a raise?" Nina asks.

"Depends on why you're asking."

"Because I just found proof that Drummond couldn't have been involved with Fish's shooting," she says. "Which would then cast doubt on Kramer's theory that he was involved with the other Chinatown murders."

A jolt of adrenaline surges through me. "Tell me."

"I pinged his phone and the GPS in his car like you asked, and unsurprisingly, they both showed he was at home all night, like he claimed. Easy enough to fake, though, as we established," she replies. "I also didn't find any other phones or cars in his or his wife's name, or in the names of any shell companies associated with him. That's not conclusive, of course, but it's something."

"Okay, so now that you've told us what you didn't find, tell us what you did find."

Nina grins. "The Councilman doesn't have a social media footprint. His office does, but I expect that's run by staffers. He's got two young kids, though, and social media is like catnip to kids these days," she goes on. "So, I went snooping through his kids' socials and found this..."

She taps a key on her laptop, and the monitor at the foot of the table lights up. A second later, a screen capture from the social media account for Drummond's daughter pops up. The first, from his daughter Lacey, simply says "Spaghetti night," and shows a picture of her posing with a plate of pasta. She's smiling wide and is holding up a piece of garlic bread. It's the background of the photo that captures my attention. Councilman Drummond is seated at the head of the table, captured mid-laugh.

"And then there's this..."

Nina pulls up another screen capture of "Family Game Night," and shows Lacey taking a selfie at the same table, but the food has been cleared and a board game has been set up. And once again, in the background, Lacey managed to capture Drummond and his wife laughing together.

"Both of these photos were taken the night Fish was shot, in the window he was shot in," Nina tells us. "I checked the metadata, and it confirms the time and location. I looked for the usual tells, and from what I can see, these pictures are authentic, Boss."

"Excellent work, Nina. Do me a favor, package that all up and send it to Kramer," I say. "Opal, since he's likely going to ignore it anyway, see if you can figure out which DA he's tight with—review old cases they've worked on together—and send Nina's package to them as well."

"I'm on it," Opal says. "And what are you going to do?"

Ironically, it was something Kramer said to me that started moving me away from a political motive for the shooting and took me back to basics. The main motives for murder are usually power, money, and lust. It took the murder of Meng, Xie, and Cao, in addition to Fish's shooting, to narrow my focus. Viewing the Chinatown shootings through that lens leads me to an inescapable conclusion… that Fish's shooting was a lot closer to home than I thought.

"Now that we've proven it's not Drummond, I'm going to see if I can find out who is really behind these murders," I tell them.

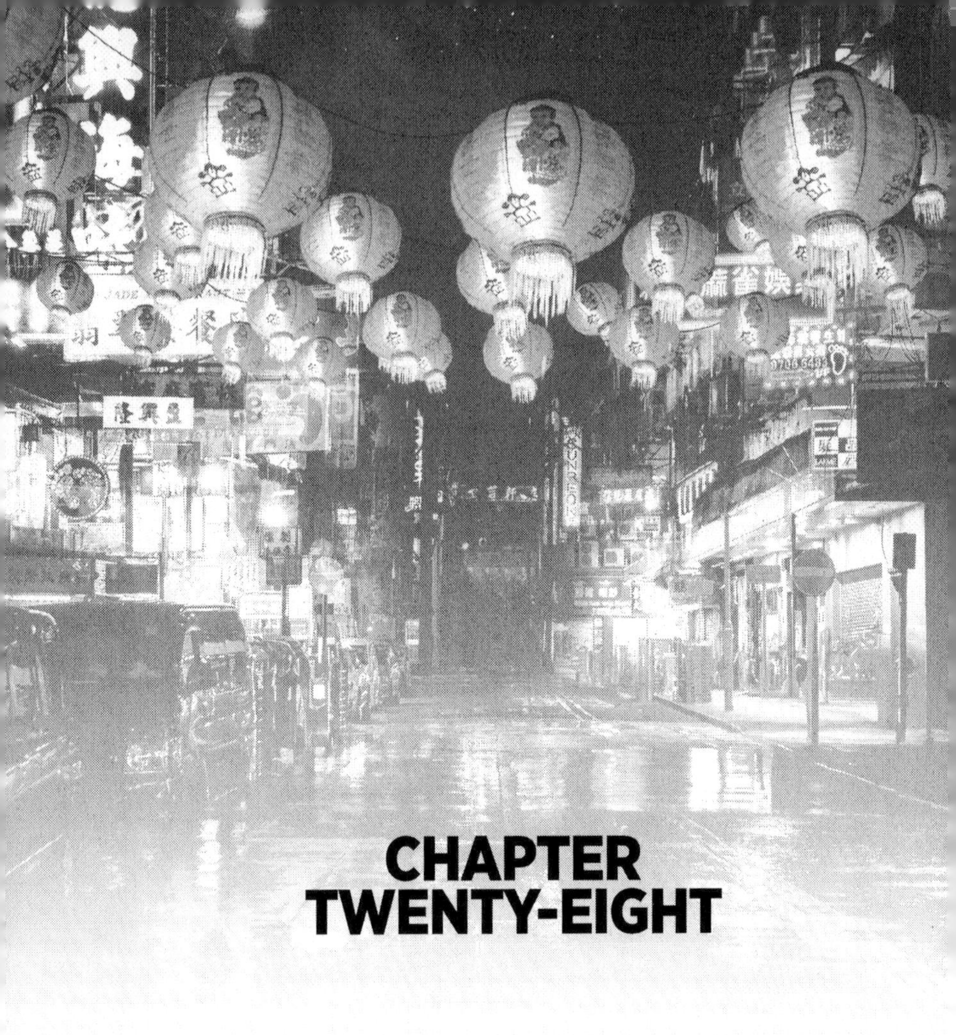

CHAPTER TWENTY-EIGHT

Jade Pearl Billiards House, Chinatown-International District; Seattle, WA

The man outside the office is one of Fish's men whom I know relatively well, so he lets me in without any question. Trevor is seated behind Fish's desk and seems to be holding court with a trio of men who are sitting in chairs before it. Conversation immediately stops, and a chill fills the air as I walk in; an expression of sheer annoyance crosses Trevor's face when he sees me. He sits back in his chair and gives the men seated in front of him a dismissive wave.

"We'll pick this up later," he says. "Give us the room."

The three men are young—they're barely men—and stand as one, glowering at me darkly as they exit the office, close the door, and leave me alone with Trevor. I drop into the chair in the middle of the trio and cross my legs as I sit back.

"You look like you're settling in well," I say.

"Somebody has to keep things running on this end."

"And by running things on this end, do you mean taking out the heads of the other families?"

His face remains stony, but I can see a giddy light in his eyes. It almost seems like he's proud of what he did. Like he wants to tell me that he ordered the hit on the other family heads. He's holding his tongue, probably only because as long as Fish remains on life support, there is a chance he'll recover, and if he does, Trevor will have to account for his actions.

"I don't know what you are talking about, Agent Wilder," he says.

"Surely you've heard that Hua Meng, Guang Xie, and Feng Cao were all shot to death today, haven't you?" I ask.

"Of course, I did. But if you believe I had something to do with it, you are sorely mistaken. I would never go against Fish's wishes like that."

I want to tell him I know he's lying, that I think he had Meng, Xie, and Cao killed as retaliation, as well as to claim his own foothold in case Fish doesn't make it. But as of yet, I have absolutely no evidence connecting him to anything, so there's no point in having that back and forth with him. It would be counterproductive.

"Trevor, the deaths of the three family heads are going to produce a lot of instability in Chinatown. I'm sure you know that already," I tell him.

"It is possible. I have already dispatched people to calm things down out on the streets—to make sure everybody knows retaliation will not be tolerated," he responds. "We are doing everything we can to lower the temperature."

I somehow doubt it. "Is there anybody you can think of who will try to capitalize on the chaos that will follow? Anybody you can think of who is looking to make a name for themselves and step into that power vacuum?"

Part of me knows Trevor fits that description. He's ambitious and wants to make his own mark. And there is little doubt in my mind that he ordered the hits on the family heads. But I think he still holds Fish in awe and loves him the way a son loves a father. In a strange way, we're almost siblings. I know he's rash and doesn't see all the angles like Fish does. But I also believe he's hurting just as much as I am by what happened to Fish.

Trevor plays the heavy and likes to think of himself as a major player just because he's served as Fish's right hand for so long, but I've never viewed Trevor as somebody with the backbone to make the moves necessary to get there. He doesn't think long term or have the sort of strategic mind that Fish does. To his credit, though, I believe he knows that. He's always been loyal to Fish, and his reach has never exceeded his grasp. That's something I've always respected about him.

"I heard you were looking at Councilman Drummond for Fish's shooting?" he asks.

He is clearly already plugged in to Fish's network of eyes and ears around the city, which shouldn't surprise me since he's been groomed for eventual command. There are still a great many lessons Fish needs to impart—obviously—which is another reason I need him to recover. Turning Trevor loose right now, without the wisdom and understanding he still needs to learn, will end in chaos. My belief that Trevor had those three killed today is proof of that.

"Not anymore. We proved it's not him. Not that I really thought it was to begin with," I respond. "But what about threats within the organization? Or from those outside the organization looking to establish themselves?"

"I am making inquiries."

"Any early thoughts?"

"As I said, I am making inquiries."

"I need you to tell me—"

He gives me a sly grin. "As you like to say, I cannot comment on an ongoing investigation."

I scowl. "Trevor, this is not the time for games."

"I am not playing a game. I am simply telling you that if we have an internal problem, we will handle it internally."

I glower at him, my frustration and anger growing. "This is the difference between you and Fish... he always knew where the line was and when not to cross it."

"Actually, that is not exactly true," he says. "Fish has always known what he can and cannot tell you. There's a difference, and that is the line he never crossed. You may not understand this, but you are on the outside of that circle, Agent Wilder. You always have been."

I don't know why, but his words hit me like a punch to the gut. Intellectually, I understand what he's saying. Yes, I'm outside the circle of Fish's organization, and I always have been. It's nothing we've ever talked about; it just is. And that's by design. But to hear Trevor, with the venom in his voice, almost seeming to be relishing the fact that he is part of Fish's life in ways that I'm not—as ridiculous as it is—stings.

"Believe me when I say that I will be investigating these murders vigorously, Trevor. And if I find any evidence that you were involved, I will not hesitate to arrest you. Do you understand?"

"Investigate as vigorously as you wish. You will not find evidence that I was involved."

It's not the same as telling me he wasn't involved, further cementing the idea in my mind that he was. Part of me wonders if he's daring me to arrest him, knowing it will hurt Fish to see me send Trevor away. But if he commits a crime, I can't just look the other way. I won't. It would be devious as hell, but part of me is wondering if Trevor is using that in an attempt to drive a wedge between Fish and me.

"I hope not," I tell him. "For both of our sake, I hope not."

"Is there anything else I can help you with, Agent Wilder?"

"You haven't helped me with anything at all."

He's unamused. "I have things I need to take care of."

"I mean it, Trevor. If you hear anything, you need to call and let me handle it."

"Sure. Of course."

I don't know what I expected out of seeing him today. I knew walking in that a confession that he'd ordered the hits was wishful thinking. But I'd hoped that he'd give me a little something to go on, if for no other reason than to help keep Fish's hard-won peace in Chinatown. It was obviously foolish to hope. I am, however, convinced that he had them killed. Now it's a matter of proving it, and when I do, hoping it doesn't break Fish's heart.

When I step into Fish's room, I see immediately that he's not alone. The woman sitting in the chair beside the bed turns to me, and I see her dark, almond-shaped eyes are red and puffy, as is her flawless, milky complexion. She gets to her feet and dabs her eyes with the crumpled tissue in her hand. She's a beautiful woman with black hair that has several silver strands and fine lines at the corners of her eyes. She's five-five and thin, her every movement is graceful, and I am silent for a moment. I have no idea who this woman is.

"You must be Blake," she says, her voice soft but musical.

I glance down at my waist to see if my badge is on my belt. It's not. After that, I rack my brain, trying to figure out where I've seen this woman before but come up empty.

"I'm sorry, have we met?" I ask.

"No, we haven't," she replies. "But Huan has shared many photos and stories with me. I almost feel as if I know you very well."

"Please don't think me rude, but who are you?"

Her smile is gentle and sweet. "My name is Reiko Huriyama. Huan and I have been together for… wow, nearly twenty years now."

My stomach drops into my shoes as I gape at the woman in disbelief. Fish has never talked about having a romantic relationship in all the years I've known him. All this time, I thought he was asexual, or perhaps even gay, which wouldn't have bothered me in the least, but isn't exactly embraced in the criminal underworld. Since he never talked about it, I didn't bring it up, thinking it's not my business. I guess I just assumed he would have told me about being with somebody. Clearly, I was wrong, and it hits me just as hard as when Trevor had made his point earlier about me not being in the circle. I just never knew how far outside of it I am.

"Don't look so mortified that you don't know who I am, dear. It's by design," she says. "Given Huan's previous business dealings and some of the unsavory characters he used to associate with, he kept me a secret to keep me safe."

"So... you know what sort of business he used to be in."

She nods. "I do. But I also know Huan. I know his heart. And he is one of the kindest, most generous men I have ever known. I fell in love with him despite all that."

She pulls a chair over next to hers and beckons me to sit down. I'm feeling a little lightheaded and out of sorts at the moment, so I do. Reiko reclaims her seat, then reaches out and cups my hand between hers. Her touch is soft. Gentle. And in her eyes, I can see a deep well of kindness and compassion.

"Don't be upset with him for not introducing us, dear."

"I'm not upset," I say. "I guess I'm just hurt. I'm learning that I don't know him as well as I always thought I did."

"You know him as well as I do, Blake. And you mean the world to him. Huan loves you like you're his daughter. But we all have pieces of our lives we keep for ourselves."

"I know. It's just... being with somebody for the last twenty years seems like kind of a big deal. It seems like something he would have shared with me."

Her smile is compassionate and kind. "He didn't want any piece of that world to touch me, Blake. And you may not be part of his dealings, but you are part of that world. I am his safe space... the place he comes to get away from all of that. I am clean and free of any of those dark entanglements. And he didn't want that to change. I hope you can understand that."

I want to object, but I do understand. I turn my gaze to Fish. His condition hasn't changed, but he somehow looks diminished.

I swallow hard, trying to clear the sudden lump in my throat. Having somebody to go to who is untainted by the things I see and do every day is appealing. And I guess I can't begrudge Fish for keeping his safe space to himself. In his place, if I had somebody like Reiko, I can't say I wouldn't do the same thing.

I turn my eyes to her as a thought occurs to me. "Why didn't he give you his power of attorney? That's a power *you* should have given the space in his life you occupy."

"Because he trusts you. Because he loves you," she replies. "And because he feared that by giving it to me, it would draw attention he didn't want me to have."

My eyes sting, and my face grows warm. "I can't do what he wants me to do."

"You can. But only you can know when the time is right. And he knew that when he gave you that power, Blake. He and I talked about it at length," she says, her voice soft. "He trusts you that you will not let him linger any longer than is necessary."

I shake my head. "That trust is misplaced. I can't..."

My voice trails off, and Reiko squeezes my hand. "He has always told me you are the strongest person he's ever known," she says. "He has faith in you, and that is why he gave you that power. You will know when it's time."

A tear races down my cheek, and I lower my gaze. He has more faith in me than I have in myself because I don't know that I'm ever going to have the strength to tell the doctors to pull the plug. I don't know that I have that in me.

"You will know," Reiko says as if reading my mind. "But I still feel him here, as I'm sure you do, which is why you have not given that order. I feel that he will come back to us."

"I haven't given the order because I'm a coward."

The corner of her mouth quirks upward. "I've heard enough of your exploits to know you're no coward. And I am confident, just as he was, that if we ever get to a point where Huan is no longer with us, you will know. You will feel it in your heart. And you will do what is right."

My phone buzzes in my pocket, and I pull it out quickly, seeing it's a message from Nina asking me to get back to the Chapel ASAP. I don't want to go. I would rather sit here and talk to this woman and learn more about Fish's life away from all the trappings of the world he created for himself. I thought I knew most all there was to know about him, and now, finding out I've been dead wrong about that all this time, I want to learn more about him.

"Duty calls?" Reiko asks.

"Always."

"Before you go, I just want to tell you one thing. All Huan has always wanted for you is that you carve out a safe space of your own. That you have somebody clean, somebody you can go to, as I am for him," she says. "He says you have too much to give to be alone, Blake, and he hopes that one day, you can overcome your fears and be open to the possibility of love."

The lump in my throat returns, and I have to blink away my tears. "Why has he never said that to me?"

"Because like any father figure, he was afraid of overstepping," she says. "As I fear I may have done by telling you all of this."

"You didn't overstep. And I am grateful you shared that with me."

"Open your heart, Blake. I know I don't know you, but I feel like I do, and I can see in you what Huan sees... you have too much to offer somebody to close yourself off."

"Thank you, Reiko."

"Of course, dear," she says. "Now, go. Do your duty."

I get to my feet and head for the door but stop and turn back. "It was wonderful to get to meet you. And thank you for loving him. He truly is a good man."

I walk out of the room and head for my car, overcome by a myriad of emotions. But the one that stands out most clearly is that I'm happy—happy that Fish has somebody so good and pure who loves him so well. Happy that he is happy.

CHAPTER TWENTY-NINE

The Chapel; SNAP Team HQ, Industrial District; Seattle, WA

"DID YOU LEARN ANYTHING USEFUL?" OPAL ASKS when I walk into the bullpen.

"Not what I was expecting to learn," I respond as I sit down.

Opal cocks her head, a curious expression on her face, but when I don't elaborate, she doesn't push the issue.

"What about the other Chinatown murders?" Opal asks. "Do we think they're connected to Fish's shooting?"

"I don't believe so. I'm pretty certain those were something else entirely," I answer. "I'm thinking that was somebody sending a message."

"Who was sending the message?"

"I'm not sure yet," I reply. "What did you find, Nina?"

I can tell Opal wants to question me further about who was behind the other murders, but I'm not ready to implicate Trevor yet… not until we have something concrete. She seems to pick up on my reluctance, and while not happy about it, she doesn't push me for an answer.

"Take a gander," she says.

The monitor at the end of the table lights up, and I see a frame of grainy, black and white footage pop up. It's a video clip.

"What am I looking at?"

"I wanted to play a hunch I had, so I called Drummond and asked for access to any footage from the security cameras at his house—"

"Wait, how did you know he had security cameras?" I ask.

"I checked to see if he had a security system and found that he does. It's a concealed system, so you wouldn't have seen the cameras if you were at his place," she replies simply.

"Way to take the initiative," I tell her. "But we've already cleared him of an involvement in Fish's shooting—"

"We did. But Opal kept going back to that parking stub found in the shooter's vehicle—"

"I wanted to find out how they got it and whether they could have broken into Drummond's car and stolen it like he claimed," she explains.

"All right. That's good stuff, guys," I say. "And I'm assuming by your text telling me to get back here that you found something."

"Indeed, we did," Nina chirps. "Feast your eyes on this."

She hits a button, and the clips starts to play. Drummond's car is in his driveway, and according to the time stamp, it's well after midnight a few days before the shooting. Nothing happens for a minute, but then a figure dressed in black from head to toe enters the screen. He has a slight build and is wearing a balaclava, so we can't see his face.

The man in black stops behind Drummond's car and surveys the street around him. Apparently not seeing anybody, he pulls something out of his pocket, and I see a light blinking on the small black square he's holding. The lights on Drummond's car flash.

"Did he just turn off the alarm?" I ask.

"That is my guess," Opal says. "There are gadgets you can buy online these days that allow you to bypass car and home alarms."

"That's disturbing."

"Yeah, just a little bit."

The figure in the video opens the driver's side door and reaches inside. He's there for a few seconds, then comes out with something and slips it into his pocket. It's impossible for us to tell what it is, but it's safe to assume it's small. The figure closes the door, then uses his gadget to reengage the alarm and scurries offscreen. It was fast and efficient. From the moment he stepped into the picture to the moment he left couldn't have been more than twenty seconds. At most. Whoever it was knew what they were looking for, got it, and got out again quickly.

"If I had to guess, I'd say he pilfered that parking stub out of Drummond's car," Opal says.

"I would say that is an excellent guess. But the question is, who was that?"

"I can't even venture a guess at that," she says.

"We know he's small," I say. "Nina, is there any sort of fancy, techy wizardry you can use to get us a height on the guy?"

Nina laughs. "Lucky for you I have a fancy, techy wizardry program in my bag of tricks."

"I thought you might."

Her fingers fly over the keys on her computer, and I watch as she pulls up a still image from the surveillance video. A moment later a white line appears above the figure's head, and one runs vertically alongside him, and a measurement of five-six flashes on the screen.

"There are a number of variables that can't be accounted for, so it's not pinpoint exact, but it's usually good within a couple of inches—meaning this guy is realistically somewhere between five-four and five-eight," she tells me.

"So, he's not an exceptionally big guy."

"Right."

"Does that tell us anything?" Opal asks.

"Nothing definitive," I respond. "But it's another data point we can use."

Opal taps her pen on the folder in front of her. "It seems like somebody is going to a lot of trouble to make us think Drummond was involved with the shooting. Why?"

"To throw us off their scent," I respond.

"But why Drummond? They could have set up anybody," Opal presses. "Why would they pick somebody with such an unproblematic background?"

"I'm not sure about that yet," I admit.

"It seems to me like somebody was just watching the highlights without knowing the players and picked him based on that," Nina says.

"What do you mean?" I ask.

"It's just... if you just looked at the clips of some of the City Council meetings where Drummond and Fish were going after each other, you might think they were like mortal enemies or something. If you didn't know they had a good relationship outside of chambers, you might really believe they hated each other."

It's an interesting perspective I hadn't considered, but it seems right. It feels like it fits. But I'm also acutely aware that I may think it fits because I'm scrambling to find an answer that makes sense and am latching onto the first thing that does. But it's an interesting thought, nonetheless.

"So, maybe it's somebody who just hates Drummond," Opal offers. "Disaffected constituent maybe? Someone opposed to one of his projects?"

I close my eyes for a minute, and for the first time since this whole mess began, feel a sense of calm descend over me. The conversation with Reiko offered me an unexpected peace in my heart. It was as if her words and her faith in me helped settle my soul. It's helping me to see and think more clearly and without the emotion that's clouded my mind from the start.

In my mind's eye, I see the video footage of Fish's shooting again. I see the car roll up, the figure lean out the window, and the shots that tear through Fish's body. Then I add the video Nina just showed us to the brew already bubbling around in my head and start letting the pieces of the puzzle fall together.

"It's possible," I say. "But even if that's true, I'm getting a sense that this is transactional."

"How so?"

"The shooting was cold. The shooter remained at a distance. Removed from the attempted killing," I say, thinking back to the video. "There was nothing personal about the shooting."

"How can you know that?" Opal asks.

"Typically, if there is a personal motivation, the killing will be up close. Bloodier. Vicious. In personal revenge killings, you will usually see the killer get directly involved and not hold themselves at a distance the way this shooter was. And oftentimes, if the motive is personal, overkill is common. This wasn't like that. This was several shots, from a distance, with an immediate exit when it was done," I say. "This one feels more like a business transaction to me. A hit. Somebody hired our shooter to take Fish out."

"Well, isn't it likely one of the main families in Chinatown wanted to take over what Mr. Zhao has and finally made that leap?" Opal asks.

"You'd think so. But if one of the families was making a move, they wouldn't be shy about announcing it. They would need to tell everybody they were taking over," I respond. "And as of yet, none of the families has said a word."

"What does that mean?" Nina asks.

"It means they're terrified of what comes next if Fish survives. It also tells me this wasn't any one of them—or anybody else trying to stake a claim," I answer. "Nobody has stood up and claimed the credit. No, somebody else hired that shooter."

"Who?" Opal asks.

With the emotional blinders finally off and my brain working as it should, I'm seeing the bigger picture. Or at least, the outlines of it. I still need some of the remaining puzzle pieces to fall into place before I have the full scope of it, but I can see it trending in a direction that weighs my heart down with a darkness I was not expecting. I hope I'm wrong. I want to be wrong. But with the way things are starting to line up in my mind, I'm not expecting to be.

"Blake? If it wasn't one of the families or some outside group looking to gain a foothold in Chinatown, who hired the shooter?" Opal asks.

"I'm not sure yet. But the better question we should be asking ourselves is, why? Why did somebody hire a shooter to take Fish out?" I respond. "Answering the why is very likely going to lead us to the who."

"All right, then not to ask the obvious question... but, why?"

I drum my fingers on the tabletop and try to quiet the voices echoing through my mind. There are still a lot of pieces that need to fall into place to validate the theory that's developing in my mind, and I'm making a lot of logical leaps, but I can't deny the ring of truth developing. However, I am very cognizant of the idea that this could once again be me wanting to find answers so desperately that I'm clinging to theories that have more holes than a piece of Swiss cheese. I need evidence. I need something that will either validate this theory or debunk it entirely.

I get to my feet. "I have to go."

"Go? Where?" Opal asks. "And what about the why? Shouldn't we—"

"She does this," Nina says. "She sometimes gets a wild idea and goes out hunting answers. It usually works out, so we've all learned to just let her roll."

I flash them a grin. "I'll be back. And hopefully, with answers to the why."

My feet feel heavy as I walk out of the Chapel, but not nearly as heavy as my heart. The fog is lifting from the path before me, and I find myself confronting things I haven't let myself see yet, and I have a feeling I'm not going to like what I find when I get to the end of this path.

Not at all.

CHAPTER THIRTY

Brunson Professional Building, Downtown District; Seattle, WA

"CHIEF WILDER, GOOD TO SEE YOU AGAIN," Roy Odell says.

He comes around his desk and shakes my hand like we're long-lost friends rather than two people who met less than a week ago.

"Please, have a seat," he says.

He leads me over to the sitting area in his office and motions for me to take a seat in one of the plush, oversized chairs while he perches on the edge of the one across from me.

"Can I offer you some coffee?" he asks.

"No, thank you. I'm fine."

"All right then," he replies.

Odell sits back and crosses his legs, resting his hands in his lap, and waits for me to begin. Frankly, I'm not sure exactly where to start since the theory developing in my brain seems a bit out there. But if anybody is going to have answers for me, I'm confident he'll have some. Hopefully enough to validate my thinking.

"So, what can I do for you, Chief Wilder?"

"I wanted to talk to you about… about what we talked about last time I was here."

"Huan's will. Yes, of course."

Just the words send a jolt of pain shooting through my heart. I stuff it down though, forcing myself to focus on the task at hand, seeing everything as an investigator rather than somebody who is intimately involved with a victim. I run a hand over my face.

"Yes. His will," I force the words out of my mouth. "In addition to the power of attorney, you said he's leaving everything but the Jade Pearl to me."

"That's correct."

"May I ask why he didn't leave anything to Reiko?"

"Ms. Huriyama has been provided for… separately. Huan didn't want that made public for obvious reasons, as I'm certain you can understand."

"Of course," I respond. "May I ask when he drafted this version of his will?"

Odell cocks his head. "Does it matter?"

"It might, yes."

"How so?"

"I'm curious about the timing of everything."

"What are you looking for here, Chief?"

I sit forward. "Can you just tell me when Fish put this will together?"

Odell frowns, obviously not believing this has anything to do with anything. He can't understand what I do or why. But then, as a lawyer and not an investigator, I guess maybe he wouldn't.

"Mr. Odell?"

"Well, Huan and I sat down a few weeks ago and put this together. But I'm not sure what it is you're looking for here."

My stomach lurches, and my mouth grows dry as an important piece of the puzzle snaps into place. I lick my lips and lock my hands together to keep from fidgeting. Fish is a planner. He always makes sure to see all the angles and accounts for everything. He doesn't do things on a whim. So, I know beyond the shadow of a doubt that he didn't just put together a will a few weeks ago. The document he had Odell work up is a revision of an existing will. I know it deep in my bones.

"This will you worked up with him a few weeks ago—it's a replacement for an existing will?" I ask, needing to confirm my thoughts.

"Well... yes."

"And did Trevor know about this change to Fish's will?" I ask.

"Not at first," he replies. "But once we had the framework in place, Huan invited Mr. Kondo to sit down with us to discuss the changes."

"And under the previous version of Fish's will, did Trevor stand to inherit... more?"

Odell's frown deepens as he finally seems to latch on to where I'm going with this line of questioning. And the expression on his face makes it clear he disagrees.

"Well, yes, I suppose so," he admits. "But when we sat down with Mr. Kondo, he was very understanding and said all he wanted was the Jade Pearl anyway. He was very adamant about wanting to build on Huan's legacy. There was no animosity."

I pull a face. "You have to admit that having one's inheritance reduced so drastically probably has to sting a little bit."

He shrugs. "I imagine for some it might be a problem. But Trevor made a point of saying he came from nothing and would have nothing if not for Huan. He was grateful for the leg up having the Pearl would give him but seemed genuinely eager and excited to earn his way—as Huan has taught him to do."

For being a lawyer who began his career dealing with some of the lowlifes he's defended, I'm frankly surprised by Odell's naivete. He should know, better than most, just how deceitful people can be and just how much greed can drive them to do the unthinkable. However, it's not a point I want to argue with him right now since it would do nothing to advance my theory, and I have more pressing questions to ask.

"Mr. Odell, what spurred Fish to change his will in the first place?" I ask.

He pauses and seems to consider his answer. "I'm not sure I can answer that question."

A frustrated breath escapes me. "Fish trusted me with his power of attorney—with making literally life and death decisions on his behalf. And I'm investigating his shooting, so I doubt he would be upset if you shared that bit of information with me."

Odell still seems hesitant, as if he's having some sort of internal debate. If I'm going to solve this and find Fish's would-be assassin, I need to know what he knows.

"Mr. Odell—Roy—I know you and Fish are close. I know you care for him," I start.

"We are. And yes, I do."

"Then help me find the person responsible for him being laid up in that hospital room on death's door. Help me find the person who is threatening to take him away from us."

He runs a hand across his face. "I can see where you're going with this, and I have to be honest: I think you're barking up the wrong tree. I don't think Trevor is involved. He seemed genuinely sincere in his understanding of why Huan changed his will."

"And maybe I am. But I want to be able to prove that so I can move on to the next line of inquiry," I tell him. "This is important, Roy. I need to know."

Odell sighs and gives himself a small nod. "Huan had originally divided his assets—those he didn't allocate to Reiko—between you and Trevor. But my understanding is that Huan and Trevor had a bit of a falling out. They had a disagreement. What that was about, I was not told. I just know that it was serious enough that it prompted Huan to make some changes to the allocation of his assets," he tells me. "But he and Trevor talked about it, and like

I said, by the time they were here to discuss those changes, they seemed just as close as they ever had. Everything between them was good, and Trevor understood. It was why Huan relented and allocated the Pearl to him again."

I silently groan to myself. This was definitely heading down the path I wouldn't let myself see or even consider before. Odell may truly believe that things between Fish and Trevor were good again, but that doesn't actually mean they were.

"I know how that sounds," Odell adds. "But it's not what you're thinking—"

"It's motive, Mr. Odell. It's motive."

"You're on the wrong path."

"Maybe. But I am still obligated to follow that path to its end."

"Huan himself told me he and Trevor had a heart to heart about it all and that he was on board with the changes."

"And I have no doubt Fish believed that. Just as you do. But I know Trevor, and he is not a man who takes slights very well. And being essentially cut out of Fish's will, after how many years he's been with him, is about the biggest slight I can think of him receiving."

"I think you're wrong about this."

"To be honest, I hope I am. I really do," I respond and get to my feet. "Thanks for your time, Roy. I'll be in touch if I have any other questions."

"Before you go, there's one more thing you should know."

The chasm that opened in my gut yawns even wider as I sense that I'm not going to like whatever it is Odell is about to tell me.

"What is it?" I ask.

"I only just finished drafting Fish's will. I still don't have Fish's signature, so technically, until he signs it, the will can't be executed," he says.

"So… if Fish were to die without being able to sign the current version of his will, everything would revert back to the older version?"

He nods. "Yes. That's what I'm saying. But if it comes to that, and I truly hope it doesn't, as Mr. Zhao's attorney, I know his desires, and I will fight to ensure his wishes are fulfilled. I just wanted to be transparent with you."

I take a moment to absorb the information and nod. “Okay. Thank you, Mr. Odell.”

“Of course.”

I walk out of Odell’s office not feeling very good about what I learned. Nor do I feel very good about the fact that Dr. Azar was right about me wearing blinders when it comes to people I care about. She told me I tend to keep myself from seeing things that may be right in my face. Not that I care about Trevor the way I care for others, but in a way, I suppose I do consider us family. We are the children Fish never had. And maybe because of that, I kept myself from seeing what should have been obvious all along: Trevor has motive to kill Fish… he’s got it in spades.

But motive without evidence is absolutely meaningless. Now that I believe I’m sniffing around the right tree, I have to find what I need to chop it down. If Trevor had anything to do with Fish’s shooting, as I now believe he did, I am going to make him pay for it.

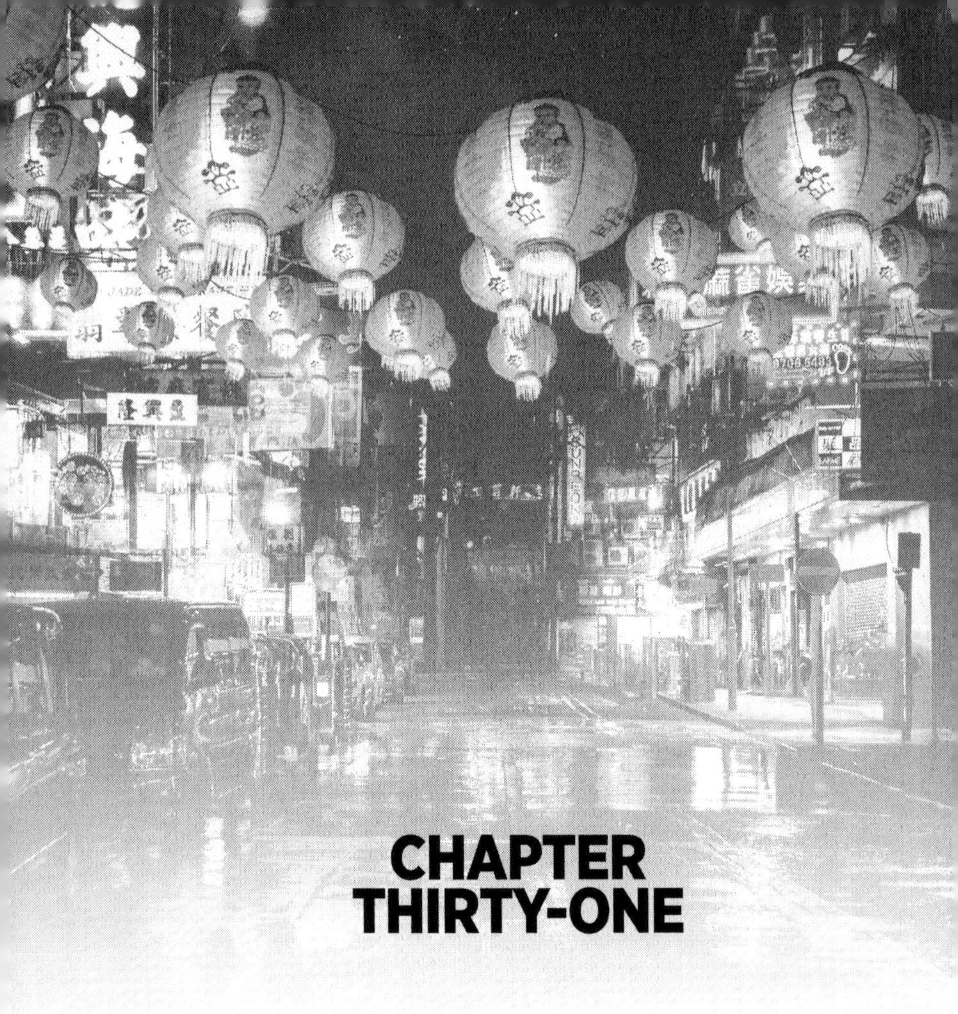

CHAPTER THIRTY-ONE

The Chapel, SNAP Team HQ, Industrial District; Seattle, WA

"WAIT, WAIT, WAIT... SO YOU'RE TELLING US YOU think this man Mr. Zhao has practically raised as his own son is behind the shooting?" Opal asks incredulously.

"That's what I'm telling you."

"Because he was cut out of the will."

"Right."

"Except that he wasn't cut out of the will," Opal counters. "He was, according to you, given control of Mr. Zhao's empire."

"If he can hold it, sure, I guess," I respond.

"Which is why you think he orchestrated the murders of the other family heads. To solidify his power and control," Nina says.

"Exactly."

"That's… ruthless. Seriously cold-blooded," Nina grouses.

"It's how he plans on ruling Chinatown," I reply. "But I also think it's why he's been pushing me so hard to take Fish off life support. With Fish out of the way, his path to the crown is open and clear. And the new will Fish had drawn up can't be executed. At least, not easily. Odell assures me he'll fight that if it actually happens."

"Jesus," Nina groans. "I'd say that's one hell of a motive. To get cut out of millions of dollars in assets… yeah, that's motive all right."

"So, why make the move now? Mr. Zhao isn't dead. He's still clinging to life with a chance of recovering. Why would he risk it?"

"I don't think he expects Fish to survive, so he's making moves now to not only consolidate his own power but to preemptively cut the heads off the other snakes who might be tempted to step into the power void."

"This seems like a bit of a stretch," Opal says.

Nina frowns. "I actually think it makes sense. The picture is starting to take shape."

"One thing you need to understand about Trevor is that respect is one of the biggest things to him. And nobody's respect means more to him than Fish's. He has been chasing Fish's approval as long as I've known him," I add. "So, to have Fish essentially cut him out of the will and leave everything to me, of all people, had to feel like the biggest slap in the face to him."

"What do you mean, you of all people?" Opal says.

"Trevor hates me. Always has," I tell her. "He's always thought by associating with me, Fish was weakening his own position within the community—that people didn't respect him because he was close with a cop. With a Fed—a Fed who'd locked up a lot of heavy hitters in Chinatown's underworld, no less. He thought it made Fish look like a sellout and that nobody respected him because of it."

"Have you shared any of this with Detective Kramer?" Opal asks.

I give her a face. "He fired me from the case, remember? Speaking of which, did he respond to the package you sent him clearing Drummond?"

Nina rolls her eyes. "He said he would take it under advisement."

"Wonderful," I say. "Opal, did you happen to find the ADA he's tight with?"

"I've identified three," she replies. "I'm trying to narrow it down, but all three have been on a large number of the cases he's closed."

"If you can't narrow it down, send the package to all three of them. Send it to the DA herself if you need to."

Opal frowns. "Do you really think given the information we sent him that Detective Kramer would really keep going after Councilman Drummond?"

"If it gets his name in the papers, yes. The man chases glory harder than an Olympian chases gold. The headlines will all announce the arrest of a sitting councilman, and his name will be attached to it. It would add to his legacy," I tell her. "Nobody will ever read the eventual retraction when the charges against Drummond are dropped. That's best-case scenario."

"And the worst-case scenario?" Opal asks.

"The worst-case scenario is that an overzealous ADA chasing glory like Kramer takes the case and runs with it," I respond. "And the most catastrophic scenario is they get an indictment then a conviction."

"With nothing but a parking stub."

"And a lot of innuendo and conjecture," I respond. "I hate to say it, but juries can be incredibly easy to manipulate. I think they get it right far more than they get it wrong, but the fact remains that they sometimes get it wrong."

"Yeah," Nina says glumly.

"Which is exactly why we need to nail the right guy," I tell them.

"And how are we going to do that?" Opal asks. "Right now, all we have are your theories, gut feelings, and I hate to say it, a lot of innuendo and conjecture."

It's a fair statement. I know I'm making a lot of leaps of logic, and deep down I wonder if my inherent dislike for Trevor is fueling this drive. Still, there's a small part of me that wants to reject the notion that Trevor would actually try to kill Fish, a man who really has been a father to him, over something as simple and stupid as money and possessions. There's a part of me that wants to deny the idea that Trevor would ever do anything to the man who took him in and raised him—the man who has given him everything he has today. If not for Fish, who knows where Trevor would be right now? Although I can say with certainty, it wouldn't be anywhere good.

But my experience on this job and with the people I've chased down for all these years tell me it's not outside the realm of possibility. I've seen people kill someone they claimed to love for far less. Then there is the respect factor to consider. The assets I am set to inherit should Fish pass aren't inconsequential, but it's what Fish turning it all over to me represents to Trevor that may have caused him to turn on the only father figure he's ever known.

"All right, so how are we going to go about proving Trevor is the man behind the curtain who's pulling all the strings?" Opal asks.

"I'm still trying to figure that out. Fish has taught him everything he knows, so he's probably going to cover his tracks well," I say.

"I have a question," Nina asks. "Why did Fish cut Trevor out of his will in the first place?"

"Odell said they had a falling out about something. It was obviously pretty serious if Fish reorganized his will," I respond. "But he wasn't sure what the nature of it was. All he knew was that they had reconciled by the time the draft of the will was finished. They met in his office, and Odell said everything between them was hunky dory again. He said Trevor was on board with Fish's changes."

"But you don't believe that."

"Oh, God no," I respond. "Trevor isn't the type who lets himself be disrespected and just lets it go."

"Then it seems to me if you can figure out the why of that, why Fish cut him out," Nina says, "you'll be a lot closer to proving the who. Isn't that what you always say?"

I chuckle. "Something like that. But it's a good point. Understanding why Fish cut him out might lead us down the right path that allows us to nail him."

"Or prove he's not involved at all," Opal points out.

"Or that," I reply without much conviction.

"So, how are we going to figure out what went down between them?" Nina asks.

I tap the tip of my finger against my lips, racking my brain. If they had an argument, it's because of something Trevor did—something that would have made Fish angry. Something serious enough that it made him lose faith and trust in him.

"Nina, you and Opal start looking at police reports from Chinatown over say… the last month," I say. "Fish had his will reworked a few weeks ago, so whatever caused the rift between him and Trevor likely would have fallen in that time frame. Look for murders, drug busts… anything big that got some public attention."

"I'm on it."

"Also, take another look at the footage of the person who broke into Drummond's car," I say. "Scrutinize it and see if you can find anything that tells us anything about who they are."

"Copy that."

"Good. Thank you," I respond. "I'll be back."

"Where are you headed?" Opal asks.

"I'm going to see if I can find more proof that Trevor is the man behind the curtain."

Opal turns to Nina. "This is one of those wild ideas again?"

Nina nods. "Just roll with it."

"Copy that. I'm rolling."

I give them both a smile then head out, not sure if I'm hoping to find proof that Trevor is guilty or proof that I'm wrong.

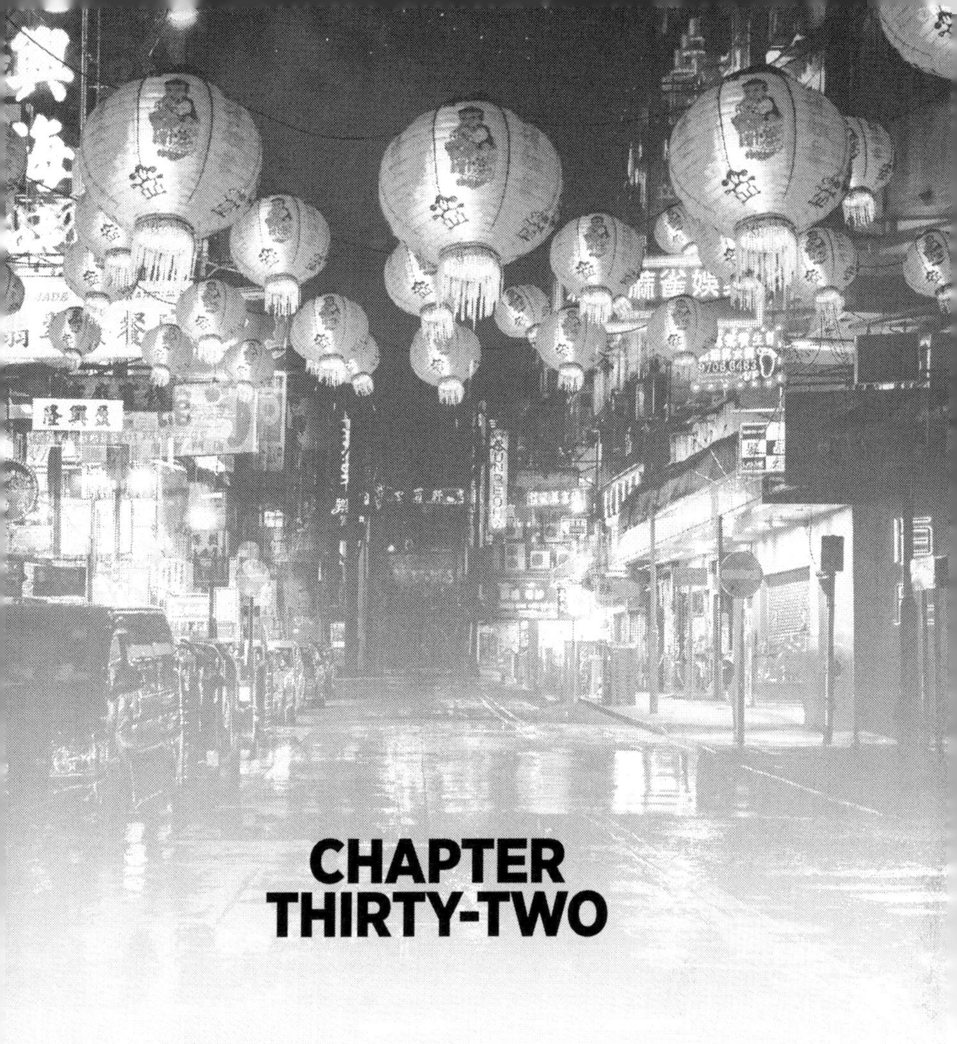

CHAPTER THIRTY-TWO

Sound View Luxury Condominiums, Downtown District; Seattle, WA

FISH HAD GIVEN ME A KEY TO HIS PLACE A LITTLE WHILE ago, but I've never actually been here. He moved out of Chinatown and got this condo after winning his seat on the City Council, telling me he thought it would "look" better. Fish normally isn't bothered by the opinions of others, but he really wanted to put his best foot forward in the eyes of his constituents and separate himself from his past and the niche he'd forged for himself in Chinatown.

It makes me wonder if that was where the friction between him and Trevor started. Trevor is an absolutist, and watching Fish move into the tonier, upscale Sound View probably felt like a betrayal to him. Like he was "forgetting where he came from." Fish never has forgotten where he came from. He continues to do good work for the people of the community, and though he has softened and isn't the hardline crime boss he once was, he still manages to maintain the peace and order he worked hard to establish.

Not that Trevor would see it that way. To him, moving out of Chinatown and into the upscale neighborhood is probably proof that Fish sold out. I'd go so far as to say he is probably more upset about that than about Fish's relationship with me. But I'm a convenient target, and Trevor can't help himself from lashing out, so I am the target for all his slings and arrows.

"Hello?" I call as I step inside.

The condo is silent and dimly lit. I close the door behind me and stand in the small foyer, looking around, but the place just has the feeling of being empty. I doubt there's anybody lurking around the corner, ready to pounce on me. All the same, I keep my hand near the weapon on my hip and move through the entire place, clearing every room before I finally let my guard down.

Fish's place is quite understated and unlike the flamboyant showman he usually is. And yet, despite the lack of the normal flourishes I associate with the man, I can still feel Fish's presence hanging over the place. It's like his energy has seeped into the very walls of the condo. It's comforting and makes me smile.

"You better snap out of it and come back here. That's an order. Do you hear me?" I say, my voice thick with emotion, as if he can hear me.

The kitchen is large and modern, and there is a formal dining room with a long table that would comfortably seat eight. Behind it are glass doors that open onto a balcony that offers a breathtaking view of Puget Sound. In the distance, the sun is slipping toward the horizon, making the waters of the Sound sparkle with a golden light. Opening the doors, I step out onto the balcony and listen to the sounds of the city for a moment. A cool breeze sweeps in from the water, raising goosebumps on my body and making me shiver. It's peaceful and I can see why he always told me how much he likes the place.

Stepping back inside, I close the balcony doors and walk to the sunken living room. Plush, comfortable seating surrounds an onyx-colored coffee table on three sides with the fourth side being a large gas fireplace with a large flat screen television mounted to the wall above it. It's not hard to picture Fish holding court there, glass of wine in hand as he waxes philosophical on any number of topics. The man knows a little bit about everything.

I don't know what I was expecting Fish's place to be like—maybe something colorful—but it wasn't this. The color palate in his condo is cool and decidedly... bland. The floors are light wood, the walls are an eggshell shade of white, and the art is tasteful, modern, and with a strong Asian influence, provides the only splashes of color. It's elegant, but the whole place has a sterile, almost art-gallery feel to it—all except for the closet where he keeps his expansive wardrobe, which is an absolute riot of color. It's almost like the clothes in his closet have leeched the color out of the rest of his place or something.

Not finding anything in his bedroom, I move to the guest room and don't find anything particularly useful in there either. The third room in his place has been converted into a home office and is the polar opposite of every other room in his condo. This is the kind of room I associate with Fish. Like him, it's loud, flamboyant, and colorful. It's vibrant and full of life. And if his presence were a whisper in my ear in the other rooms in his place, it's a full-throated shout here. Vivid reds and oranges mix with turquoise and bright lime green, but somehow, it all comes together.

There is a large desk, ornately carved out of a dark wood to my right, and the wall behind it is lined with shelves that hold a plethora of photos and knickknacks. I'm amused to see that Fish has a surprisingly large collection of pop-culture bobbleheads. I see everyone from Superman to Scooby-Doo to Spock to the Simpsons. It's as random as he can be. A pair of chairs sits before his desk, and a large, overstuffed couch that looks comfortable sits on the wall to my left. A beautiful woodblock painting that looks very old hangs on the wall above it.

On the wall beside the door is a large television that sits on a swivel. It's currently swiveled toward the desk, allowing Fish to watch as he works, and the wall across from the door has three large panes of glass offering the same view I saw while standing on the balcony. Walking over to the desk, I lower myself into the captain's chair. A soft smile touches my lips when I see the framed picture of Fish and Reiko that sits on the corner of his desk. I pick it up and look at it closely. It's more than obvious that they're happy and in love, which makes me happy to see. He deserves the sort of love I see in her eyes.

Setting the picture back down, I turn to the piles of papers and files neatly stacked and organized on top of his desk and start to rifle through them. I don't know what I'm looking for exactly and am just hoping to find something that will lead me to the reason for the rift between him and Trevor. What I do know is that Fish documents everything. He writes everything down on the off chance he forgets something.

"Come on, Fish. Where are you keeping your journal?" I ask the empty room.

I rifle through the desk drawers, then through the tall filing cabinet tucked away in the corner of the room. Nothing. I know firsthand that he's got a black, leather-bound journal in which he writes things down. He's probably got dozens of them by this point in his life. And I just know that one of those books holds the key to his rift with Trevor and the current state of their relationship. It's going to have all the information I could ever want. While perhaps not proof that Trevor was involved with his shooting, it's going to tell me if I'm on the right track. More than that, depending on what it says, it could give me some leverage I can use against Trevor.

Leaning back in Fish's chair, I scrub my face with my hands and let out a long, frustrated breath. Where are his journals? As I sit there, I notice the table beside the sofa on the wall across from me sits on rollers. Getting up, I cross the room and roll the table aside to find a safe with an electronic keypad mounted into the wall.

"You're kidding me," I mutter.

I run through all the obvious numbers—birthdays, the day he was elected, the day he took office—punching them into the keypad, hoping one of them will be the combination. None of them are. Frustrated, I let out a sound that's half-scream, half-animalistic growl as I yank on the handle and beat on the safe door. Not surprisingly, that doesn't open it either. I just know the journals I'm looking for are in there, but I have no way of getting into that safe to get them.

I stand up and resist the urge to kick the safe door knowing it will do nothing but make my foot hurt. I give myself an internal high five for my self-control. Pacing the room instead, I rack my brain, trying to remember if Fish ever gave me the combination. I'm not nearly as obsessive as he is, but I do write things down, so I pull out my notebook and flip through the pages, looking for a set of numbers I jotted down seemingly at random. I find nothing. If he gave me the combination to his safe, I don't know what I did with it.

"Dammit," I growl.

There's really only one choice. I'm going to have to get somebody over here to crack open that safe for me. Good thing I know plenty of people with the skills to do it. I hope Fish doesn't get too upset when he wakes up and finds out what I've done, but I have to believe he'll understand. My decision made, I walk over to the desk and grab my bag and am just about to leave when I happen to turn and look at the pictures on the shelves. I honestly hadn't given them a thought, but when I started to head out, it's almost as if some unseen force is compelling me to see them. Clearly, my subconscious had registered something my conscious mind didn't and is urging me to see it now.

Most are like the photos he keeps in his office down at City Hall—Fish posing with various city dignitaries and groups of children positively impacted by the programs he's championed. And there are a few of him with Reiko in various spots around the world. But there are some I haven't seen before. Candid shots. Fish knows like everybody in this city, but he has very few in his orbit I would call real friends. He doesn't trust easily and tends to keep his intimate circle very small. Some of the people in those candid shots I recognize, but some I don't.

As my gaze slides from one photo to the last one in the row, I notice a Batman bobblehead next to it. Suddenly, my eyes widen, and my heart turns a somersault as a flood of adrenaline hits my veins. Picking up the last photo, I stare at it in dumbfounded disbelief for a long, silent minute as I try to convince myself this is real and not some figment of my imagination. When the photo remains in my hand, unchanged for a solid two minutes, I start to tremble with excitement as I finally accept that this is real.

"You have got to be kidding me," I say.

Tucking the framed picture into my bag, I sling it over my shoulder and head out, the feeling of puzzle pieces finally snapping into place and giving me a glimpse of the completed photo. There are still a couple more pieces that need to be added, but I'm finally seeing it all clearly.

"I've got you," I say as I lock Fish's door behind me. "I've got you."

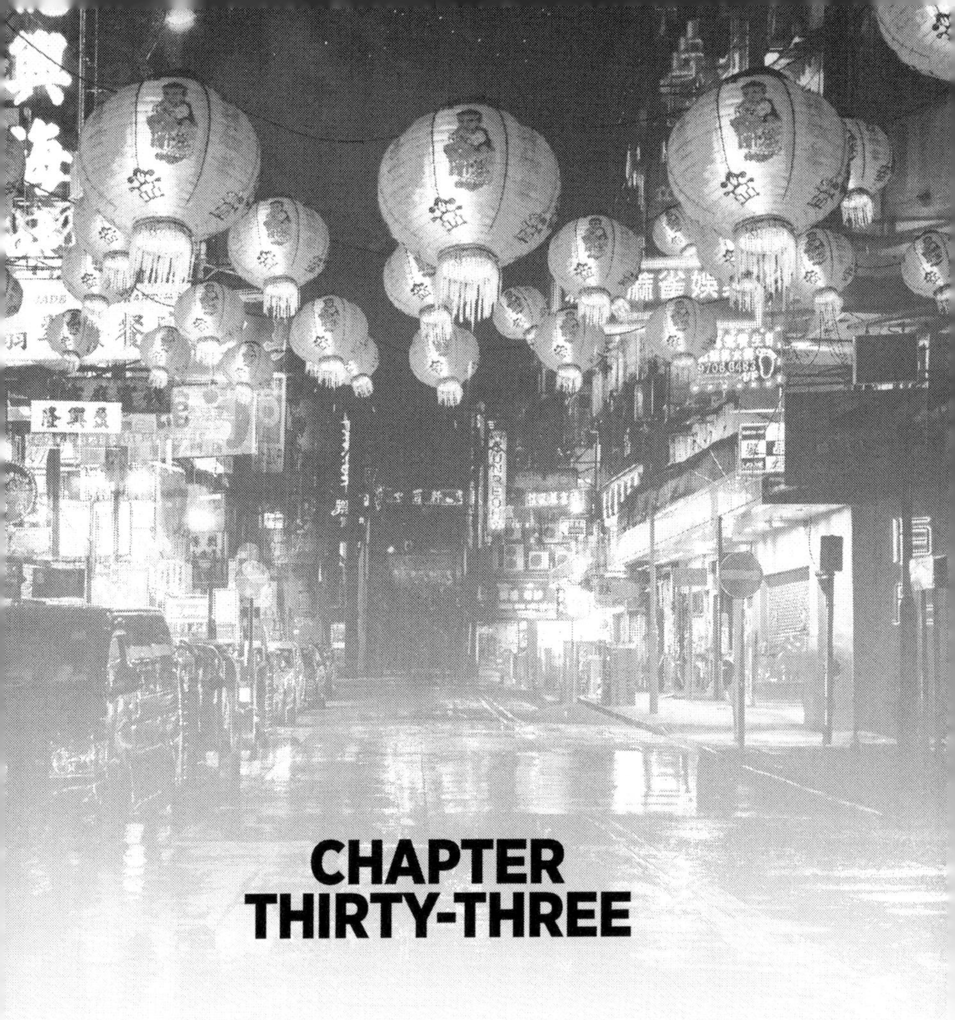

CHAPTER THIRTY-THREE

The Chapel, SNAP Team HQ, Industrial District; Seattle, WA

"No way," Nina says.

"I'm… surprised," Opal adds.

"And you had no idea they all knew each other?" Nina asks.

"None. And neither Kramer, Ma, nor Trevor saw fit to mention that little factoid to me," I say as I shake my head. "Fish is a man of two worlds. I occupy one of those worlds, but I'm learning there's a world I'm not part of."

"And never the twain shall meet," Opal quotes.

"Pretty much, yeah," I reply. "I know it's to protect me, but ..."

"But it still stings to be reminded of that," Nina finishes.

"Silly, I know."

"Your feelings aren't silly," she says. "But I've got a feeling it's better for you that you're not part of that world."

"Yeah. I know you're right," I reply and glance down at the photo in my hand. "But we're getting off track here. All that matters is this."

The photo I took from Fish's office was probably taken a few years ago at some sort of dinner party at a restaurant, which judging by the decor, I'm guessing is in Chinatown. Fish is at the head of the table, but around him are other faces I recognized instantly: Trevor, of course; across from Trevor is Detective Scott Kramer; and to Kramer's right is Henry Ma, the man whose SUV was stolen and used in Fish's shooting. They're all laughing and looking quite chummy.

I turn to Opal and give her a grin. "Still think my theory sounds outlandish and crazy?"

She laughs. "It seems a little less so right now. But I'm not quite there yet."

"Nina, we need to know what the connections between Fish, Ma, Kramer, and Trevor are," I say. "Dig through their socials, financials, phone records—anything you can to prove the link between them."

"On it," she says.

"So, walk me through your theory again and get me there," Opal says. "As you see it, how do all the players fit into their slots?"

"Okay, so Trevor finds out that he's being cut out of Fish's will. He obviously doesn't take it very well, but he swallows it down and bides his time. Frankly, it's a level of self-control I didn't think he possessed, but he's apparently learned a lot from Fish," I say. "Anyway, knowing the revised will hasn't been signed yet, he hatches a plan to get what he wants—which is everything. If he can remove Fish, he still gets the full inheritance as outlined in the original will as well as operational control of Chinatown."

"The broad strokes sound fine so far, but I'm still not quite there. Keep going."

"Right. So, Trevor contracts Ma to carry out the hit. He does. But they don't plan on me jumping in and getting involved, which frankly, was stupid on Trevor's part and shows the lack of foresight I usually associate with him," I say.

"Wait, this is where you lose me," Opal says. "Henry Ma, the mild-mannered dry cleaner… in this scenario, you think he's a hitman?"

"It makes sense. I knew the first time I talked to him that he wasn't on the up and up," I tell her. "And now, finding out he's close enough to Fish and Trevor to be a guest at one of their dinner parties? That tells me he's not just a mild-mannered dry cleaner."

"That doesn't necessarily mean he's a hitter," Opal points out.

A small grin creeps across my lips. I actually like that Opal is pushing back on me. It's a role that Astra normally fills and something I've been missing. Having somebody question me and force me to think through my rationales for various positions is helpful. It sharpens my focus, which is something I appreciate.

"You're right, it doesn't," I tell her. "But we can get back to that—"

"I have another question," Nina chimes in. "Where does Kramer fit in with this?"

"My theory is that Trevor got Kramer, who is obviously on the payroll, to jump on the case so he could steer it however he wanted," I say. "And when I got involved, he directed Kramer to feed me bad intel and get me looking the wrong way. Think about it… where did we get the lead on the parking stub? Where did we get all the information we've been working with?"

"Kramer," Nina says.

"He's been steering the direction of this case from the start—and steering us where Trevor has wanted us to go: away from the actual answers."

"That makes sense," Nina agrees.

"Turning back to Ma, my belief is that he is the man we saw in the video breaking into Drummond's car and grabbing the parking stub. He then gave it to Kramer who planted it in the SUV for the forensic techs to discover," I go on.

Opal frowns. "The idea that Ma would use his own SUV to pull off the hit though… that bit doesn't make sense to me."

"I can't answer that. Knowing Trevor's impatience, maybe it needed to be done quickly, and they didn't have time to get a clean car. They did stage a theft, then planned for the vehicle to be parted out and made to disappear, after all," I respond.

"That's true," Opal says.

"So, all of this because Trevor has his feelings hurt about Fish cutting him out of his will?"

"That's my theory, yeah."

"But do we know what precipitated the change to his will?" Opal asks. "What was the reason they had a falling out?"

"That much I don't know. Yet. I found his safe, and I'm sure he keeps his journals inside. The answers will be found in them," I say. "But I don't know the combination to get into the safe, which is why I'm here. It's got a digital lock, so I was hoping you might be able to crack it, Nina."

"Oooh, I've never cracked a safe before," she says excitedly. "Rick is going to be so jealous."

"Don't make a habit of it," I respond and hand her a slip of paper. "I wrote down all the information of the make and model I could find on the type of safe Fish has."

"Sweet."

"There are still a few too many holes for my liking, but it's a good theory. I'm almost there," Opal says. "But we still don't have much in the way of actual evidence. Unfortunately, even if we are able to get our hands on those journals you mentioned, that doesn't constitute proof."

"No, but I'm hoping it will give us something to use against Trevor," I tell her. "My hope is that we can leverage Trevor to get him to roll on Kramer and Ma. He's always had a strong sense of self-preservation, so I'm hoping he'll give them up to save his own skin."

"And we score a hat trick," Nina says.

"Exactly."

"Oh, I got so caught up, I almost forgot. This came for you today," Nina adds and slides a manila folder to me.

"What is it?"

"The stolen car report that Ma filed."

"Great. Thanks."

"I'm going to need a few minutes before we head to Fish's," Nina says. "I want to do a little bit of research on the safe beforehand—see if I can get more familiar with it."

"Take your time."

As Nina does her research, I open the file she gave me, not expecting to find anything of value in the report. As I read, though, something catches my eye. It doesn't seem right, so I go back and read it again. And then again. And as I do, a ball of lightning forms in my belly and sends its electric tendrils crackling through my veins. Gripped by excitement, I raise my head.

"Keep researching," I tell her. "I have to go have a chat with Mr. Ma."

CHAPTER THIRTY-FOUR

Residence of Henry Ma, Lower Queen Anne District; Seattle, WA

"Agent Wilder," Ma says with surprise on his face.

"Mr. Ma."

He stands in the doorway of his home and for a moment, looking as if he's thinking about bolting. The man gets himself in check, though, and an expression of composure crosses his face as he once again slips into his mild-mannered persona. Watching the transformation, as quick as it was, is fascinating and only reinforces my initial read on him. There is far more to this man than meets the eye. He is not what he seems.

"How may I help you?" he asks.

"I just had a couple of follow-up questions about your vehicle," I respond. "May I come inside and talk to you for a couple of minutes?"

He catches himself before he can frown and nods. "Of course."

I follow him back into the living room, and he offers me a seat as he perches on the edge of his sofa. I notice he keeps his distance from me and sets himself up in a position that he can move quickly if needed. Believing he's a professional hitter, I silently chastise myself for not thinking this through a little better in my rush to prove myself right. I have no way of knowing where he's got his weapons stashed and can't reach the Glock on my hip without giving the game away and perhaps making him act before I'm ready or able to defend myself.

"So, what can I do for you?" he asks again.

Keeping an eye on him, I decide to roll with it and deal with whatever comes. I don't like being in a position where I'm reacting to him and not dictating the terms of the encounter, but there's not much I can do about it right now.

"Right," I say. "I was reviewing your stolen car report—"

"I was told by the SPD that they'd found my vehicle."

"They did. It was in a chop shop."

He nods. "That's what they told me. And they said they would be able to return it to me once they'd finished processing it."

"And I'm certain they will."

"Then what is this about? The matter seems to be resolved," he asks quickly.

"Except that it's not."

"How so?"

Now we're at the tricky part. Moving deliberately and without provocation, I reach into the messenger bag at my feet, moving as subtly as I can to open my jacket enough that my weapon is available to me. Pulling the file that Nina had given me, I retrieve the report.

"This is the report you filed, Mr. Ma," I say and show it to him. "Is that your signature, attesting that your report, under the penalty of perjury, is true and accurate?"

He looks at it, then nods, but I can see the wheels in his head starting to turn. He knows he's caught because he can't deny that it's his signature, but without knowing where I'm going, Ma doesn't quite seem to know what to do.

"Yes. That's my signature," he finally says. "Again, what is this about?"

After gaining his confirmation, I close the file and slip it back into my bag, then settle myself on the chair, feeling a bit steadier and more comfortable that I can reach my weapon if this goes sideways. And if it's going to, this is probably when that would happen.

"Well, as you're aware, your vehicle was used in the drive-by shooting of a City Councilman, is that correct?" I ask.

"As I said when you were here and told me the last time, I am aware, but obviously had no part in it because I'd already reported my vehicle stolen," he says, growing agitated.

"Then I wonder if perhaps you can tell me why you didn't actually file your stolen car report until the day after the shooting?"

Ma's face blanches, and his body stiffens as his worst thoughts become his reality. Hoping to head off any potential for violence, I sit forward, pinning him to the sofa with my gaze.

"Mr. Ma, I know you didn't do this alone. Maybe you didn't even want to do it but were forced to," I say. "I know that somebody directed you to shoot Fish. If you cooperate with me to bring those other people in, I will speak to the DA personally about cutting you a deal."

Ma slides his hand slowly and subtly, but inexorably toward the cushions, making me worry about what he might have between them.

"Please, stop moving, Mr. Ma. I don't want anybody to get hurt here today," I say. "Least of all me. So, please, just... calm down, and let's talk this out. Let's talk about getting you a deal."

"I don't want a deal, Agent Wilder."

His movements are cat-quick and in one fluid motion, he pulls something out from between the couch cushions. I barely have time to register that it's a throwing knife before it's slicing through the air, heading straight toward my face. I throw myself to the side, but not before my cheek explodes in pain as the edge of the blade slices into my skin. The blood flowing down my face is warm and thick as I hit the ground with a hard grunt.

Before I can get to my feet, though, Ma is on me. He maneuvers himself behind me and wraps his arm around my throat and cuts off my air. He's wiry and strong, and as he applies even more pressure, trying to choke the life out of me, I feel myself growing lightheaded. My vision begins to waver as his warm breath washes over the back of my neck. If I don't get out of this hold, I'm dead. But still on my butt, I don't have much leverage, so I do the only thing I can think of. Mustering all the strength I can manage, I thrust my head backward.

Ma grunts in pain, and I feel something crunch as the back of my head connects with his face. It's enough. His hold on my throat loosens, allowing me to slip out of his grasp and leap to my feet. I take several deep breaths, trying to clear my vision, and see the lower half of Ma's face is slicked with blood; it appears that he's missing his two front teeth. He glares at me for just a moment before launching himself at me again.

This time, I'm on my feet and am able to step aside, getting out of the way of his bull rush. Before I can reach for my weapon, though, I'm forced to play defense again as he hurls a glass vase at me. I dodge the projectile but can already see him rushing toward me again. Thankfully, I'm prepared for it this time. Reaching back, I propel my fist forward with as much strength as I can. It connects with the side of his head, and Ma crumples to the floor.

He's not done, though, as he springs back to his feet like a damn Jack-in-the-box from hell. Ma comes at me again with a dizzying flurry of punches, most of which I'm able to block, but he catches me across the chin with a blow that snaps my jaw shut so hard I hear my teeth clack together, catching my tongue in between. The coppery taste of blood fills my mouth, and I wince as I stagger backward. My foot catches the chair I'd been seated in just moments ago. I lose my balance and pinwheel my arms as I fight to stay upright.

Ma, having produced another knife from God knows where, charges at me again. As he closes in, he brings the blade down in a murderous arc that, if he connects, will surely slice straight through me. I throw myself to the side again, the edge of his knife narrowly missing me. I hit the ground and roll as I've been taught. Ma is already swooping in for another chance at disemboweling me. I surprise him, though, when I close the distance and get inside his reach and deliver a hard chop to his throat.

The force of my blow sends him reeling, and the blade falls to the floor with a hard clatter as he reaches for his throat with both hands. His face red and eyes bulging, he coughs and hacks as he tries to regain his air. Not waiting for him to recover, I wade in and throw a flurry of vicious punches to his face. His nose breaks with an audible snap, sending scarlet streaks across his face, adding to his already bloody, nightmarish visage.

Ma doubles over, still hacking and wheezing from the blow to his throat, and I drop him face down onto the floor with a savage kick to the back of his knee. Moving swiftly, I pull the cuffs off my belt, wrestle his arms behind his back, and secure him. That done, I slide off and sit down, leaning against the back of the chair. My breathing is ragged, my face is ringing with pain, and I know I'm a bloody mess. I'm sure I don't look much better than Ma does right now.

Ma is still gasping as he turns his head, staring at me with eyes filled with rage. Being the petty person I am, I blow him a kiss.

"Thank you, Mr. Ma," I say. "You've just given me what I needed to tear this place apart. And what do you think I'm going to find?"

As if confirming my thoughts, he turns his head away, unable to look at me any longer. Pushing myself back to my feet with a loud, pained groan, but feeling better than I should, I pull my phone out of my bag and make the call to get a forensics team from the Seattle FO, rather than the SPD, down here to process the place.

CHAPTER THIRTY-FIVE

The Chapel, SNAP Team HQ, Industrial District; Seattle, WA

“HENRY, IT WOULD BE TO YOUR BENEFIT TO TALK TO me,” I say. “I know you didn’t do this alone. I know you were hired to do it. I’ve got your phone proving that. Don’t take the ride for this by yourself. Tell me who paid for the hit.”

Ma sits across the table from me in one of the Chapel’s three interrogation rooms. Like most other interview rooms I’ve been in, it’s small, windowless, made from concrete painted with a thick layer of industrial gray over it, and designed to be uncomfortable. A camera is mounted high in the corner recording the interview, and I'm sure Nina and Opal, who had been aghast at my appearance when I returned, are on the other side watching intently. Our entire case against Kramer and Trevor hinges on what Ma tells us. Or, as I'm now seeing, doesn't tell us.

After calling into the FO from Ma's house, a forensics team and paramedic was dispatched. While the techs did their thing, the EMTs patched the two of us up. He was fit enough to be turned over into my custody, so I planted him in the interview room, and the man has not said a single word in the three hours he's been here. He's just sitting on the other side of the table, his hands chained to the bar in the center, sitting as quietly and serenely as a statue of Buddha. If it weren't for the cameras, I might give into the sudden urge to beat an answer out of him.

"Henry, come on," I say. "This is the time for you to help yourself. Do you really think anybody else is going to help you out here? You're on your own, and you need to look out for yourself. You need to do right by you."

Ma just sits there, staring straight through me in an almost Zen-like trance. Before I do something I'm going to regret, I get to my feet and exit the room, slamming the door behind me. I storm down to the kitchen and grab a bottle of water, downing half of it in one swallow as Nina and Opal walk in. Nina grabs a soda, and Opal grabs an apple from the bowl. We stand together in an awkward silence for a moment. I drain the last of the water, throw the bottle away, then grab another out of the refrigerator.

"Three hours," I finally seethe. "Three hours and the man hasn't said a word. Hasn't asked for a lawyer, hasn't told me to get stuffed, nothing. It's like he's completely checked out. He's giving me absolutely nothing to work with. Speaking of which, Nina, have the techs gotten back to you about the burner we found in Ma's house?"

She nods. "They were able to trace it back to where it was purchased and confirmed it was purchased by Ma," she replies. "Also, there is only one stored number in the phone. It's actually the only number that phone has ever contacted."

"A single-use burner. Not surprising in his line of work. That's SOP," I say.

"They also uncovered some text messages that Ma had deleted," Nina adds. "It proves he did take the job to kill Fish. Between that and the weapon they recovered, there's no doubt that Henry Ma is our shooter."

If not for a sharp-eyed tech who realized the closet seemed to be too small, we might not have had anything on Ma at all. But the tech discovered Henry's workshop behind the false wall in the closet. The room was filled with all the tools of the trade a professional hitter would require: weapons, electronics, false IDs, ammunition, and more than a few large stacks of cash. And among the paraphernalia, we found an AR-15 and a burner phone.

I might say it was sloppy of him to have not disposed of those things after the attempted hit on Fish, but Henry strikes me as a smart man who plans for a rainy day. Something tells me he kept them as insurance. Why he's choosing to not play that card and remain silent, though, I'm not sure. He could easily play it and save himself a little time and trouble, but he seems content to ride it out on his own and not give up his co-conspirators. And I don't know why.

"Why hasn't he asked for a lawyer?" Opal asks.

"I don't know," I answer. "I know he wants something; I just don't know what it is."

"Maybe it's something we can't give him," she offers.

"If he's waiting for Trevor and Kramer to come through for him, that's going to be a long wait for a bus that never comes. Those two won't lift a finger to help him and will be happy to just hang him out to dry."

Opal pauses and seems to consider something. "What if it's leverage?"

"What do you mean?"

"It seems odd to me that a professional killer would leave evidence lying around out in the open like that for you to find."

"I thought that too."

"What if he has other evidence that he's stashed away somewhere—evidence that directly ties Trevor and Kramer to the shooting?" she goes on. "Maybe he knew this would eventually come back to him—probably because of the car, I'd assume—and he left the phone to let us know he didn't do this on his own but is keeping the other evidence hidden as a break-glass-in-case-of-emergency sort of thing. Maybe he has somebody who will then release that evidence in case something ever happens to him while he's in prison. Maybe he's loyal enough that he's willing to remain silent and take the ride on his own so long as he's left alone."

"Like a life insurance policy."

She nods. "Like a life insurance policy."

"That's a really interesting thought."

The buzzer sounds, snapping the tension in the air. Nina turns and darts over to the security monitors and hits the button to open it.

"Hey, Boss, it's Kramer," she calls across the bullpen. "And be advised: it looks like he's coming in hot."

"Noted. Thanks, Nina," I say and groan inwardly.

"Good news travels fast," Opal says.

"Even faster when you're on somebody's payroll."

After Nina opens the door for him, Kramer comes charging through the bullpen, face red, lips drawn back, and nostrils flaring like a bull in an arena. I feel like all I need is a funny hat and a red cape. He storms into the kitchen where Opal and I are standing and eyes us both.

"I heard you have Henry Ma in custody," he says.

"Hi, Detective Kramer. Good to see you again too. And don't worry. It's just a little cut, I'm fine. Thanks for asking."

Unamused, he glowers at me. "Why in the hell did you pick up Henry Ma?"

"Why do you care?" I ask.

"Because he's part of my case."

"He's not. You said so yourself. You said he's some poor schmuck who got his car stolen at the wrong time," I remind him.

He crosses his arms over his chest. "He's still connected to my case—a case I revoked your access to, if you recall."

"Oh, I recall just fine," I say. "I went to speak with him about a different matter entirely, and he attacked me. It seemed like a red flag to me, so I went ahead and arrested him, then authorized a search of his place—"

"Then you are going to turn over whatever evidence you found to me. Need I remind you this is my case, Wilder."

"Actually, given the fact that he attacked and injured a federal agent, that makes it our case now," Opal tells him. "But we'll keep you in the loop as our investigation progresses."

I want to hug her for that, but I hold off. For now. Kramer is apoplectic, and if he gets any redder or tenser, I'm half afraid he's going to stroke out right here on the kitchen floor.

"Blake, turn Ma and all the evidence you gathered over to me right now!" he hisses through clenched teeth. "This is my case!"

"No."

"I swear to God, I will call your superiors. I'm not going to stand for this—"

"My superior is Deputy Director Lauren Church," I say and pull my phone out of my pocket. "Did you want her number, or do you want me to dial for you?"

"I am not screwing around."

"Neither am I," I tell him, matching his sneer with one of my own. "And while I have Church on the line, we'll talk about the rampant corruption within the SPD. One of my favorite subjects."

"What the hell are you talking about?"

"I know, Kramer," I say simply. "I know about you and Trevor Kondo. I know all about what you've been up to. I know everything."

He seems to bite off his next words and grows pale. Kramer quickly recovers, though, and puts the sneer back on his face.

"You don't know anything because I haven't done anything," he says.

"You think I'd really tell you that I knew if I didn't have something to back it up?" I ask. "I happened to find a picture of you, Trevor, and Henry Ma looking very friendly and cozy at a dinner party. How do you think that's going to play with a jury?"

He grimaces. "If you had anything I'd be in cuffs right now."

"We'll get to that," I respond. "But right now, I think you better start looking out for yourself because I can promise you that Trevor won't."

I can tell this whole conversation has not gone the way Kramer had envisioned it. He obviously never expected us to ever uncover his role within Trevor's schemes. We've caught him completely flat-footed, and he suddenly looks like he wants to be anywhere but here. But he knows he can't leave just yet without losing face and casting more suspicion on himself. Not that I think that's even possible at this point.

"You've got nothing on me because I haven't done anything," he growls.

"And if you tell yourself that often enough, you might eventually believe it," I fire back.

"This isn't over," he says.

"No. It's not," I tell him. "But you'll know it's over when I put you in cuffs."

Turning on his heel, Kramer storms out of the Chapel the same way he stormed in—in a huff. He slams the door behind him, and I let out a breath.

"You know we've got nothing on him," Opal says.

"I know," I respond. "Not yet. But we will. Like he said, this isn't over."

Opal turns to me. "Something just occurred to me."

"Yeah? What is that?"

"You knew we had nothing on Henry Ma and would never be able to search his house unless he did something drastic to give you cause. Like attacking you," she says. "Did you go to his place specifically to get him to do something like that which would give you cause?"

I shrug. "I just tried to ask him a couple of questions."

"Uh-huh," she replies. "You're just lucky that cut on your cheek is all you got."

"No risk," I tell her. "No reward."

CHAPTER THIRTY-SIX

Jade Pearl Billiards House, Chinatown-International District; Seattle, WA

My first thought was to do this alone. It somehow feels like I should. But the bandage on my face—along with Nina and Opal—reminded me that I'm human, that I'm probably too emotionally invested in this case, and that I have been prone to doing stupid things because of it. So, after sending a couple of agents to the hospital to secure Fish's room—nobody in and nobody out—

to make sure Trevor didn't catch wind of what I'm up to and take measures to finish what he'd started, I had a couple more agents accompany me to the Pearl. It's time to bring this to an end.

Thankfully, the illegal gambling lounge is empty and doesn't seem to be open today, which is one less thing for me to worry about. Fish's man on the office door gives me and my escorts a nod, then steps aside. We walk into the office to find Trevor in another meeting with two of the three young men I saw him with the last time I was here. He glowers at me, then tells his men to bail. They do. As my agents close the door again, then post up beside it to keep an eye on things, I drop into the chair in front of Fish's desk. Trevor and I engage each other in a silent standoff for a moment as the air in the office crackles with growing tension.

"What happened to your face?" he finally asks.

"Your friend Henry Ma gave me a little something to remember him by."

"Henry who?"

I chuckle softly. "Really? That's the way you're going to play it?"

He shrugs. "What do you want me to say? That I know somebody I do not?"

I gaze at him for a moment, almost impressed with his brazenness. Surely, he can't expect me to make an accusation like that without having something to back it up. But then, like I've said many times before, the power of foresight is not one of Trevor's gifts, so maybe he does. I reach into my bag and pull out a copy of the dinner party photo I made and fling it across the desk. It lands face down in front of him.

"What is this?" he asks as he picks it up.

I say nothing, giving him a minute to look at the photo, and realize just how deep the hole he's in actually is. Though his face remains smooth and passive, I see it dawn in his eyes. It's a slight, brief widening before he gets himself back under control again, but it's there all the same. Clearing his throat, Trevor drops the picture, doing his best to look unimpressed and uninterested.

"It was a dinner party," he says. "You cannot expect me to know everybody—"

"Except that I can, Trevor. You can't BS your way around me. I know the things you do for Fish, and I know that nobody gets close to him without you vetting them first—or having them on the payroll," I tell him. "You know everybody in that photo because you vetted every single one of them including Detective Scott Kramer and Henry Ma, your hired hitter."

Trevor scoffs and shakes his head but says nothing. The silence in the room lingers, and the atmosphere around us is growing tenser by the second. I watch Trevor closely, making sure I keep track of his hands. As if reading my thoughts, the two agents near the door move, flanking the desk and keeping Trevor between them with a clear line of sight. He raises his hands with his palms facing me, then lays them flat on the desktop.

"Why did you do it, Trevor? Why did you try to have Fish killed?"

"I do not know what you are talking about."

"I've got my techs poring through your financials right now. It's only a matter of time before we find the transaction between you and Ma," I say. "Save us all some time and just tell me why."

"As I said, I do not know what you're talking about," he repeats. "You and I have never gotten along, that is no secret. But I never thought you would stoop so low as to try to frame me for a crime I did not commit. Are you so desperate for Fish's attention that you would do this?"

"Trevor, the game is over. You lost. We know you conspired with Ma and Kramer to hit Fish then control the subsequent investigation. I also know you had Meng, Xie, and Cao murdered to solidify your place of power," I tell him. "I just want to understand why. Why would you do this when Fish has given you everything?"

His lips curl back, exposing his teeth. "Everything? No. He gave *you* everything! *I* had to work for every scrap he threw me, but you? He gave you everything on a silver platter!"

"So, that's it then. You weren't as okay with the revision to the will as you made Fish and Odell believe. You've been planning this since you found out about the change."

As if realizing he'd already said too much, Trevor leaves his hands palms down on the table but leans back in his chair and takes a moment to gather himself.

"As I said, I do not know what you're talking about," he says with a forced calm.

My gaze lingers on him for a moment longer, giving him one last chance to bring this farce to an end. He doesn't take it though. Letting out a long breath, I reach into my bag again and pull out the phone I confiscated from Ma. The techs have already processed it and downloaded everything; it is of no more use to them, so they gave it back to me. I open up the old-school flip phone and call up the only number in the memory and raise my gaze to Trevor again.

"Last chance," I say. "Tell me why you did it."

Trevor doesn't say a word. He just sits in Fish's chair and stares at me gloomily with pure contempt in his eyes. When I say nothing, he slaps his palm against the desk.

"And what is that? I do not have time for games, Agent Wilder," he practically shouts.

"Oh, this? This is Henry Ma's phone, and it only has one contact number in it," I tell him. "What are the odds that when I press this button, you're going to get a call?"

Trevor sits stoically and seems to swallow down whatever acidic reply was sitting on the tip of his tongue. He raises his chin defiantly, but I can see in his eyes that he knows he is screwed six ways to Sunday. Shaking my head, I hit the call button, turn on the speaker, and hold the phone out in front of me. After a moment of dead air, it begins to ring. And a moment after that, I hear the muffled ring of a cellphone in one of the desk drawers.

"Well, I'd say we have a winner," I say.

"I don't know what that is," he protests. "That must belong to Fish."

"Save it, Trevor. Once my techs get the serial number off that phone, they're not going to have any trouble tracing it back to you. This is over."

He glares at me icily. "This is far from over. Far, far from it."

"Keep telling yourself that," I say, then turn to the agent on the right. "Can you please arrest Mr. Kondo, then get a team down here to process the office?"

"Right away, Chief."

As the agent starts to move in, Trevor leaps to his feet, his hand moving toward the small of his back. I'm ready for it, though, and this time I'm quicker. Leaping up, I pull my weapon in one motion and level it at Trevor's face. His eyes grow wide as he stares down the barrel of my Glock. The two agents flanking him also have their weapons drawn and trained on him. Trevor licks his lips and swallows hard.

"You might want to rethink that," I say.

Moving cautiously and with care, Trevor raises his hands. I keep my weapon trained on him, my jaw clenched, and my eyes narrowed to slits. As this all plays out, I'm overwhelmed by a sense of sadness. Not for Trevor. For Fish. When he wakes up and finds out what happened and who did that to him, it's going to devastate him. Trevor has been like a son to him, and I wish it hadn't gone down like this. But Trevor let his greed and sense of entitlement get the better of him. This isn't my fault. This is his.

My agent moves in, and Trevor lets himself be cuffed. Once his hands are secured behind his back, the agent disarms him, dropping the nine-millimeter tucked into a holster at the small of his back onto the desk, then searches him for any other weapons. He has none.

"You do not deserve anything Fish gives you," Trevor hisses. "Who in the hell are you, anyway? You are not one of us, and you never will be."

"No, I won't ever be one of you. I'm okay with that," I tell him. "But more importantly, Fish is okay with that too."

"You are a cancer, Blake Wilder. You rot and kill everything you touch. Including Fish," he growls. "You will be his downfall one day. *You* will be the reason he is killed."

"I pity you, Trevor. You really had it all, and you threw it all away because you thought you were owed something. Because you thought you deserved more," I say. "You're like the dog with a bone in its mouth who happened upon its own reflection in a pond and was so desperate to get what it thought was a second bone, lost the first and ended up with nothing. There's a lesson in that story that applies directly to you."

He glares at me hatefully but says nothing. Perhaps my words sunk in… and perhaps they went in one ear and out the other. It doesn't matter. More importantly, I don't care. I won't feel guilty about somebody else's actions. I won't let myself carry that weight. It's something Dr. Azar has been trying to get me to understand and apply to my life. It's unfortunate it took this to get me there simply because of the impact this will have on Fish when he wakes up, but there isn't anything I can do about it.

"Take him out of here," I say.

As the agent leads him away, my phone buzzes with an incoming text. I pull it out and feel my heart lurch when I see it's a message from Reiko.

"Get to the hospital right away. It's Huan…"

CHAPTER THIRTY-SEVEN

Mountainview Medical Center, Downtown District; Seattle, WA

I MUST HAVE BROKEN EVERY TRAFFIC LAW AND SPEED LIMIT ON my way to the hospital, but I managed to get here twenty minutes after Reiko's text. My heart thundering, I nod to Fish's men who are standing discreetly but watchfully off to the side, then badge my way by the two agents on the door. And when I walk in, my stomach turns over as my heart swells, and I can't control the tears that flow down my cheeks.

"Fish," I say.

He's sitting up in his bed, looking haggard and weak, but very much alive. He offers me a weak smile as I rush over and take his hand, giving it a gentle squeeze.

"You're back," I say.

"For the most part," he replies, then looks at me worriedly. "What happened to your face, Blake? Who did this to you?"

"Nobody. Well, I mean, a suspect did this to me, but it doesn't matter. I'm fine."

He purses his lips and frowns for a minute before seeming to accept my answer—or at least, accept the fact that it's the only answer I'm going to give him, so he doesn't push. If he had his usual strength, he would hound me as badly as Astra until I told him what he wanted to know, so lucky for me, he's not operating at optimal capacity.

"My memory of what happened is missing, and the doctors are not sure if it will return. It's a wait-and-see thing, but they say cognitively, I seem all right. For the moment," he says.

"I hope it doesn't come back. You don't need to remember that."

"I disagree. I do need to remember that," he replies softly.

Fish's face is grizzled and dotted with salt and peppered stubble. His skin is sallow, and his eyes are puffy and bloodshot. He looks horrible. Fish is a man who prides himself on his appearance, and he would no doubt be mortified if anybody saw him in this state, but he's alive. And that's all that matters. That's all I care about.

"I could use a shower. And some fresh clothing," he says, making me laugh.

"I can't do anything about those items right now, but is there anything else I can get you?" I ask. "Something to drink, something to eat—you must be starving—"

"I am fine for the moment," he says, and his face fills with something that looks like regret. "I understand you met Reiko."

"I did. She's lovely, Fish—"

"I am sorry, Blake. I never wanted to keep her from you, but—"

"She's your safe space. Your bit of clean in this dirty world," I say. "Believe me, I understand. I really do. And I'm not upset about it. You deserve to be happy, and you deserve to be loved. I'm so glad she can be those things for you."

His smile, though subdued and weak, still lightens my heart. I'm sure it will take some time before he has his strength back. It will be even longer before he's back to his normally energetic, flamboyant self. But those things will come. All that matters is he's alive.

"Thank you for that," he says. "She is very fond of you as well. And since the secret is out, at least to you, I suppose there is no harm in letting you two interact with each other."

"If our paths cross, certainly. But right now, all you need to be focusing on is healing and getting better. That's it. That's your job."

I pull a chair to the side of the bed, then sit down and take his hand between mine again. His face clouds over as a sober expression crosses it. He's troubled.

"Blake, Reiko mentioned that you are investigating what happened to me," he says.

"I am. Was. It's over now."

"Tell me everything."

I shake my head. "It doesn't matter right now. You need to rest and regain—"

"I need to know who did this to me, Blake," he says, his voice surprisingly firm. "Please."

"I don't want this weighing on your heart right now. It can wait."

"It can't. Not for me," he says. "And I will not be able to rest until I know who put me in this bed and why."

As much as I'd like to convince him that now is not the time for it, I can see that hard gleam in his eye that he gets when he will not relent on something. He wants to know, and he wants to know now. I can't say I blame him. In his position, I'm sure I'd be just as unyielding. But the truth is, I don't want to tell him because it's going to break his heart into about a billion pieces.

"Blake, please," he says.

And so, I tell him everything. As he listens, his face grows paler and more drawn. It's like I can see his soul fracturing right before my eyes, and it breaks my heart. It takes me about half an hour to summarize the investigation and the arrest, and when I'm done, the grief I see on Fish's face makes me want to crawl into a hole.

"Are you okay?" I ask.

"I am fine," he replies. "I just... I truly believed Trevor when he said he understood and that we were all right. He seemed so sincere."

"Sometimes we have a blind spot when it comes to people we care about. We want to see the best in them," I tell him, recalling Dr. Azar's words to me. "Believe me when I tell you I understand that completely."

Fish settles back against his pillows, his expression shifting from heartbroken to angry. I don't begrudge him his anger.

"Fish, what happened between you two? What made you change your will in the first place?"

"Trevor's reach far exceeded his grasp," he tells me. "I discovered that he was making side deals with some very bad people—people I had worked hard to run out of the community. He knows I will not tolerate human trafficking of any kind, but he saw there was money to be made and, well... he made some very poor decisions."

"But you were going to let him take control of the organization anyway?"

"We had a long talk, and I believed we had arrived at an understanding," he tells me. "He wouldn't assume control for many years yet, I hoped, and I wanted to believe in that time, he would grow, mature, and learn from me. I wanted to see the best in him. I was wrong to do so."

"It's because you have a good heart," I tell him. "And because you care about him."

"It was a mistake. And one that I need to rectify."

His voice is low and menacing, sending a chill rushing through me while leaving me no doubt as to the meaning behind his words.

"Fish, you need to leave this alone. Trevor is going to prison for a very long time—"

"That is the funny thing about our justice system... simply because I did not die, he will be out again in the not-too-distant future. And when he does get out, he will be angrier than before. I have little doubt he will come for me again."

"Then we can deal with that when the time comes. But you have worked so hard to step out of your past life to build something better. Something cleaner. Please, don't go back. I am begging you," I plead.

He is silent for a minute, then offers me a smile. "Don't worry, Blake. I'm not going back. And I will trust that these things sometimes have a way of working themselves out."

His words don't make me feel the least bit better, and I'm already making plans mentally to have Trevor moved into protective custody. I want to believe that Fish has evolved from what he used to be. But maybe that's my blind spot because I care about him. He has evolved. He has built something better. He *is* better. But somewhere inside, I also know that he's never left that shadow world behind entirely. He still straddles that line simply because he must in order to maintain the balance and order in Chinatown.

"Please, Fish," I say again. "Just let me handle Trevor."

His smile is enigmatic, but before I can say anything more, the door to his room opens, and a man in a white coat sweeps in. He pulls up short when he sees me though.

"I'm sorry, you can't be here right now," he says. "Mr. Zhao needs to rest and is not allowed visitors. I'm afraid I'm going to have to ask you to leave."

I quickly badge him. "I'm Unit Chief Wilder—"

"I don't care if you're the Queen of England; no visitors means no visitors."

My cheeks reddening, I get to my feet and quickly stow my badge as Fish's eyes sparkle with amusement, giving me the first glimpse of the man I've always known peeking through.

"Sorry," I say, then turn to Fish. "We'll talk about this later—when you're rested."

"Of course."

I head for the door, but before I can open it, Fish's voice stops me.

"And Blake… find your safe space," he says. "You, more than anybody I know, deserves that clean and free space in this dirty world. Find it, grab hold of it, and don't let it go. You deserve to be happy and loved. Let yourself be."

I turn to him, my vision blurring with tears as I smile. "I'll talk to you soon."

"Yes," he says. "You will."

CHAPTER THIRTY-EIGHT

The Emerald Lounge, Downtown District; Seattle, WA

After getting back to the Chapel, I send Nina and Opal home. It had been a long several days, and they needed some rest and time to unwind. Astra and the rest of the team are still in Ohio and won't be back for a few days yet. Their case is more difficult than expected, so I may need to go out there to lend a hand. I'll know more in the next day or so.

While I've got some time alone, I want to take advantage of it. I put on some music and write up all the after-action reports and send them away to DD Church for review. I am exhausted and yet, I'm restless at the same time. I would like to go sleep for the next three days, but I'm also wired, not ready to go home just yet. At the same time, I'm also not in the mood to be especially social.

My mood is as chaotic as my heart is troubled, so, unsurprisingly, I opted for the Emerald. Seated in a booth in the back, I listen to some music, unwind, have a few drinks, and nobody bothers me. I guess it's just what I need. I'm on my third scotch and enjoying a slight buzz that's mellowing me out when he slides into the booth across from me. Raising my gaze, I offer Sonny Garland a smile.

"I was surprised to hear from you," he says.

"It seemed like a good idea after my second," I respond, raising the glass in my hand.

"Ah. So, I'm what, your drunk booty call?"

"Something like that."

"And if I'm not in the mood to put out?"

I shrug. "Your loss. I'm sure I can find somebody who is."

He grins. "Lucky for me I know you're not like that."

"I'm trying to make some changes in my life."

He chuckles and signals to the waitress for a drink. It's not my usual girl, but she's friendly and efficient. Her eyes linger on Sonny a little too long when she drops off our drinks, and I feel a flash of jealousy shoot through me. It's got to be the booze because I'm not a jealous kind of girl. She flashes him a wide, enticing smile just before she departs, leaving me with the aftermath of that jumble of stupid emotions swirling around inside of me.

I blame Dr. Azar for this. She's the one who told me to get in touch with my emotions and to let myself experience them. Let me just say, experiencing them sucks. Sonny's cool, blue eyes search mine, and I must look awful or something because concern crawls across his face.

"You okay?" Sonny asks.

"Yeah. I'm fine," I croak. "Just been a long week."

We're silent for a couple of minutes, and it feels like we're trying to find something to talk about. It's a strained, awkward feeling, which I guess is my fault, considering how I left things with him the last time we talked. Oh, and probably because I tried to sneak out of his hotel room without waking him. That was kind of a jerk move.

"I heard you closed your case. Caught the guy who shot your friend," he says. "Congratulations on that."

"Thanks."

He motions to the bandage on one cheek, then to the bruise on the other. "That where you got those battle scars?"

"Comes with being an idiot. I never should have taken this case because I knew I was too close to it, and it wasn't letting me see or think clearly. This," I reply and gesture to my face, "is a direct result of my idiocy."

His smile is small and warm. "I wouldn't call you an idiot. I'd call you a good friend. I know if somebody had shot me, I'd want you on the case simply because you are relentless. Passionate. And you do not give up. Not for anything."

My face reddens, and I shift in my seat, uncomfortable beneath the weight of his praise. Most of me feels like I don't deserve it. I never do. That, too, is something Dr. Azar is encouraging me to work on. I swear to God, it seems like the more I see her, the more I find there's something wrong with me. It makes me feel defective, and there are days I don't want to confront those broken pieces within myself and think maybe if I don't go, I can just ignore them, pretend they don't exist, and everything will be okay.

Unfortunately for me, I know it doesn't work that way in the real world. I went to Dr. Azar in the first place because I couldn't ignore those broken pieces any longer.

"So, what did you really call me down here for?" Sonny asks. "Not that I mind. I've been wanting to see you."

"I just… I guess I didn't want to be alone tonight."

He frowns. "Seriously, are you all right, Blake?"

"Yeah, I'm fine. I think. I just… there's a lot going on in my head, and I guess I'm just looking for a quiet space. A… safe space."

Sonny's gaze lingers on me as if he knows there's more meaning behind my words than I'm saying. Which, there is, of course. I like that he can read me that well already and like even more that he seems to instinctively know not to push me until I'm ready to talk about it. I drain the last of my scotch and set the glass down.

"You want to get out of here?" I ask.

"You sure that's not just the booze talking?"

"Might be."

"Am I going to wake up tomorrow to you sneaking out on me again?"

A lopsided grin creases my lips. "No promises, but I don't think so."

He stares at me. "What's going on with you? Something seems different."

"Like I said, I'm trying to make some changes in my life."

"So, I'm your practice run?"

"Something like that."

He laughs, then swallows down his drink. "Come on, let's go. We should talk."

"We should."

As I'm sliding out of the booth, my phone buzzes with an incoming text. It's from Opal, and when I see her words, I feel a gaping chasm open in my belly.

"Trevor Kondo was killed in county lockup."

Sonny cocks his head. "You all right? What's up?"

I shake my head. "I guess things just sorted themselves out."

Questions light up Sonny's eyes, but I shake my head, not ready to talk about it yet. Instead, I take his hand and lead him out of the Emerald... filled with uncertainty, but hoping this path is leading to a safe space of my own.

AUTHOR'S NOTE

Thank you for embarking on another exhilarating journey with Blake Wilder! I'm thrilled to have shared this story, as it offered both Blake—and you—a deeper glimpse into Fish's former world more than ever before. Through her investigation, Blake uncovered a side of Fish she never knew existed, one that resonates with her own struggles. This discovery deepens her appreciation for him in unexpected ways, even as it sharpens the pain she feels in the face of his ordeal. I loved delving into these layers of Fish's character, his past choices, and the fine line he's walked for so many years. I hope this glimpse into his world added new dimensions to his role and enriched your connection to him, just as it did for Blake.

If you enjoyed A SHOT TO KILL, I would be grateful for your reviews and recommendations. Your support is invaluable to indie writers like myself, helping to spread the word and keep these adventures alive.

If you're on the hunt for another exciting mystery, I'd love for you to check out the latest book in my Sweetwater Falls series, WHISPERS IN THE FALLS. In this story, former FBI Agent Spenser Song, now the town's Sheriff, takes on a chilling case that cuts to the core of Sweetwater. When a grieving mother pleads for answers about her daughter's tragic murder, Spenser faces a tangled web of lies, high school grudges, and threats meant to silence the truth. With the whispers of secrets swirling through town, Spenser is drawn into a mystery that could devastate Sweetwater if it ever comes to light. If you enjoyed Blake's relentless pursuit of justice, I think you'll find Spenser's journey just as gripping—with new dangers and twists that keep her world and story intriguingly unique.

Thank you again for joining me on this exciting journey. I can't wait for you to join Blake and her team on their next adventure!

By the way, if you find any typos or want to reach out to me, feel free to email me at egray@ellegraybooks.com

Your writer friend,
Elle Gray

CONNECT WITH ELLE GRAY

Loved the book? Don't miss out on future reads! Join my newsletter and receive updates on my latest releases, insider content, and exclusive promos. Plus, as a thank you for joining, you'll get a FREE copy of my book Deadly Pursuit!

Deadly Pursuit follows the story of Paxton Arrington, a police officer in Seattle who uncovers corruption within his own precinct. With his career and reputation on the line, he enlists the help of his FBI friend Blake Wilder to bring down the corrupt Strike Team. But the stakes are high, and Paxton must decide whether he's willing to risk everything to do the right thing.

Claiming your freebie is easy! Visit
https://dl.bookfunnel.com/513mluk159
and sign up with your email!

Want more ways to stay connected? Follow me on Facebook and Instagram or sign up for text notifications by texting "blake" to 844-552-1368. Thanks for your support and happy reading!

ALSO BY
ELLE GRAY

Blake Wilder FBI Mystery Thrillers

Book One - The 7 She Saw
Book Two - A Perfect Wife
Book Three - Her Perfect Crime
Book Four - The Chosen Girls
Book Five - The Secret She Kept
Book Six - The Lost Girls
Book Seven - The Lost Sister
Book Eight - The Missing Woman
Book Nine - Night at the Asylum
Book Ten - A Time to Die
Book Eleven - The House on the Hill
Book Twelve - The Missing Girls
Book Thirteen - No More Lies
Book Fourteen - The Unlucky Girl
Book Fifteen - The Heist
Book Sixteen - The Hit List
Book Seventeen - The Missing Daughter
Book Eighteen - The Silent Threat
Book Nineteen - A Code to Kill
Book Twenty - Watching Her
Book Twenty-One - The Inmate's Secret
Book Twenty-Two - A Motive to Kill
Book Twenty-Three - The Kept Girls
Book Twenty-Four - Prison Break
Book Twenty - Five - The Perfect Crime
Book Twenty - Six - A Shot to Kill

A Pax Arrington Mystery

Free Prequel - Deadly Pursuit

Book One - I See You

Book Two - Her Last Call

Book Three - Woman In The Water

Book Four- A Wife's Secret

Storyville FBI Mystery Thrillers

Book One - The Chosen Girl

Book Two - The Murder in the Mist

Book Three - Whispers of the Dead

Book Four - Secrets of the Unseen

Book Five - The Way Back Home

A Sweetwater Falls Mystery

Book One - New Girl in the Falls

Book Two - Missing in the Falls

Book Three - The Girls in the Falls

Book Four - Memories of the Falls

Book Five - Shadows of the Falls

Book Six - The Lies in the Falls

Book Seven - Forbidden in the Falls

Book Eight - Silenced in the Falls

Book Nine - Summer in the Falls

Book Ten - The Legend of the Falls

Book Eleven - Whispers in the Falls

A Chesapeake Valley Mystery Series

Book One - The Girl in Town

Book Two - The Lost Children

ALSO BY

ELLE GRAY | K.S. GRAY

Olivia Knight FBI Mystery Thrillers

Book One - New Girl in Town

Book Two - The Murders on Beacon Hill

Book Three - The Woman Behind the Door

Book Four - Love, Lies, and Suicide

Book Five - Murder on the Astoria

Book Six - The Locked Box

Book Seven - The Good Daughter

Book Eight - The Perfect Getaway

Book Nine - Behind Closed Doors

Book Ten - Fatal Games

Book Eleven - Into the Night

Book Twelve - The Housewife

Book Thirteen - Whispers at the Reunion

Book Fourteen - Fatal Lies

A Serenity Springs Mystery Series

Book One - The Girl in the Springs

Book Two - The Maid of Honor

Book Three - The Girl in the Cabin

ALSO BY

ELLE GRAY | JAMES HOLT

The Florida Girl FBI Mystery Thrillers

Book One - The Florida Girl

Book Two - Resort to Kill

Book Three - The Runaway

Book Four - The Ransom

Book Five - The Unknown Woman

Made in United States
Troutdale, OR
11/30/2024

25501309R00139